W9-BZU-513

GAP
YEAR in
GHOST

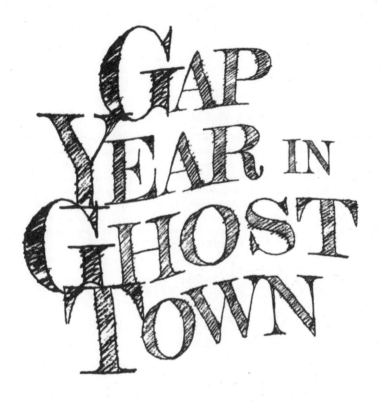

GAP YEAR IN GHOST TOWN

MICHAEL PRYOR

ALLEN&UNWIN
SYDNEY•MELBOURNE•AUCKLAND•LONDON

First published by Allen & Unwin in 2017

Allen & Unwin
83 Alexander Street
Crows Nest NSW 2065
Australia
Phone: (61 2) 8425 0100
Email: info@allenandunwin.com
Web: www.allenandunwin.com

A Cataloguing-in-Publication entry is available from the
National Library of Australia
www.trove.nla.gov.au

ISBN 978 1 76029 276 8

For teaching resources, explore www.allenandunwin.com/resources/for-teachers

Cover and text design by Ruth Grüner
Cover illustration by Craig Phillips
Set in 10.8/16 pt Caslon 540 by Midland Typesetters

Printed and bound in Australia by Griffin Press

3 5 7 9 10 8 6 4

MIX
Paper from
responsible sources
FSC® C009448

The paper in this book is FSC® certified.
FSC® promotes environmentally responsible,
socially beneficial and economically viable
management of the world's forests.

To Jacinta di Mase, with many thanks

CHAPTER 1

Let's get this straight – ghosts are everywhere. I can see them. You can't. And, see them or not, they're dangerous.

This is why my family has hunted ghosts for hundreds of years: to protect people like you.

And don't forget that this whole thing is abso-freaking-lutely serious, so whatever you do, don't mention any of those movies. Or sing the song. Especially don't ask me who you gonna call.

Just don't.

As part of a great 'Try Before You Buy' gap year experiment, I was out hunting ghosts one night. I was concentrating on one ghost so hard that I didn't realise another was sneaking up behind me.

The ghost in front of me was a Lingerer. When I first saw it, I thought it was a Weeper, but I was wrong. No tears, no sobbing. It was elderly – no surprise there, most ghosts are – male, and had those old Victorian clothes on. A bowler hat, a longish coat, high collar and tie. Nice moustache, too, as 'taches go. Melbourne has plenty of ghosts like this, being a great Victorian-era city.

You pick up a bit of history when you hunt ghosts.

Okay, so details like this would be tricky to make out at night, even on an ordinary living human being. That's where the benefits of being in the family business come in.

I can see in the dark, as long as I'm wearing the family-heirloom pendant that also helps me track down ghosts. It's not as clear as daylight, but it's a lot better than those night-vision goggles the military use. The world is made up of greys, blacks and silvers, but hi-def enough for me to get to work.

The Lingerer was skittish, and I was having trouble rounding him up. Anyone watching would have thought I was having some sort of attack, standing all by myself in the darkness of the old Conservatory surrounded by fuchsias, hydrangeas and begonias (I read the signs), waving my arms around like a traffic cop on a really bad day.

The Conservatory is a big, pink, 1930s building in the Fitzroy Gardens near the middle of the city, something like a cross between a wedding cake and an old-style fun palace. It's heated and steamy, good for growing and displaying plants. Lots of windows, including three big arched windows at either end, meant shadows everywhere.

And it smells. Not a bad smell – flowers and greenery and damp earth – but it's all around, wrapping everything like a spongey blanket.

It's good, really, that ordinary people can't see what I can see. Nothing would get done, otherwise. With all the ghosts around, ordinary people would be driven half out of their minds. Me? I'm used to it. I've been raised to be a ghost hunter. Some kids are raised to be doctors, some are raised to be firefighters. Dozens of generations of Marins behind me meant I had no real choice. It's ghost hunting for me, like it or not.

At least, that's the family plan.

This Lingerer was pretty docile, but even so, I was having to work hard to hold him there. I had my arms spread wide, hands extended, as if I was trying to herd him, which I was. I inched forward slowly so I could reach out and touch him. The thing shivered, cowering, tucking his head in and trying to cover it with an arm.

I had to touch him. That's how I do the easing.

You see, my family doesn't just hunt ghosts. We ease their passage. With a special touch, we release them, let them move on.

Where do they go after we ease them? No idea. That's for priests and shamans and theoreticians to argue over. We just do what we can to stop their suffering by letting them depart this place. For somewhere better? Let's hope so.

I crept closer, trying to hold the ghost there and stop him from vanishing. Maybe I mightn't have been totally alert. I was pretty new to going solo, after all. I was concentrating, which was meant to be good. I was deeply into the moment, imposing myself on this ghost, preparing to help him on his way – also good. The result, though, of all this focus was that I mightn't have been one hundred per cent keeping an eye on my surroundings.

'Stay aware of your surroundings,' my dad had drummed into me. 'An unaware ghost hunter is a dead ghost hunter.'

Eek.

A noise came from behind, which is always the way with ghosts. It must be in their job description that they can't announce themselves by marching up and waving both hands in your face. It's all noises from behind you, slight gusts of cold air and/or a feeling of impending doom.

It could have been the scuff of a footstep, or a rustle of clothing, but it was enough to make me break off and whirl around.

A ghost was drifting towards me. This one was from the 1920s or '30s – the clothes the giveaway again, particularly the hat. She was youngish, though; mid-thirties, maybe? Too young to die, and that's what could have spawned a ghost, and an angry one at that. You see, her demented, furious face told me she was a Rager.

She slapped at me with a clawed hand that had enough substance for me to feel the wind as it barely missed. I yelped and staggered backwards, nearly tripping over the neat brick border of the flower bed. She surged forward, both hands raised, her face a twisted mask underneath a turban-style hat. Her long, sleeveless dress was tattered and streaked with mud. And, Rager that she was, she was mad as hell.

So this Rager lurches at me, full of spite and fury. On top of that, she was giving off the standard ghostly waves of fear. Even though I knew what I was dealing with, I felt the effects. With the first ghost, my heart had already been doing a good gallop, but now it upped its rate to the red zone. I bounced on my toes in classic fight-or-flight adrenaline overdrive, because this ghost was substantial enough to do me some serious damage.

Once ghosts manifest themselves, you see, their one aim is to stay here. When they do, some of them have enough determination, or need, or longing to start gaining solidity. And the more solid they get, the more they can hurt us – in a real and physical way.

The Lingerer wasn't a worry. He was a cream puff compared to this newcomer. I had to get in a state to control the Rager; herd her into a corner, calm her down, then get to work on easing her the hell out of here.

'Hey!' I danced back out of her reach. 'What's up? Why so mad?'

Most ghosts don't retain much intelligence at all, being just fragments of the original person spun off at the moment of death. I didn't really expect an answer, but talk can sometimes engage them, distract them a little.

'Come on,' I wheedled. 'Take a deep breath or two. Count up to ten, slowly. What about meditation? Tai chi?'

She came at me again and I wasn't totally happy to see that she had teeth. Big, nasty, sharp ghost teeth.

Ghosts. They mess themselves up, then they mess you up.

The Rager hissed at me. I started looking around for a shovel, a hoe, but the parks people had been annoyingly responsible and not left anything lying around.

I began to see headlines. 'Vandal Youth Found Dead in Fitzroy Gardens', 'Prank Gone Wrong Results in Death', 'War Erupts in Middle East'. That last one was a media default, but if things went really bad for me I'd give it a nudge in Trending lists, surely.

Really bad? Huh. Things got worse.

The Rager advanced until we were only a metre apart and then the possum appeared.

So it seems the Conservatory had at least one resident possum. I mean, the Fitzroy Gardens are full of the critters, so it's no wonder that one found its way into the building, looked around, took in the warmth, the space and the quiet and said to itself, 'Home sweet home!'

The thing is, the Rager and I had disturbed the quiet. Lots of noise, possum gets grumpy. Grumpy possum wants to get away from the noise. Grumpy possum can't just call a cab and so grumpy possum gets grumpier.

Besides, animals are often sensitive to ghostly presences. So Mr Grumpy Possum feels ghosts are about, decides enough is enough and makes a break for it – only to freeze on a windowsill when he sees the Rager and me.

So, a small furry animal, grumpy and paralysed with fright, catches the attention of a raging, snarling ghost. What's going to happen next?

The Rager swiped at the cowering beastie, and I moved fast.

I darted under the Rager's arm and scooped the possum from the windowsill. Oh so grateful, the possum decided I was a tree, dug its claws in and scooted up my arm. It reached my shoulders and then scuttled around to cling to my neck.

Possum claws are made for the nice tough bark on trees, which meant that they went straight through my coat, my jacket, my shirt and my skin. I think they stopped when they hit the bone, but I wasn't sure because ouchie. Much ouchie.

Under attack by a furious ghost with enough substance to inflict real damage and with a frightened possum riding my shoulders, I responded pretty well, I think, by swearing, howling, and dancing a crazy jig inside a public flower house in the middle of the night.

Just to add to the moment, one of the big glass doors opened at the end of the Conservatory. Involving civilians in the affairs of the ghostly world is a big no-no. Dad had drummed this into me, in the drummiest way possible. It's tacky, for a start, and probably dangerous. And don't get me started on the consequences of police showing up while ghost hunting is going on. Instead, just imagine and double it, then double it again. Then you'll be in the ballpark. At the far end, but in the ballpark.

This responsibility is part of the family business. It's all about protecting the ordinary people, the civilians, the ones who can't see what I can see. So the appearance of this stranger coming through the door was an extra worry for me, on top of two ghosts and a panicked possum.

While I swung around, trying to dislodge my furry passenger (gently!), the newcomer came up behind the Rager, who was fixated on me.

All in all, I was grappling with a complex situation, but handling it with a fair degree of cool.

This newcomer, though, passed my level of cool easily because, in one neat move, she flung back her coat and drew a sword.

A freaking sword.

My jaw muscles gave way and my mouth hung open, Luna Park style. For a second I forgot about possum claws, which is saying something.

The Rager knew something was up. Maybe it was the bulging of my eyes, or the way I was pointing, but she twisted just in time to meet the downswing of the sword.

The sword ripped through the ghost from shoulder to hip with a sound like tearing paper. The wielder caught the movement, angled to one side, then slit the ghost horizontally so fast I almost missed it. After that, it was more like a kitchen demonstration ('It slices! It dices!') than any sort of swordsmanship. And I know swordsmanship. I've seen *The Princess Bride* about a dozen times.

Job done, the ghost in a pile of ghost stir-fry strips that were rapidly evaporating, the stranger's sword slid back into the sheath. I scanned the area for the Lingerer, but he had disappeared.

I was about to turn and run, but sword-wielder didn't really look like one of the Trespassers Dad had warned me about. The way she wasn't attacking me was a giveaway, too.

She frowned. 'Did you know you have a furry animal on your head?'

It was one of those Brit voices that made me think she'd spent a lifetime in front of bonnets-and-frocks BBC dramas. She could be earning a fortune in voiceover work, that was for certain, but it'd be upmarket stuff, no trash.

'You're not from around here,' I said, without screaming in pain, which was a win. I reached up. Gently, I freed Mr Possum's claws one by one. He wriggled, but I held him tightly until I lowered him to the path. 'It's a local custom, carrying possums around like that. It brings good luck.'

'I see.'

The possum sprinted out of the open door without a backward glance. 'Scamper like the wind, my friend!' I called. 'You don't have to thank me!'

'It didn't.'

'That's their way. Possums are shy, they live in trees, make the most awful noise in the night-time and they prefer to write thank-you notes rather than say it in person.'

She was tall. Now, I'm tall, the sort of head-and-shoulders-over-a-crowd tall that comes in handy sometimes, but she was right up there too. I couldn't make out much more in the dark, but she had dark hair tied back in a ponytail and she wore a dark overcoat. My night sight was amazing, but colours? Not exactly.

'Nice sword,' I said because I had to say something. 'Where'd you get it?'

'You'd be surprised.'

'What, the lady of the lake, her arm clad in purest samite?'

'Ebay.'

'You never.'

'Ebay has everything. Good, serviceable swords are just a start.' She studied me for a moment. Her gaze was careful, the sort that would notice a dangerous move a second or two before it happened. 'You're a ghost hunter,' she said. 'I was told I'd bump into others here.'

'What, here in the Conservatory?'

'In Melbourne.'

'I was right – you aren't from around here.'

'Rani Cross,' she said. 'I haven't been here long, no.'

'Hello, fellow ghost hunter Rani Cross,' I said. 'I'm Anton Marin.'

'Oh, you're a *Marin*.'

'No need to say it like that.'

'Like what?'

'Like being a Marin is the same as having leprosy. I come from an old and respected ghost-hunting family.'

'I know. About the old part, anyway. Look, we'd better get out of here before you set off an alarm.'

'No chance. I took care of the locks and the alarms with my magicky-wagicky ways.' Magicky-wagicky? I could have facepalmed. 'Just the same, we should leave. You don't want anyone finding us in here, especially with that sword.'

She stalked towards the door, a hand on her hip. Hilt of sword, was my guess.

Outside, she stood guard while I used my pendant to lock the door behind us and re-set the alarms. Manners.

My pendant is multipurpose. As well as the night-sight enabling and ghost detecting, it can also crack open any lock and disable alarms. You need that sort of access when you're hunting ghosts, believe me.

Yes, it could get me into bank vaults. But I don't.

'You were in trouble with that ghost,' she said. 'And the possum, most likely.'

'The Rager? Yeah, she was a handful.' I pushed back my hair. Sweaty and curly. Bad combination. 'You didn't have to chop her up like that, though.'

We were outside, in front of the Conservatory. The old government buildings were not far away. In the other direction were the gardens proper, with big elm trees looming in the dark. Plenty of lights, too, which meant that now I could see that her nose was off-centre, pushed sideways, slightly. Had it been broken at some time in the past and not fixed properly?

Her coat was stylish, offset with pegs instead of buttons, and a scarf hung over her shoulder in a way that would have taken hours to arrange in a photo shoot.

She was looking at me as if I was mad. 'Of course I had to take to it with my sword. It was a ghost. I dispatched it. It's what ghost hunters do.'

'Dispatch ghosts? Got it. You're one of them, aren't you?'

She frowned. 'It depends on which them you're referring to.'

'The thingos. The whatsit.'

'I'd never belong to a whatsit.'

'One of those ghost-hunting orders. Or fraternities. Sororities, sorry.'

'If you know that, you'll know that the Marins are the outcasts of the ghost-hunting world. I shouldn't be seen with you.'

'Outcasts?' I blinked. 'Okay, sometimes my granddad was a bit rough around the edges, but outcasts is a bit harsh.'

'It's said that you don't destroy ghosts.'

'No. We don't destroy ghosts.' I sat on the steps. It made it easier to grab my knees and stop them trembling. From tiredness, you understand; just fatigue and the after-effects of nearly being torn apart by a very angry ghost.

She stood there in ominous mode, weight on the balls of her feet as if she expected a spectral army to appear at any moment and didn't want to miss the fun. There was a whole city of lights and people behind her, but she made them seem distant and unimportant.

It was quite a trick.

'My family doesn't destroy ghosts,' I said. 'We help them on their way.'

'Marins are the ghost hunters who don't dispatch ghosts.'

'We do. We just go about it differently. We ease their passage and release them from their earthly bondage.'

'Which is what I do.'

'I'm not sure that using your sword on them is the same.'

'We sever their connection with the world and they're free.'

'Free? That wasn't what I saw. I saw a ghost being destroyed with no chance of going on.'

She took a step towards me. The hilt of her sword cleared the sheath in a move so smooth that I was still admiring it when I realised how threatening it was. 'You're wrong.'

I swallowed. 'I know what I saw.'

She thrust the sword back into the sheath and stalked away. I didn't say anything, which is a bit of a rarity for me.

This whole human/ghost thing is seriously messed up. At least, that's the conclusion I came to after Dad's years of history lessons. I don't know, but I think it was that the ghost sight/easing thing had passed over Dad, as it apparently did reasonably often, that made him determined to know as much about the ghost world as possible.

Ghost world. Messed up. Right.

Ever since humanity learned about ghosts, some of us have been able to see them all the time, and all of us have been able to see them some of the time. Enough to make everyone a bit jumpy in haunted places. The ghosts? Hard to tell what they feel, really.

It's enough to say that ghosts scare the pants off people. Partly it's to do with their association with the mysteries of death, but partly it's because of their spooky nature. Even the least of ghosts gives off waves of fear. They inspire dread in us, enough to paralyse if we let it.

But wait – there's more. Ghosts like to clamp onto humans and use our vitality to maintain their existence. Good for ghosts, bad for us.

This is why so many Companies, Brotherhoods and Orders have grown up dedicated to protecting humanity from the scourge of ghosts. Most of these top-secret bands have military origins, so their approach to solving the ghost problem is an aggressive one. Chop and hack.

My family, though, goes about things differently.

I wanted to explain all this to Rani Cross, but when I lifted my head she'd gone.

Shy, I expect.

CHAPTER 2

You might think that ghost hunting is full of glamour and excitement, international jet-setting, hobnobbing with world leaders and stuff like that. Well yeah, nah. Ghost hunting is more about mud and cold and waiting around for something to manifest.

I was homeschooled. Dad taught me, so my education was heavy on the history of ghost hunting, the methods of ghost hunters, the stylish day wear of ghost hunters, stuff like that. Oh, he had to teach English and Maths and the regular business, but Dad's conscientious. I got the lot, plus ghosts.

Socialisation with other kids? Not so much. We weren't total isolates, but I didn't have the everyday exposure to the usual mix you find in any school, from angels to psychopaths. It meant that my view of the world was largely determined by pop culture. Not in an Abed way, even though I sometimes found myself humming 'Troy and Anton in the mooorn-ning', in a sensible and not-crazy way.

But my pop culture background is erratic. I have gaps, to say the least. Lots of it depended on Dad's sensibilities. He went backwards and forwards over the whole TV thing, for instance. Sometimes we watched plenty of TV. Sometimes he went on an anti-TV binge and refused to have one in the house. Internet? Pretty much the same. Ups and downs.

So, gaps.

I had just finished Year Twelve. Dad had my future all organised, ever since I was little and had shown the family ability to see ghosts. Funny thing was that when I went all teenagery, I started to have other ideas. I didn't want to do what he wanted me to do, I wanted to do what I wanted to do.

It was just that I didn't know what I wanted to do.

University sounded like fun, but I had no idea what I wanted to study. Everything sounded good, in its own way. I'm a bit of an all-rounder, interest-wise. English, Maths, Science. Languages, not so much, but I'm happy to give them a go. Art? So-so. Music, likewise. Nothing repels me, though.

Long story short, when it came time to make up my mind about what to do after Year Twelve, Dad and I sat down and discussed it sensibly. Whoops, I left out all the arguing and slamming doors and shouting that came before we sat down and discussed things sensibly.

In the end, I applied for an Arts course. General, open, challenging, with plenty of chances to specialise later on.

I got in, and deferred. Dad's compromise was that I'd take a gap year, go into the family business full time. If I gave it a good go, Dad would abide by my decision at the end of the twelve months. With gritted teeth, maybe, but he vowed he'd support me if I still wanted to dump the ghost hunting to study instead.

He's a good man, my dad. He even let me work in the other side of the family business in the daytime.

We have a second-hand bookshop. Selling books has been in the family ever since Dad's grandfather came to Australia after World War Two. It gives us an excuse to chase up some seriously weird tomes on the subject of ghosts and the ghost hunters who police the world.

Our shop is in Thornbury, one of the hipster zones of Melbourne, which means I can get good coffee and a good haircut, and our patrons are okay with old stuff that we cunningly pass off as retro.

The shop is in a building that was once, a long time ago, two shops, before Dad converted it to one giant bookstore. It has two big window frontages under a verandah that reaches the street. The shop goes back and back and back, some twenty-five metres or more, and inside are lots of different rooms. The front part, with the counter and cash register, is the biggest. After that, a corridor up the middle leads to rooms on either side, all full of bookshelves. A few of them have easy chairs and couches so browsers can really do some quality browsing. You don't want to rush into a purchase of *Wisden Cricket Almanac 1972*, after all.

Dad is a dynamo when it comes to fitting out a bookshop. He can slap up shelves like nobody's business. Sometimes, when we go visiting other people (which is rare), I catch him studying bare walls with that 'I think this place needs more bookshelves' look on his face.

In principle, I'm with him. I always say that a house can't have too many bookshelves or too many hooks to hang hammocks.

Right at the rear is a kitchen, tiny bathroom and a crash room for when I need a place to sleep. The kitchen used to double as my schoolroom. Outside the kitchen is a small yard with enough room for our van. The bluestone-cobbled lane that gives access to this runs along the back of all the shops. It's handy, but makes the rear of the shops pretty exposed. That's why reinforced steel doors and bars on the windows are the designer items of choice in these parts.

I know that some bookshops specialise. It's a good way to corner a market. Sports books. Military books. Travel books. We're different. We specialise in everything. Dad hates to turn down a book, if someone wants a trade, or if he happens to lob into a garage sale, or if he sees a book lying in the middle of the road. The result is so many books on so many subjects that it's hard to keep track of them. Dad has a system, but it's only known to him.

In the end, I just love the place – mainly the smell when I open the door. Mmm ... book smell.

The bookshop mightn't be a super-sized money spinner, but that doesn't matter. The Marin family trust, the one set up with the gold the family managed to get out of Europe and into Australia after the war, means we're not anywhere near broke and we have enough to pay our informants, buy useful books, stuff like that. Not filthy rich, not broke.

After my encounter at the Conservatory, I went straight to the bookshop to open up. This was the routine we'd established for the gap year. I open the shop really early. Dad joins me later and I head home to catch some sleep before my night-time ghost-hunting activities.

Ten minutes after I'd settled behind the counter with a cup of coffee, waiting for my laptop to fire up, the bell over the door went.

Bec.

Bec is my long-time friend and next-door neighbour. We grew up together. She doesn't often make it all the way to our bookshop, but lately she's taken to bike-riding – with a vengeance, like pretty much everything she does. Never half-hearted, is Bec. She's probably the smartest people I know, and one of the hardest-working. Now, that's a killer combo – smart and hard-working. No wonder she gets so much done.

She stood in the doorway in her mixture of lycra and urban wear. She was having trouble with her helmet, thanks to her mass of black frizzy hair. Even tied back, it has a life of its own. It would probably save her from any serious head injury anyway, but she's a stickler for rules. Some rules anyway.

Both her eyes are dark brown, almost black. This is important, because one of them isn't real. Well, it's not imaginary, but it's not the one she was born with. Tiny Bec had an accident, a nasty one, and she had to get a replacement. The one she most often wears is really, really good. Most people wouldn't know it's a fake, as it moves around when the other one does – clever stuff – and the iris even gets bigger and smaller with the light, thanks to technology.

Bec doesn't hide any of this. She calls her robo-eye a feature, not a drawback. I used to feel sorry for her, but she told me off once, and since then I hardly even think about it. 'It's not who I am,' she said. 'I'm not defined by this. I'm Bec, and just like you have a weird ridge inside your right ear, Anton, I have one eye.'

'What's wrong with my ear?'

'Never mind. It's bizarre, but I don't sideline you because of it.'

She also gets some weird and wonderful eyes she uses on special occasions. Glow-in-the-dark eye? You bet. Eye of Sauron? If she feels like it. Cat eye? Easy.

She pointed her bike pump at me. 'What happened to you last night?'

I sighed and turned away from the laptop and the inventory.

The inventory spreadsheet was my latest crusade. Dad always says he knows every book on every shelf, which I doubt, but I'd taken on the project of cataloguing the contents of the whole shop.

I was glad of any distraction, though. 'Sorry about that,' I said to Bec. 'Couldn't be helped. Don't stand in the doorway. Come in if you're coming in.'

She looked over her shoulder. Pointedly. 'Sorry. I seem to be blocking the hordes of invisible customers who are trying to make their way into your fine establishment.'

She blinked, hard, then rubbed her left eye. With a sigh she popped it out, inspected it, and snapped it back in again. Even though I'd seen her do it a million times, and I was used to it, I was glad no one else was in the shop. It seriously freaked people out, but that never bothered Bec.

'It's Thornbury,' I said. 'It's before ten a.m. Not many people are up and about yet.'

'Hmm.' Bec looked sceptical, but she closed the door behind her. She studied the rack of 1990s pop music magazines for a while before fronting the counter where I sat.

'All right,' she said. 'Come out and tell me. You hated the football, right?'

I was near the Conservatory last night because, after years of nagging, I'd finally caved and gone to the footy with Bec, and the MCG is not far from the Fitzroy Gardens. From a distance, you wouldn't pick her as a die-hard footy fan, but she has the Melbourne disease good and proper. Since birth, when she was wrapped in a red and blue scarf, she's been devoted to the Melbourne Football Club.

Bec is a rational and reserved person, normally, except where football is concerned. Being as smart as ten smart people put together, her passion usually comes out in an amazing head for statistics, charts and data, but she is also a stubborn match-goer, rain or shine, success or failure.

Once, I made a joke about being a one-eyed supporter. Never again.

Me? I like footy, but I'd never really got into the live-match thing. Bec had nagged me for years and I'd always been able to put her off, but in a fit of weakness, I had given in and gone with her to a game. Her team – which was my team, since I was a good friend – lost.

It was when we were filing out of the ground and I was patting her on the back as she cried – what are friends for? – that I'd felt my pendant stirring, letting me know that a ghost was manifesting somewhere nearby. The crowd heading for Jolimont station was massive and gave me a chance to slip away. I think I told Bec that I wouldn't be long.

I think.

I shut the lid on the laptop. 'It was a good game. Sorry about the result.'

'That's hardly an answer,' she said. 'You hated it, right?'

'No,' I said, and I surprised myself. It was true. Bec's enthusiasm had been infectious. When she jumped to her feet, I did too. When she cheered, I joined in. When she went wild at the umpire, I pretended I didn't know her.

'If you enjoyed it,' she said, 'then why did you run away?'

'Ghost hunting.'

Dad had always stressed the secret nature of our family business. We could endanger ordinary citizens if we introduced them to the whole spirit world thing. It was pretty much an article of faith with all ghost hunters.

But Bec was Bec. Recently, I shared the whole ghost thing with her, to stop her bugging me about why I wasn't going to uni. And she's proven to be incredibly useful; having an ordinary civilian's point of view puts things in perspective, sometimes.

'Oh. That's different. What was it? A Moaner? A Growler?'

'A Lingerer, in the Conservatory in the Fitzroy Gardens.'

'Old?'

'Victorian. Eighteen-eighties, maybe.'

'I wish you could photograph them,' she said wistfully. 'I could pin down its origin era.'

'While I was concentrating on him, a Rager came up behind me.'

'No!'

'Yes. And that's when I met someone.'

I told Bec about the mysterious Rani Cross and her ghost-hacking ways. If I omitted any mention of a possum riding me like a cowboy rides a bronco, it was in the interests of economical storytelling, right?

'I think I get it,' she said when I finished. 'You're only in this ghost-hunting business because it helps you meet hot girls.'

'Well, if that's a side benefit of my noble calling, who am I to argue?'

Bec rarely teased me about my awkward and dismal romantic efforts, which was one of the things I liked about her, but she didn't mind reminding me about them – and she didn't mind listening to my tedious wonderings about what I was doing wrong and what I should do differently. No advice, but she was a good listener.

'Okay, then.' She pointed a challenging finger at me. 'I've got one for you.'

I grimaced. 'Hit me.'

'What's the capital of Mongolia?'

'Give up.'

'Ulan Bator. Coolest capital name since Ouagadougou.'

'So it's my turn now? I'll have one for you tomorrow.'

Ever since we were really little, Bec and I have taken it in turns to ask each other trivia questions. The more obscure, the more off-beat, the better. We don't keep a point score or anything like that. It's enough to dazzle the other person with bizarre facts. And if you happen to answer correctly, it's a win of epic proportions. Of course, no googling or other external help is allowed in answering. It's an honour thing.

'Take your time,' she said. She'd seen a stack of old kids' magazines and her attention was wandering.

The bell rang again, the door opened and I was sandbagged.

'I've found you.' The sword-wielding, shadowy ghost hunter from last night looked around. 'Nice shop.'

Bec looked at me. 'The mysterious stranger reappears?'

I put my head in my hands. All I wanted was a nice simple life where I could hunt ghosts, do a part-time university course, be rich and famous and happy and have a talking alpaca. Was that too much to ask?

'Stop groaning, Anton,' the ghost hunter said. 'How do you do? I'm Rani.'

I looked up, but she wasn't talking to me. She was talking to Bec.

'I'm Bec,' Bec said. 'Can I see your sword?'

Rani glanced at me. 'I can see that I've been the topic of conversation.'

I tried to look innocent. 'Sorry?'

'Look,' Rani said to Bec, 'I need to have a private word with your boyfriend.'

'He's not my boyfriend.'

'I'm not her boyfriend.'

Bang. Bec and I had said it so many times now it sounded like expert double-tracking. I was about to start on my rant about gender stereotyping and how people assumed that any boy/girl relationship had to be a romantic one and how that was both demeaning and ignorant, but Bec warned me off with a look. She'd heard it a million times before. She'd actually critiqued it until it was a smooth and irresistible diatribe. She liked to set me up and watch me crush loudmouths with the force of my argument.

Not this time, though.

'Sorry.' Rani had a different coat on this morning. Long, but in a dense herringbone pattern. The scarf was different too. Solid black.

'It's okay,' I said. 'Bec can hear what you've got to say.'

Bec looked at me, and then at Rani. 'I can go for a coffee, if you like.'

'You don't like coffee.'

'I'm trying to learn. Cool factor.'

'No,' I said. 'Don't go.'

Bec slapped her pump in her other hand. 'It looks like something's going on between you two. He—' she pointed at me with the pump, 'doesn't want to talk about it while you—' she pointed at Rani, 'do.'

Rani spread her hands. 'It's rather delicate.'

'What? Since when are ghosts delicate?'

Rani started. 'You're a civilian.'

'I don't have the ghost sight, if that's what you mean.'

Rani turned slowly to me. 'I don't believe it. You've told a civilian. You've broken one of the fundamental principles of our calling.'

'Well, there it is, then. We Marins, right out there on the edge, ghost-business-wise. Show me a rule and I'll break it.'

Rani fumbled for words for a moment before she gave up. She threw her hands in the air, then paced up and down the length of the front room.

She stopped and pointed at Bec. 'I've changed my mind. I think you could be useful.'

'You want me to stay now?'

Rani crossed the room, flipped the lock of the door. She turned the dangling card from 'Open' to 'Closed'. 'Let's talk.'

CHAPTER 3

The kitchen, right at the rear of the bookshop, has an actual window to the outside world (well barred, of course), a sink, some cupboards and room for the Gaggia espresso maker. No automatic settings on this venerable machine. It's *mano a mano* coffee making in our bookshop.

The kitchen also has a round table with chairs. None of the chairs match, but we sat on them anyway.

Rani cut to the chase. 'I want to know more about you.'

'I'm flattered.'

'Don't be. I used the plural "you". I want to learn about the Marin family.'

'Burn,' Bec said. 'Nice one, Rani.'

My mouth runs away with me sometimes. Most times. All the time. For some reason, this irritates some people. Mostly those with no wit of their own. Jealous, I suppose.

Rani pointed at me. 'I want to know about what you were trying to do with the ghost last night, before I saved you.'

Bec said to Rani, 'Please tell me there was sword work.'

I had to squirm a bit when Rani recounted her version of last night's events to a rapt Bec. I mean, the outline was consistent, and most of the details. Let's just say that the emphasis was different. In my version, I was calm, self-possessed, elusive and attractively mysterious. In Rani's version, not so much.

'That's one evening chock-full of ghosts,' Bec said when she'd finished. 'It's not usually like that, is it, Anton?'

'Not that I have a lot to go on, but no. And what about you?' I asked Rani.

'It was sometimes like that during my training in London.'

'You trained in London?' Bec rubbed her hands together. I nearly groaned. London is Bec's favourite city in the world, and she was planning to get there soonest. In the meantime, she collected any traveller's tales she could.

'That's where I was living before the Company sent me here,' Rani said.

'The Company?' I echoed. Alarm bells were ringing, great big ones.

'The Company of the Righteous. That's the ghost-hunting organisation I belong to.'

I'd been half-expecting it, ever since she said the word 'Company', but it still hit me like a sock full of gravel. 'You're a member of the Company of the Righteous?'

'On probationary assignment here in Melbourne.'

'This is the same Company of the Righteous that the Marin family split from a hundred years ago?'

She nodded slowly, never taking her eyes off me. 'We're taught that they were expelled for heretical approaches to ghost hunting.'

'Yeah, well, I was taught that the Marins couldn't stand the close-mindedness of your Company and they had to go their own way to preserve their integrity.'

'Point of view,' Bec said.

We both looked at her. She shrugged. 'You're both right, depending on your point of view.'

I let out a breath I hadn't realised I was holding. My shoulders were tense, too, and I rolled them, stretching. 'Okay, I can see that. It doesn't explain why you, Rani, Company operative and all, are hanging around with a nasty heretic Marin.'

'I came to see if you'd come back to the Conservatory tonight.'

'With you?'

'There's still a ghost roaming about. I want to see what you plan to do with him.'

'You don't want to just charge in and chop him up?'

'If you're not interested, just say so.'

'Oh, I'm interested. I just want to make sure I know what I'm getting into.'

Bec nudged Rani. 'London must be full of ghosts, right?

Rani smiled. 'They're thick on the ground, especially around places like the Tower. I've got a link to a special Google Maps overlay somewhere. I'll show you if you like.'

'I'll hold you to that,' Bec said, with one hand on her heart.

Rani pushed her hair back. Today it hung loose on her shoulders. 'When I took up the Melbourne posting, I hoped I might meet someone from your family.'

I nodded at Bec and pushed my chest out. 'Famous.'

'Or infamous, really, in Company terms,' Rani said. 'The Marins and their unorthodoxies were mentioned, in passing, in our history lessons. A footnote to something else, really, but it was enough to intrigue me. Our training emphasises that we should observe as well as act.'

'Gather intelligence.' Bec nodded. 'Good field practice.'

'It underlines that your club is a quasi-military gang,' I said. 'Explains a lot.'

'So who's right?' Bec asked. 'Destroy ghosts or ease their passage?'

Rani and I looked at each other. She spoke first. 'I was taught that destroying ghosts was the only way to protect humanity.'

'There is another way,' I said. 'The Marins have been doing it for a long time now.'

'Show me, then,' Rani said. 'Show me tonight.'

'You're serious.'

The rear door swung open. Rani was on her feet and had flowed – that's the best word for it – so that her back was against the wall behind the door, and she had the sword half-drawn.

Dad staggered in with a large cardboard box. He dropped it on the table as we jerked back, then he stumbled, panting, to the sink.

Dad is old, as fathers tend to be. He's tall like me, but he's gone through the filling-out stage and passed through to the other side, where he's getting a bit gaunt around the neck and cheeks. Most people wouldn't see it, though, because of his beard. Black and grey, reasonably close, with short straight hair to match. Sad eyes, and large-knuckled hands. He was wearing one of his waistcoats over one of his T-shirts atop one of his pairs of jeans. He has other outfits, but the never-ending combination of waistcoats, T-shirts and jeans takes care of ninety-five per cent of his clothing needs.

'Anton,' he wheezed. 'More boxes in the van. Hello, Rebecca. I like your helmet.'

'Hello, Anton's father Leon,' Bec said distinctly enough for Rani to hear. 'You want me to help?'

'Sit, sit. Anton can manage while you introduce me to your fierce friend behind the door.'

Rani slid the sword home and stepped out into the room. 'I'm sorry, Mr Marin. Forgive me.'

Dad straightened – at some cost to his chronic bad back, I knew. 'Welcome to our biblio-emporium,' he said as he flicked some dust off his waistcoat. 'But I'm afraid I didn't catch your name.'

'Rani Cross. And I was just about to go.'

'Go? No, don't do that. I haven't had a chat with a member of the Company of the Righteous for ages.'

Rani speared me with a look, and all I could do was shrug. 'I didn't say a word. He's just sharp. And he can spot a sword a mile away.'

'Boxes, Anton,' Dad said. 'They won't shift themselves.'

By the time I'd carried in the six boxes of books, Rani and Dad were getting on as if they'd known each other for years. Dad can really turn on the charm when he wants to.

Then Rani was up and on her way. 'I'll see you tonight, then, Anton.'

Dad's eyebrows rose but before he could get in with one of his supposedly suave observations I just nodded. 'Sure.'

'I left my number for you, just in case.'

A slip of paper sat there. I grabbed at it, decided that was a bit needy, let go and it fluttered to the floor. Cool as, I pretended it wasn't there. 'Great. Tonight then, at the Conservatory.'

'Time?'

'I'll text you.'

Rani smiled a little and then left.

The straightforward world of ghost hunting that Dad had promised me had become just a tiny bit complicated.

'So,' Dad said, 'she doesn't seem like a representative of the oppressive organisation that nearly killed all our ancestors, does she?'

'You talked about that while I was carrying boxes?'

'We talked about Melbourne. And London, didn't we, Bec?'

'She lived in Bayswater,' Bec said. 'That's right near the Peter Pan statue in Hyde Park.'

'This statue is on your list of places to see in London?'

'It's about number sixty-three, from memory. It doesn't mean it's not important.'

Dad straightened his waistcoat. 'Be careful with this Rani,

Anton. The history between our family and her organisation ...
Now, Rebecca, tell me what you've been up to lately.'

I thought I'd better do some catch-up reading on our family story. I had a feeling I'd missed the juicier details.

Bec happily told Dad about her uni studies, her bike-riding regime and the cosplay convention coming up in a few weeks. Bec's a mad-keen cosplayer as well as a mad-keen football follower.

'Dad,' I said, slipping into a conversational pause just like a dancer into a revolving door, 'I was thinking that Bec could help with our business.'

'The bookshop? I'm not sure if we need any extra help.'

'I meant the other business – the ghost-hunting business.'

Dad put a hand to his chest, almost as if he'd been shot. Even if he didn't have the family gift, he'd been brought up in its principles. And, probably to make up for his shortcomings, he adhered to them extra hard. 'Careful, Anton, careful.'

'It's okay, Leon,' Bec said. 'I know about the ghosts.'

Dad immediately went stony-faced. 'I don't know what you mean, Rebecca.'

'Anton told me all about it. The ghosts, the family business hunting them down, the protecting and all that. I think it's cool.'

'Cool,' Dad repeated in a voice of doom. 'Rebecca, I think you had better leave us now. I need a private talk with Anton.'

Bec blinked. She looked slowly at me, then back to Dad again. 'Leon?'

'Now, please, Rebecca.'

Bec swallowed, stood, fumbled for her pump and left with a few dozen looks back over her shoulder. I mimed 'I'll call you'.

After Bec closed the door behind her, Dad sighed. He spread his hands palm down on the table.

'Tell me, Anton, tell me everything. Company of the Righteous? Rebecca knowing about our calling? What's next? You'll meet up with the Ragged Sisters and then open a twenty-four hour Ghost TV channel?'

I have to hand to it to Dad. For someone who's proudly Stone Age when it came to technology, he can cut a pretty good hi-tech reference when it suits him.

Where to start? You see, Dad takes the ghost business seriously. That's not to say that I don't – hard not to, the way I was raised – but while I had my doubts, Dad was one hundred per cent committed to it.

Dad's grandfather brought the family out to Australia after the war. Apparently he'd been concerned that he'd have no work to do here, but the situation in Europe was so bad that Australia was the lesser of two evils. He needn't have worried, though. One hundred and sixty years of European settlement meant one hundred and sixty years of European ghosts. He had plenty of business on his hands easing the passage of the lost, distressed, traumatised fragments we call ghosts. His son, my grandfather, took up the calling and continued the family tradition.

Then came Dad. He didn't inherit the talent for seeing ghosts, let alone for helping them leave this earthly plane, and it was a tragedy. He tried, and I can imagine how hard he tried, but nothing happened.

Now, this would have been hard. Dad would never talk about it, really, but from stuff his sister Tanja had told me, it was really, really tough for him. She had the sight, so she was respected, like a true Marin. He wasn't mistreated or abused, but he was made to feel deficient.

To show that he *was* a true blue Marin, Dad turned his energy to learning; he constructed family trees, studied the theory of ghost hunting, collected books and anecdotes – anything he could do to be connected to a world that he was barred from by his genetics.

So when I came along and the talent showed itself in me nice and early – scaring me half to death, I might add – he was relieved. Aunt Tanja had no kids before she disappeared when I was fourteen, so I was in line to keep the family calling alive.

The trouble was, Dad was also jealous. Not that he'd say so, but every so often I could see his wistfulness when I reported on my fumbling efforts to intersect with the world of ghosts.

He was a hard taskmaster, too. He was upholding the family name and he wasn't about to let me do otherwise.

And here I was, breaking one of his prime commandments. Ghosts were not to be discussed with ordinary civilians.

Why don't we tell civilians all about it and enlist their help? Believe me, it's been tried. Have you heard of the Spanish Inquisition, the Salem witch trials? That's the sort of reaction we get when we share. So excuse me if we're a bit wary of going public.

And by now my brief mention of 'a hundred and sixty years of European ghosts' has really been getting to you, hasn't it? You've been agog, wondering about the other forty thousand years people have lived on this continent and what's going on there, right?

Nothing. There's nothing going on – at least that I know of. I don't see any Aboriginal ghosts. No one in my family has. It made my Aunt Tanja wonder if this whole ghost business isn't a cultural one where we're attuned to the death rituals we're bound up with, and we're locked out of those we aren't. Different traditions of death and afterlife spawn different ways as beliefs and traditions and stories combine. The people who've lived in this wide brown land longest have their own way and we simply don't intersect.

It's sensitive. I'd like to discuss it with someone who knows what they're talking about but it's a great taboo. I wouldn't know where to start without putting my foot in it.

'Dad.' I studied my hands. Book dust all over them. 'It just came out.'

'You wanted to talk about it to two pretty girls to impress them, you mean.'

Ouch. Low blow. 'I'm happy to impress pretty girls. Any girls at all, really, as soon as I find out how to impress. But that wasn't it.'

I explained that I had to tell Bec. She didn't believe me when I told her I wasn't going to uni because I needed time to find myself. In fact, she nearly laughed herself to death.

'Hm.' Dad rubbed his beard. 'I suppose it could be worse. Rebecca has kept you out of trouble in the past. Remember when you were little and you lost your swimming costume?'

I hurried on to my encounter with Rani.

'Did Rani tell you much about her Company of the Righteous?' Dad asked.

'Not exactly.'

'An old outfit, very old. I haven't heard of their being in Melbourne before.' He tilted his head back and stared at the ceiling. 'I wonder what they're doing here now.'

Slicing up ghosts, to judge from last night. 'What do you want me to do about Bec?'

'Rebecca? She can keep a secret, can't she?'

'Well, she didn't tell you about our love child, did she?'

That got me a startled look before he recovered. 'Rebecca has better sense than to partner with you. I hope that's a way of pointing out that she has the good sense to keep a secret.'

'Of course.'

'I'll want to talk to her.'

'I'll get in touch. Tomorrow?'

'Not tomorrow. I have someone coming.'

'Here? Someone with books?'

'Someone.'

Sometimes I think Dad overdoes the mysterious occult guy thing. One day, he'll trim his beard into a goatee and start shaping up a wicked widow's peak.

CHAPTER 4

It's funny, but real down-to-earth practicalities are as much a part of ghost hunting as any spooky supernatural stuff. Sleep, for instance; sweet, sweet sleep.

I generally catch some sleep time in the afternoon and evening. I used to come home after a night of tracking down ghosts and try to sleep then, but the adrenaline buzz kept me wide awake.

Another advantage of homeschooling, this was. I couldn't imagine a regular school letting me lie down for a snooze in the afternoon. Damn that inflexible education system. Build sleeping time into the regular school day, I say.

So my usual daily schedule is this. I get up at around eleven at night, prepare, then head out into the world to hunt ghosts. Mostly, that means following up on leads that have come Dad's way, to which I've added the much more efficient scanning of social media, mostly Twitter, for bizarre and unexplained sightings.

On top of that, there's a fair bit of wandering around the city. I've got to know the gloomy and suspect places, the ones that spawn or attract ghosts, and I have a schedule for checking on these regularly. Hospitals. Old buildings. Cemeteries. Stations. You'd be surprised how many ghosts cluster around stations. Waiting for that train that never comes, I expect.

Since ghosts can't usually be seen in daylight, most of my work is over when the sun rises. This means I can get to the shop in Thornbury and open it at eightish. I front the shop until Dad gets in around midday. Then I head home. Once I get there, I prepare some stuff for the next scouting trip, do household maintenance stuff – washing, cleaning, cooking, the usual – and try to relax before I haul down the blackout curtain I installed in my bedroom and try to get some sleep before rising and repeating.

This might sound like a finely tuned ghost-hunting machine, complete with 'hut, hut, huts', 0400 hours, and stuff like that, but it's really just something that Dad and I stumbled onto. All his figuring of ghost hunting was based on his father's and uncles' notes, and what he observed of his sister.

To tell the truth, I hadn't really done any concerted, systematic ghost hunting until this year, this gap year. Oh, I'd done a bit, either with Dad tagging along or observing Aunt Tanja, but nothing serious, nothing solo. So this year has been the king of ambivalent years. I'm not sure I want to carry on the family tradition and become a Big Bad Ghost Hunter, but I've sort of been itching to get into it having heard so much about it. I've been at it for about three months, and it's been a gentle start, I'd say. I've managed to find and ease the passage for a few dozen ghosts, mostly Weepers and Lurkers, nothing too confronting. This all means that I've had a taste of what Fulfilling My Destiny (it always had capital letters when Dad said it) is all about, and it's pretty cool.

But I'm still not sure if I want to dedicate my life to it.

So after the action-packed morning of Rani's visit, Dad took over the shop and I headed home. A tram, then a bus, then a tram, got me back to Parkville, which was, as usual, swarming with uni students and medico people, none of them aware of ghosts – except maybe as that uneasy back-of-the-neck prickling shivery feeling, or an unexplained headache, or a feeling of unearned sadness and loss. All these are ghost signs, possibly, and if I spot enough people feeling poorly for no reason, it's a hint that I need to start sniffing around for malignant spooks.

We couldn't afford our house if we had to buy it today. It was only my great-granddad's smuggled gold and his eye for a useful location that got it for us. And no one since has been stupid enough to sell such a prize, no matter how many cheesy estate agents have begged us to.

'Rambling', that's what these estate agents would put on the sign if it ever came up for sale. 'Federation charm', that'd be there too, and 'unique opportunity', in big bold letters.

Parkville is an old Melbourne suburb; tiny, really, full of grand Victorian terraces and other big houses, plus lots of smaller historic cottages on small blocks. Our house is one of the rare ones with a huge block of land, big enough for massive front and back gardens with some big old trees. It's usually under some sort of agriculture or other, growing much of the food the Marin family eats. Chooks, too, not that we have any now, but the chook shed and yard are still there if we ever have the urge to get into poultry again.

Get home. Eat. Sleep. A simple life is a good life, sometimes.

My body knew when Dad got home, even though I was still sleeping. He rattled around in the house, doing some cooking, picking up books from bookshelves and putting them back again, a noise that I knew well.

The house is too big for the two of us. Even when Judith, Dad's second wife, is in the country, it's still too big. That gives us plenty of storage space, though, and some of the bedrooms are full of stuff that has accumulated over the years.

I dragged myself out of bed some time later, showered, climbed into jeans, a T-shirt and a black woollen jumper. I selected a dark navy pinstriped jacket to go over the top.

In the kitchen, Dad was cooking one of his wintery stews with peppercorns and plenty of bay leaves. He loves bay leaves.

He looked over his shoulder. 'Won't be a minute.'

'Not for breakfast, thanks. I'll save it for later.'

I went to the fridge and grabbed a bottle of orange juice.

'Use a glass,' Dad said without looking.

I stopped with the bottle halfway to my lips and started to argue. A reflex. I knew that. I found a glass in the overhead cupboard and filled it.

I was getting good at this maturity thing.

Dad added his finishing touches to the stew, filled the stove-top espresso maker, put it on, then joined me at the kitchen table. It's an old, battle-scarred lump of wood that's seen a thousand thousand meals, arguments and emotional scenes.

'You're ready?'

He often asked if I was ready, before I went out. Partly it was a genuine desire to see if I was as prepared as possible. Partly it was to reassure himself that he'd done all he could.

Dad came with me when I first started confronting ghosts. Fifteen was the magic age when he first allowed me to do what our family heritage, my observing of Aunt Tanja, and his training had pointed me towards. As hard as it was to stand back while I went in to grapple with ghosts, he did it. But he was always there, until this year, when he said I was ready to go solo.

Dad stood, and the chair was noisy on the slate tiles as it scraped back. 'I'll drive you, if you like.'

'Coffee and toast first,' I mumbled. 'Then I'll make my own way. Thanks.'

He glanced at the stove top. 'Coffee's ready. Bread's in the pantry.'

He patted me on the shoulder as he left the kitchen. To work on the family tree some more, would be my guess.

As I headed out into the night – right after midnight – I had my backpack with me. Last night I hadn't taken it to the football and felt naked without it. It contains my essential ghost-hunting gear and I've gradually refined its contents.

If you're thinking stuff like holy water, crucifix and stake, you're way off the mark. And you'd be thinking vampires, anyway. What the twenty-first-century ghost hunter needs is pretty much what a twenty-first-century guy needs. I have a phone charger, my pro standard GPS unit, a water bottle, a book and an e-reader just in case I finish my book. Can't be without a book. Ghost hunting sometimes means hanging around waiting for something I've felt to manifest itself enough so I can tackle it. Waiting = reading. There is no substitute. Apart from Facebooking and Instagramming and Twittering, maybe.

Just before I caught one of the last trams for the night I did the three-way slap, checking my phone, wallet and keys were all there in my pockets. All set, all secure, all systems go.

When I got to the Fitzroy Gardens, I didn't see Rani until she stepped out of the shadows of one of those giant Moreton Bay figs.

'I wasn't sure you'd show up,' she said.

I shrugged. 'Unfinished business. I don't like to leave ghosts hanging.'

'I heard you whistling.'

'Sometimes I whistle when I'm nervous. Don't even realise I'm doing it.'

'Don't be nervous. This should be a doddle,' she said.

I followed in Rani's almost silent footsteps, avoiding patches of light. She paused some distance away from the Conservatory and pointed.

The Lingerer from last night was drifting along under the

trees that lined Lansdowne Street, then he turned towards the Conservatory. He was wandering, head down, shuffling along, soundless. Once he reached the building, he began to circle it, wafting through the benches, pots and even the fountains in his way in the best spectral fashion. No sounds of mourning, no scary sobbing, just drifting along like a bored emo waiting for something to be disappointed with.

A couple of laps, then he propped himself up against the wall, as if he was tired.

'Yup, plenty dangerous,' I whispered to Rani.

'Appearances can be deceptive.'

'True. Sometimes I look like a complete idiot when the reverse is true.'

'You're an incomplete idiot?'

'Very snappy. Remind me never to hand you an opportunity like that again.'

'You won't have to hand them to me. I make my own.' She frowned. 'It's going through the wall.'

One of the hardest things to deal with about ghosts is their neat trick of insubstantiality. Mostly this means they can pass through solid objects like walls and floors. It makes following them a nightmare.

'Something inside the Conservatory must be attracting him,' I said. 'He keeps going back there.'

Rani touched me on the arm. 'Now it's your turn. Show me your tricks.'

Does everyone get all fumbly when someone is watching them closely, or is it just me? Instead of the casual moves I was aiming for, I ended up groping for my pendant under my jacket and T-shirt in a way that was possibly indecent. Then I nearly dropped it before I could manoeuvre it to the lock.

Smooth, that's me, all the way through.

Inside it was steamy and fragrant with growing stuff, just like before. The whole place isn't much more than twenty-five metres end to end, so it didn't take long before I saw the ghost huddling in the corner. He was crouched against the wall, almost sitting on the ground behind a spreading hydrangea.

Remembering the debacle of last night, I did a quick one-two glance over each shoulder. Rani nodded. 'Don't worry. I have your back.'

The 'shhk-snik' sound of her pulling her sword part-way out of the sheath and then settling it back home was reassuring. A friendly face with a quality weapon in hand does that to me.

I spread my arms and advanced on the ghost. 'Hey there, matey,' I said. 'Why so blue?'

The ghost looked up. His eyes were empty wells that went on and on and on, opening on something that wasn't here and wasn't there. I'd learned not look into ghost eyes. Too easy to get lost, and get trapped in a place of horror and despair with no way home.

I kept up my soothing patter.

'It's all right. I'm here to help. Turn your frown upside down. Chin up, tiger.'

When I first started, Dad presented me with a long list of ritual phrases that were meant to be helpful in calming ghosts, to reassure them and stop them fleeing. Trouble was, they were all so olde worlde that I couldn't use them without cracking up. They made me sound like a cut-rate Hamlet, all full of 'prithees' and 'hearkens'. I tried, really I did, but I couldn't take them seriously. Then I got thinking, and decided that it wasn't so much about the words as the sounds and the attitude they conveyed. If I was calm, if I spoke gently, I figured that was the crunch. After all, ghosts aren't champs when it comes to intelligence. They probably wouldn't be able to tell a prithee from a yo.

So I made it up as I went along. If nothing else, it kept me amused.

'Hush, hush, don't cry. Momma will buy you an apple pie.'

I moved in, arms extended, then knelt when I was close enough. The ghost continued to shy away from me, trembling, eyes averted. The creature was lost and confused, forlorn and tormented, not remembering how he had come here but knowing that he was hurting.

Not really the unexploded bomb that Rani thought all ghosts were.

I reached out with my palms foremost, fingers upwards. Slowly, I pushed forward until I made contact with the ghost. This superficial touch is where I always run up against some resistance, and I had to push harder until my hands sank into his chest.

Then I gathered myself and twisted my hands in an action like wringing out a wet cloth.

Even though I was prepared for it, I rocked backwards when the ghost flew apart. For a few seconds it was like being caught in a wind tunnel, but instead of wind, I was buffeted by visions: a dog, slobbering with joy; the coldness of water at a beach; children of my own; working, digging away at what had become the Fitzroy Gardens; a scrape, a cut, an infection; pain and sickness and distraught people all around.

Then the finality, a moment of gratitude when the ghost finally let go and moved on. It was a moment that made me want to cry.

And that was it. I opened eyes I hadn't realised that I'd shut.

'It's gone,' Rani said softly. 'And you're shivering.'

I rolled my shoulders and neck. I got to my feet, every joint creaking like I was four hundred years old. 'The poor thing.' I rubbed my face with both hands. 'I just helped him leave.'

'That's what I do,' she said carefully. 'My way is just a little more abrupt.'

'And violent,' I said. 'Don't forget violent.'

'It's the right way.'

'That's what you were told.' I tugged my jacket around me, straightening the lapels. 'It's the hammer problem.'

'The hammer problem?'

I pointed at her sword. 'When the only tool you have is a hammer, every problem looks like a nail.'

She narrowed her eyes. 'You do understand that you're insulting four hundred years of dedicated service to humanity?'

'What can I say? I call 'em as I see 'em, and if the Company of the Flightless thinks chopping up ghosts is the best way to deal with them, then I'm seeing stupidity.'

Her grip tightened on the hilt of her sword. 'What did you say?'

I nodded at her knuckles. 'Hammer problem?'

She glared at me.

'Look, I'm insulting you deliberately,' I went on, 'and instead of arguing rationally you're getting set to make me a head shorter.'

'Insulting *and* condescending,' she said. 'You obviously don't mix with people who carry swords.'

'I was demonstrating my proposition. That sword is a two-edged sword, so to speak.'

She let go of the hilt and crossed her arms. 'All right, convince me. I'm now rationally asking for an explanation of that tosh.'

'That sword is all sorts of awesome, but when it comes to ghost hunting I think it makes the people from your organisation see things too simply. See ghost, chop ghost. See ghost, chop ghost. See ghost—'

'Enough. You're labouring the point.'

I'd taken a chance. I'd prodded this spooky ninja warrior girl because ... Because why? Because I was jealous of her style and swagger? Because I honestly thought she was wrong? Because I thought she'd listen?

I clapped my hands together. 'Right, who's hungry? I don't know about you, but I'm always famished after dealing with a ghost.'

'You insult me, you insult my heritage, you insult my beliefs and now you want to go out to eat?'

'Or we could skip eating and go straight to dancing. How's your tango?'

You know that line, the one that when you've crossed it you've gone too far? Yeah, I've always had trouble seeing it early enough.

The sword was part-way out of the sheath. She stopped, thrust it back, took two steps and grabbed my earlobe. Really, really hard. She twisted, and it was like a squadron of wasps had decided to test their stings on the side of my head.

A jerk, and I fell to my knees.

'You think you're an expert on ghosts,' she said through clenched teeth.

'Well, I did ace that online "What Ghost is That?" quiz. Yipe!'

'I can tell you you're not,' she said. 'You've handled a few lesser ghosts, that's all. You haven't seen what they can do.'

'I don't know about ...'

She let me go and stepped away. I'd been leaning in her direction so hard that I fell over.

She stood in the doorway, CGI dramatic, with the coat swirl and all. 'I've seen what you can do, now, and my instructors were right when they said that the Marins have fled from the battle, that they've resigned themselves to confronting the most paltry of ghosts.'

'Paltry? Who are you calling chicken?'

'Go back to your books. Leave the real ghost hunting to those who understand the challenge.'

Then she was gone.

I dusted my hands, eased out of the Conservatory and locked it behind me. I headed through the gardens, kicking myself for being smart when serious was called for.

CHAPTER 5

Let's face it, she was right. There was a whole lot I didn't know about ghosts. In some ways, that's because there's a whole lot that *no one* knows about ghosts. Of course, that hasn't stopped all sorts of people in this ghost-hunting business from having opinions – which means there have been some slam-bang arguments over the centuries.

Three ghost-hunting theoreticians battle it out IN A CAGE! I'd pay good money to see that.

Try a question as simple as 'Where do ghosts go in the daytime?'. You'd think that would have been sorted out right at the beginning of time, when people first started being aware of ghosts. The standard answer, out there in ghost-hunting land, is that full-on sun is bad for their insubstantial being, so they slide onto the ghost plane, their natural resting place, and they emerge again at night. But, thanks to the Marin family archive, I've read a few dozen other opinions. Some say that ghosts don't go anywhere in the daytime – we just can't see them because of the sun. Others say that they hide in the darkest place they can find. My favourites, though, are those who use the favourite New Age buzz word and blurt 'quantum', even though they have no idea what it means.

And then there are puzzles; for example, why do some ghosts lapse into an inactive state, going dormant for years, decades, even centuries? One line of thinking says that these are ghosts who shun preying on people for one reason or another. Rather than continue their existence at the cost of pain and suffering, they just sort of go to sleep. Another bunch of eggheads say these ghosts haven't been able to leach enough energy from people and as a last-ditch effort at self-preservation go into a sort of hibernation. Yet another group of boffins have gone right out on a limb and insist that these inactive ghosts are in deliberate hiding, although from *what* no one knows. Other ghosts? Ghost hunters? Something else really ghastly? And that's a scary thought. What would make a ghost frightened?

And then there's the Big Question of Recent Times – why are there so many ghosts nowadays? Reports from Europe and the Americas suggest that the rate of ghost spawning is increasing. As usual, there are lots of opinions, ranging from the obvious ('More people now, more people dying, therefore more ghosts') to the thoughtful ('Perhaps death is becoming more traumatic as religion declines and people lack its comfort, thus spawning more ghosts') to the lunatic ('Maybe Death is getting grumpy at so many deaths and he's throwing some back at us') and everything in between.

Me? I admit I don't know everything about ghosts. I'm learning, and I just hope I'm learning fast enough.

I have picked up one thing, though, in my time. Just because people can't see ghosts doesn't mean that they're harmless. Give them half a chance and they'll latch onto you, unseen, whispering away underneath your notice, and they'll drain you in an effort to keep themselves around. Mostly, you won't die – although it depends on how healthy you are to begin with – but they'll definitely affect your quality of life. You'll get sick easier, you'll find things harder, you'll get less joy out of things you used to love. On top of that, the stronger ghosts will do you more harm, in nasty ways, just because you're real and they're not.

The next day, when Dad arrived at the bookshop, I was ready to give him my report. I wasn't going to mention much about Rani apart from the fact that she'd been there and she was interested in the Marin approach to ghosts.

I admit, her words had stung. I was ready enough to doubt the Marin family cause, but I wasn't ready to agree with strangers who doubted the Marin family cause. Were we just paddling around the edges of the ghost business? Were we really doing anything much to help the fight?

I moved on pretty quickly to the details of the ghost encounter itself.

This was an important part of the whole gig. Dad had a big notepad and jotted down the details of the location, the time, and the ghost itself. He drove particularly hard on details of clothing and then the memories that I'd experienced at the moment the ghost dissolved. He made me go over that four or five times, each time extracting a little more that I hadn't remembered first time around.

Since I'd started ghost hunting seriously, I'd added a couple of things to the project. In lots of ways, Dad was old-fashioned. Technology had never really made it onto his radar, since he didn't understand radar.

Joke.

One of the first things I'd done when we'd agreed to my ghost-hunting gap year was to add GPS coordinates to every ghost location I came across. Explaining GPS to Dad took some time, but he got it in the end, and actually became a fanatic for exact coordinates. He insisted that I buy a top-of-the-line unit to carry with me (Spectra Precision!) and he started insisting on the same level of accuracy from his network of informants.

And so we took ghost hunting into the twenty-first century with tiny baby steps.

He studied his notes when we finished. 'A straightforward enough encounter, Anton.'

'As straightforward as an encounter with a ghostly groundskeeper can be, I suppose.'

'And you're sure that not a hint of a name came to you?'

'Nothing. Sorry.'

He tapped his teeth with the fountain pen he'd been using. 'Still, I have enough to work with. Good.'

Dad stood, patted me absently on the shoulder, and wandered out of the kitchen. After a minute or two, I followed.

Dad was nowhere to be found.

I grinned. This was my favourite thing in the shop.

Now, just having a bookshop was pretty cool in itself. But having a bookshop with a secret room was even better. And best of all, this secret room was reached through a <Emperor Palpatine voice> Revolving Bookshelf Wall!

I got to the room – the last one before the kitchen, on the right – and heard the 'snick'. I ignored the sign over the door ('Philosophy, Eastern. Railways, European') and entered the room that was just like all the others in the shop. No windows, but a skylight let in murkiness enough. Bookcases lined the walls, and four rows of free-standing shelves filled the middle of the room.

I went to the far corner of the room. Being as tall as I am, finding the catch isn't hard. The shelf is so well balanced, thanks to Dad's clever carpentry, that all it takes after that is a gentle tug and a metre of bookshelf, hinged at the far end, opens enough to slip behind, into the secret room that holds the Marin archives.

In some ways, the secret room is the heart of the Marin ghost-hunting enterprise. It's long and skinny, running behind three whole rooms on the right-hand side of the shop. It's chock-full of tables, desks, filing cabinets and map cabinets (those sets of really slim drawers). Some of these cabinets are spanking-new space-age metal, probably titanium or beryllium or something, and some are wood milled from trees that suffered from dinosaur nudges. Oh, and there's everything in between.

Dad had a bunch of new index cards – we have a stationery supply – and sat at a very small desk. He began to turn his notes about my encounter last night into official Marin family records. When he was done, they'd become the latest addition to the archive, an archive that goes back to the early nineteenth century, documenting all the ghost encounters Marins have had.

On top of that, the room is also a repository for all the texts Dad has assembled about ghost hunting. There's a small publishing industry among ghost hunters for thoughts and observations about the business. Not blockbuster bestsellers, maybe, but they've always found a ready readership among those who are in the know.

I like to wander around this room, pulling out records and reading them at random. Sometimes when Dad's here, I'll ask him about his grandfather, or go even further back in family history. It depends on his mood what sort of answer I get.

The most complete records only go back to the 1940s, when Great-granddad came to Australia. He wasn't able to bring much from the old country, and this caused him much heartache.

Now, I'm not saying that Dad was over-compensating for the incompleteness of the old records by being extra, extra obsessive about the most recent ones, but someone else might. If I told them about it, which I wouldn't. Not straight away, anyway.

Lately, I've been going through the journal Aunt Tanja left behind. She was right out there on the edge of ghost studies, in thinking and experimenting. Dangerous stuff, but the more I read the more I want to read, you know? I just wish she was still around to help me with it all.

I left Dad happily recording away and went back to being bookshop guy. This meant sitting at the front counter and answering questions like 'Biographies of Jazz Musicians?' with questions like 'Continental or North American?' and 'Have you found our Lord and Saviour?' with 'Why? Have you lost him?'

Small things can make life worthwhile.

I gave Aunt Tanja's journal a rest, and started poring over some stuff about the Company of the Righteous that I borrowed from the archives. When it got too baffling, I plugged away at the spreadsheet. The whole paper-based system was an omnishambles, but I wasn't going to let it beat me.

When the telephone rang, I was so engrossed in rows and columns that I didn't grab it straight away. When it cut off, I guessed that Dad had grabbed the extension in the secret room.

It wasn't long after that when Dad emerged, looking thoughtful. That's not unusual for him, so I didn't give him a second glance. That is, until he came and stood behind me.

I looked over my shoulder. He wasn't looking at me. He was looking at the front door.

'That was the phone,' he said.

'Looked like a white station wagon to me.'

'Before,' he said without a trace of impatience, which started alarm bells ringing. Dad didn't have a great record of appreciating my sparkling wit. In fact, phrases like 'Can't you be serious for just a minute?' and 'Was that meant to be funny?' were on high rotation in the Marin household.

I'm undervalued, I tell you.

'When it rang,' he said without taking his eyes off the door and the world outside. 'That was the phone.'

'Uh huh.'

'It was Grender. He's late, but he's still on his way.'

'Ah. Oh.'

Now, I may have given the impression that seeing and hunting ghosts is a thing that solely belongs to certain families bound together by centuries-old traditions in this liminal world. Well, that's not the whole picture.

Think of ghost sensitivity as a spectrum. Me, I'm right up one end where I can see them, interact with them and, hem, hem, ease their passage to the next world. Rani and her like are up at this end of the scale, too.

Right down the other end is the bulk of humanity. You could hit them over the head with a soggy ghost and they wouldn't have a clue.

Now, between the bulk and the big cheese ghost-hunty types is a range of people with a range of abilities. Just like some families will throw up a redhead without any redheads on either side of the family, sometimes someone will be born who has a level of ghost sensitivity. Ah, the wonderful world of genetics!

Grender was one of Dad's most useful informants, and he was one of those with a tad more ability than most. He could see ghosts, dimly, and could sense when they were about. Of course, it helped that he hung around a lot in the sort of places ghosts congregated. Basements. Subways. Underground lairs. Graveyards. Which should give you a clue as to his sparkling personality.

'Grender has a sighting for us,' Dad said.

'And he wanted to share it with us through sheer generosity?'

'Cash,' Dad said. 'Half now, half when confirmed.'

'The usual, then.'

A shadow fell on the window. A few seconds later, it was followed by a roughly human shape that waddled to the door, hesitated, looked around, then squeezed into the shop.

Grender was as avocado-shaped as a human being could be without being declared a new species of fruit. He looked as if a massive three-metre-tall bald guy had been compressed until he was about a metre and a half tall, with most of the compression bulging out around waist level.

He wore a black jacket, black trousers, black knee boots, a chinstrap beard (black), sunglasses and a black beret.

There is such a thing as trying too hard in this quasi-occult world we work in.

'Marin,' Grender said after he'd closed the door and put his back to it. He grinned. His teeth were surprisingly small for such a bulky man. 'And Marin Junior.'

I leaned back in my chair. 'Hey, Grender, nice beret. You mug a poodle?'

Grender worked his mouth for a while but all he could come up with was 'Yeah, as if.'

Score: Anton, about a billion. Grender, zero.

Dad put his hand on my shoulder. 'What do you have for us, Grender?'

Grender shoved his hands into the pockets of his jacket. 'Wouldn't you like to know?'

He looked positively smug. One of his many business ventures must be paying off for him, in money or in chuckles. Grender's idea of chuckles, though, made me shudder a little.

'Yes, we would like to know,' Dad said. 'You did call us, after all.'

'Oh, yeah. Right.' Grender pulled a hand out of a pocket and consulted his phone. 'This is a hot one, okay?' He glanced right, then left. 'You interested in an asylum ghost? I've got information about an old one taking shape.'

'Asylum ghost?' Dad made a face. 'Some dreadful deaths in those asylums.'

'Yeah, you bet.' Grender was cocky. Grinning, he consulted a little black notebook while he held his phone in the crook of his arm, then clasped his hands behind his back and rocked on his heels. That cocky. 'You heard about Yarra Bend Asylum?'

I flipped my gaze up to the ceiling as I tried to see a map in front of me. I mean, I couldn't exactly nip into the secret room and grab a map while Grinning Grender was here, could I?

Right, Kew is over there, across the Yarra. Downstream is Clifton Hill and Collingwood. Too far. Back up a bit. Yarra Bend.

'Fairfield?' I asked.

'That's right. An asylum used to be there, near where the Merri Creek runs into the Yarra. Up from the golf course, down from the TAFE.'

'Right where the freeway goes through,' Dad murmured.

'Pretty much.' Grender put his phone away. 'I heard there's a Watcher there. Normally, I'd go and check it out first but I thought you might like it quick smart, right?'

I nearly groaned. Watchers are pretty common, for ghosts. They rarely pester people and often go unnoticed, even by super-sharp pros like us. They haunt places in the most ghostly sort of way, almost invisible, hardly pressing themselves on the fabric of this world, which means they don't need a lot of life to stick around.

Small stuff. Rani's words came back to me and made me wish Grender had brought us a Growler, or a Thug, maybe. Something more sinister, more challenging.

Dad's eyes went distant. 'I'll have to check the records, but I don't think anything's been seen in that vicinity for decades.'

'No idea about that,' Grender said. 'All I know is I've found one, and it's an earner for me.'

He held out his hand.

'You're sure about this?' Dad said.

'You doubt me?' Grender spread a hand on his chest. It left plenty of chest uncovered. 'I have a reputation to uphold.'

I snorted at that. I had suspicions that these days Grender subcontracted all his ghost spotting to lesser talents, no doubt skimming off the fat part of the money for himself.

Dad paid Grender after a bit of haggling. Grender handed over a scrap of paper with the location on it, then left.

'He's had good information in the past,' Dad said before I could express any doubts.

'Maybe, but remember that Mocker he sold us a couple of months ago? The one near Spotswood station? Turned out to be a bust but he claimed someone must have got in before us?'

'So he isn't one hundred per cent trustworthy,' Dad said. 'Still, you should investigate tonight.'

'Sure. Investigate, and scratch one Watcher.' I flexed my shoulders. 'It's a big night coming up for Anton Marin, Ghost Hunter.'

'Wear something warm.'

'Will do.'

I'd only been home for a few minutes and was preparing for my sleep, when Bec came over.

She barged straight in, a new board game in her hands. 'Telestrations,' she said. 'You'll love it.'

Bec is the queen of board games. We've spent hours and hours absorbed in them at my place, her place, on holidays, when it's raining, when it's not. Even though she's always getting me to play new ones she's picked up – I don't think I'll ever get over my first game of Cards Against Humanity – we often go back to old favourites, like Catan, just for nostalgia's sake.

'No,' I mumbled. 'Not a game. Not now.'

'Good,' she said. 'I won't need it as an excuse to talk to you about stuff that's been on my mind.'

'Bec. Sorry. Don't get me wrong, but I have to go to—'

She kept marching down the hall, leaving me at the door, and kept talking as if I was trailing behind her, which I was forced to do by the momentum of her entrance.

'This whole ghost thing is pretty interesting,' she was saying. 'It could open up entire new areas of science.'

'Well, I'm not sure if it is science,' I said.

'Everything is science,' she said. 'If you look hard enough.'

'Well, yeah, maybe. Is that the time?'

Bec reached the kitchen and went straight for the tea-making facilities. We had lots of them. She'd made sure of that.

I'm not a tea drinker. I have nothing against tea, mind, apart from it tasting like a bunch of wet leaves, but I'm quite happy to have it around, instead of in a special tea-drinking bunker some distance from any inhabited area, as many sensible people have suggested.

The result of this is that Bec, like many tea drinkers, has built up a huge stock of boxes, sachets, packets and bottles that hold the makings of a cup of tea. Despite the fact that some of these vegetative conglomerations have nary a trace of actual tea, she is quite happy to swap from one to the other, according to mood.

She saw my face while she was adjusting the water level in the kettle. 'The trouble with you, Anton, is that you laugh at anything you don't appreciate.'

'That is so true,' I said. 'I also laugh at lots of things I appreciate.'

'So,' she said, sitting down with her concoction du jour and interrupting my almighty yawn. 'I thought I'd help you out with your ghost hunting.'

I sat opposite her, put my elbows on the table and rested my head in my hands. 'I'm not sure that's a good idea. Wait – I actually know it's *not* a good idea.'

'And why not?'

'It's dangerous, for a start. Actually, that's for a finish, as well. Ghost hunting is dangerous.'

'I've gathered that. Some of the stories you tell ...'

Well, maybe I'd exaggerated when re-telling some of the stories Dad had told me, but only a little. Still, it wouldn't hurt if it kept Bec at a distance from ghosts.

'You know that ghosts want to latch onto people and draw off any vitality they can.'

'It's such an old-fashioned word, "vitality".'

'It's what the books use. I guess you could substitute "essence" or "soul" or "cosmic energy". The result's the same.'

'I know – lethargy, weakness, increased susceptibility to disease, headaches, skin rashes, ringing in the ears.'

'And stuff that's even harder to pin down, like paranoia, irrationality, vague feelings of being unwell. People can die from a ghost attachment, though most don't.'

'So that's why I thought I could help out in a back-room capacity.'

'Who's the what?'

'I'm going to work out the best way to digitise your family's record-keeping and archives. That stuff's too valuable to leave lying around on paper.'

'Bad idea.'

'Explain.'

I ran both hands through my hair. I needed to get some sleep, but I also needed to sort this out with Bec. 'One: Dad won't let you touch his precious records and archives. Two: there's so much there that it'll take you forever. Three: some of the records are likely to drive you insane.'

'Oh. Magic stuff that'll eat my brain?'

'No. Just really bad handwriting. Awful. Like a drunk spider fell in an inkwell and staggered across the cards.'

'I can cope.'

'How?'

'How does anything monumental get done? By doing it a little bit at a time.'

'When?'

'I'll fit it in. I'll make it turquoise on my timetable.'

'Aargh.'

Bec's time management was legendary. Her schedules were things of beauty. Her diary was god-like. Her timetables used colours that would fall outside a Pantone chart.

'And how is uni working out for you?' I asked.

'I love it. I'm sciencing all over the place with other people who are doing the same thing. Heaven.'

'Must keep you busy.'

'That's why the timetable.' She frowned. 'I'm thinking of moving out, though, getting a place of my own.'

'Why? Can't be to save travel time.'

'Independence. Growing up. Rite of passage. A chance to have houseplants of my own.'

'And so the world changes,' I intoned.

'In little ways and big ways.'

'With all this, you still want to organise our archives?'

'It should make your job more efficient, and it should help your dad.' She sipped from her mug. It had a picture of a bunny on it. 'It'll make things easier for him. He'll be able to cross-reference, make connections, construct graphs.'

'Your eye is starting to glow.' I had to be straight. It was Bec I was talking to, after all, and we told each other stuff. 'Look, you know that Leon hates computers. And he doesn't understand them. Hatred and lack of understanding. Put them together and that's how wars start.'

'Leave him to me. I can handle Leon.'

I sighed. 'Go ahead. No skin off my nose. I'm going to bed.'

'You're being unusually evasive,' Bec said. 'It's that girl, isn't it?'

'What? Who? Rani?'

'If I take that last one as a question, that's three questions in a row. Nice going. I must have hit a sore spot.'

'No sore spot here. I checked.'

'So what's going on between you and hot sword-toting babe?'

I sniffed. 'That's a horribly gendered description.'

66

'So what's going on between you and strong female role-model babe?'

'Better. Nothing.'

'Nothing? What, did she suss you out that quickly?'

'What? Cut it out, this is purely professional.' I tried as hard as I could to look dignified. 'Not that it's any of your business, but we decided that our approaches to ghost hunting were incompatible.'

'You came on too strong, hey? Not strong enough? You offered to buy her a hamburger and she turned out to be a vegan?'

'She thinks all ghosts are dangerous and need to be hacked to pieces upon sight, and I don't.'

'A basic incompatibility. Don't worry about it. Great relationships have been built on less.'

'What is this, Bec's Romantic Advice?'

'You could do worse.'

'Than her, or your advice?'

'Both.'

'I can't handle this now,' I mumbled. 'I need to get some sleep before I start to hallucinate.'

'Oh.' Bec hesitated and, tired though I was, I frowned. Bec was rarely hesitant. She was assertive, certain, sometimes blunt, but rarely hesitant.

'Something's bothering you,' I said. 'Spit it out.'

She let out a long breath. 'You're right. Something has been nagging at me for ages, and now is a good time to get it out in the open.' She put her fists on her hips. 'What exactly *are* ghosts?'

Pow. 'Are you sure you don't want to start with an easy one? I mean, this is one of the biggies in ghost-hunting circles.'

'Since I'm coming on board as part of Marin Ghost-hunting Enterprises, I figure I need to know stuff like this.'

That sat me back a bit. 'Yeah, you're right. And I know that you have a habit of being right, so you don't have to tell me again.'

'Just as long as you don't forget.'

I linked my hands behind my head. 'So, you want the official version or the Anton version?'

'There's an official version?'

'There are about a hundred different official versions.'

'And the Anton version?'

'Is my take on the hundred different official versions.'

'Hit me with it, then.'

'Okay.' I leaned forward. 'Have you ever tried to do a scan, or make a photocopy, but you accidentally moved the document while it was happening?'

'Sure. It went all weird and smeary.'

'But you could recognise that it was a copy of the original.'

'Well, if I looked at it hard enough.'

'That's ghosts. They're created at the moment of death – some deaths – and they're like a bad copy of the original.'

'They're not us?' Bec asked a small un-Bec voice.

'No,' I said. 'And let's sort this out now. Ghosts aren't us. They're independent creatures that are based on us. Badly.'

'And that's why they retain some memories?'

'Fractured, fuzzy, unreliable memories.'

She chewed this over for a while. Three sips of tea, it took, and a couple of dozen frowns. 'This prompts more questions than it answers, you know.'

'I know, but in my state, I think I've done pretty well on this one. Enough for now.'

'Okay.' She looked at me. 'Thanks.'

'Don't mention it.'

She finished her tea. She reached around and put the mug on the sink drainer. 'Lemons. I need some lemons.'

'A top-secret science experiment?'

'I'm making lemon delicious pudding.'

'Plenty on the tree out the back. Help yourself.'

'I usually do. I just thought I'd ask this time.' She gave me a look. 'You don't have one?'

I smacked myself in the forehead. Forgetting was a sign of how tired I was. 'Okay, try this one. What's a printer's devil?'

'Give up.'

'A printer's devil, in the old days, was an apprentice to a printer, a youngster who used to mix the big tubs of ink, run messages, that sort of thing.'

'Good enough. Just wait, though, I've got a special for you next time.'

'Good. Great. Whatever. Just make sure the door's locked behind you when you leave.'

CHAPTER 6

That night, I had to catch a bus and face a fair stretch of walking to get to the area of Grender's tip-off. One does not simply walk to Yarra Bend, after all. A licence and a car was on the drawing board, but they were only rough sketch outlines.

I don't mind the night, which is lucky for a ghost hunter. But add the dark to some of the out-of-the-way places I have to visit and it's enough to make wariness a way of life.

It was cold enough that I'd worn my old grey greatcoat, an ex-army number complete with brass buttons, that I'd found at a school fete. It was heavy but like +5 magic armour against wind. I had gloves and a scarf, too, over an old black suit jacket with extra-wide lapels that was my current fave. It was hard to get my backpack on over the top, but I was used to it.

Hat? A woollen footy beanie Bec had given me as part of her stealth campaign to make sure I stuck with her team. Good colours.

No rain was forecast, which was a good thing. Ghost hunting in the wet was a pain. I'd done it, and I'd learned that the non-solidity of ghosts was never more obvious than when cold rain dripped down the back of my neck but passed right through a moaning spectre. There weren't many benefits of being a ghost, but not being bothered by rain was one of them, I expect.

The solid mass of cloud overhead was low, which meant it caught the lights of the city, turning the greys orange and yellow. It was a little nauseating, to tell you the truth; sort of like looking at the innards of a giant animal.

After getting off the bus, I had to walk down Yarra Bend Road towards the freeway. The area is a funny bit of open space, almost wilderness on one side and the NMIT campus and psychiatric hospital on the other side.

Finding the location of Grender's ghost was as easy as he'd claimed.

The pillar was standing just off the road, right on the edge of the huge cutting of the freeway. It was the last remnant of the original asylum, a part of the main gate to the facility, and was now a lonely prop for a brass plaque that very few people read, most likely.

Grender said that the pillar was the site of the ghost's manifestation.

I took off my pack, found myself a nearby tree, and sat against it while I waited.

It was a weird sort of double state I found myself in. On one side, I could imagine I was in bushland, with plenty of young gum trees, the smell of fallen leaves, the sound of foliage shifting and moving in the irregular breeze. On the other hand, the nearby Eastern Freeway meant I was fully aware that the city had a claim to this part of the world.

Finally, my pendant started humming. I had that itchy, prickly feeling and saw the ghost making an appearance.

The Watcher faded into existence, a bit patchily, and I had to strain to see it. It wore old, old clothes – a long, grey, high-necked dress with a tiny lace collar. Round spectacles. Bare feet hovering just above the ground. It had one hand on the pillar, anchoring it there.

I stood and brushed myself off, moving slowly. The Watcher bobbed there, waiting as she must have done for more than a hundred years, in front of what had once been a major asylum full of unhappy souls.

As I approached, I kept up a soothing monotone. 'It's okay. Nothing to worry about. I'm not here to hurt you. It's okay.'

I guess some people would have called it a ghastly stare, but all I saw was a lost and lonely thing that was here long past her due. I got the tiniest touch of fear, but no chilling horror. Whatever death had spawned this ghost was long ago and probably unremembered.

I held up my hands, palm outwards. 'Time to go.'

As gently as I could, I pressed forward, right into the Watcher's chest. She didn't flinch, didn't recoil. Instead, she folded her shoulders inwards, as if welcoming what I was doing.

I nodded, then twisted, and the Watcher vanished. I staggered as I was buffeted by visions of a large kitchen, heat and steam that became an even larger laundry full of the same. Then, last of all, startling and unexpected, a parrot on a windowsill. A galah, all pink and grey and perky. Then there was nothing.

'Whoa.' I sagged against the pillar and tried to stop my knees from trembling. A successful easing, but it still took it out of me.

I rubbed my hands together, then my face. My stomach growled. 'Food,' I muttered aloud. 'I need food.'

Another ghost appeared.

I didn't have to strain my eyes to see this one because it snapped into existence like a searchlight coming on. And it had so much presence I could barely see the pillar through it. It was wild, with floating hair that moved as if it was underwater, and staring, flashing eyes. When it drifted against the pillar I heard it rasp against the stone.

Zowie. I had a Rogue on my hands. A freaking Rogue. Terror planted a flag inside me and said, 'I claim this territory in the name of Utter and Outright Fear!'

Despite what I may have said – and what Ms Rani Cross might have said – no ghosts are exactly a walk in the park. There's the fear, for a start. Even if you know what they're doing, the fear they create usually gets at you. You find yourself sweating, maybe trembling, and jumping at noises.

Then there's the danger of them attaching themselves. Civilians get it bad enough, and they can't see the awful thing that's doing the attaching. Ghost hunters can, and it makes it double-plus awful.

And, of course, there's the physical danger. The more solid the ghost, the more hurt it can do.

I'd heard about Rogues – tall tales from Aunt Tanja – and read about them too. I knew that they were a whole different kettle of horrific. They're ghosts pumped up on steroids, with enough solidity – when they choose it – to do plenty of damage.

This Rogue was tall and he had shoulders like two bags of cement. He was wearing an all-over apron sort of thing, stained white trousers and a close-fitting white cloth cap. Had he been spawned by an orderly? A doctor?

He flew straight for me, his heels a few centimetres above the ground, his toes making furrows, hands extended like claws.

Standard-issue ghosts want to latch onto people. Rogues, however, are more ambitious. After they maul you, physically, they want to possess you. Their greatest desire, and it's a burning, hungry need, is to merge with us and take us over. That way they have an ongoing existence of a solid and fleshly kind, which is like the ghost equivalent of nuts *and* sprinkles.

Oh, and Rogues are insane, too, which doesn't add any attractiveness points.

The only good thing about Rogues is that they are rare, and that they're even more closely bound to a location than an ordinary ghost. That's why running is a useful tactic with Rogues. You hope that it's like running from a guard dog with a very strong chain. Get to the end of the chain and it's sore neck time, poochie.

That's the theory, anyway. With a Rogue you can't take a squiz at the chain around its neck and get an estimate of how far you have to run before it's brought up short.

At first, I just ran, heading back down the road away from the pillar. The trouble is, that went right against the Marin family grain. Leaving the Rogue around wasn't an option. It had to be dumb luck that no one had stumbled on it. The remoteness, the relative isolation of the location must have helped, but sooner or later someone would come close enough while the thing was manifesting and then it'd be bloody mess time. Or, even worse, possession time.

I had to do something.

I took a quick look over my shoulder and the Rogue was still after me. I slewed sideways off the road, across the path and into the trees. I kept going, trying not to trip in the dark and hoping to find the end of Rogue Boy's home range.

It didn't help that the apparition made a hideous whistling through his teeth, like drawing a knife across a blackboard.

Solid worked both ways, of course. If he could claw and bite me, that meant I could return the favour. Not clawing and biting, of course, but something a bit more stylish, a bit more intelligent, a bit more like something a panicked and skinny eighteen-year-old could manage in the dark.

I sorted through the options as I wove around a tree that was determined to get in my way. I could trip him, then jump on his back and pummel his skull with my fists. I could scoop up a nice heavy branch and smash his face in. I could flick up a rock with my heel so that it caught the

Rogue right in the gut. I could jump over a park bench, roll, come to my feet and give him such an uppercut that he'd be no good for anything.

In my dreams. Actual combat isn't my strength. I work in other, more subtle and less bruising, ways.

Out of the corner of my eye, I saw someone standing in the shadows of a clump of tall gum trees just off the bike path I was now hurtling along. A bad situation was getting worse. Even if I got away, the Rogue had a civilian victim nice and handy.

The whistling ghost noise behind me changed abruptly, becoming more of a high-pitched scream. If a screechy noise can sound triumphant, this one did, probably at the prospect of two warm and live humans to wreak its revenge on. Believe me, Rogues like nothing better than a good wreaking.

I skidded to a halt. The Rogue had swung around towards where the civilian was. I had to make it centre on me so the civilian would have a chance to escape. At my expense, but I had a few tricks up my sleeve.

I could see him, for one, and I could taunt him, for two.

'Hey,' I yelled to his back. 'Big bad and crazy! This way! Come on, try tangling with someone your own size!'

My gestures were obscene. I hoped they'd translate down the years.

Something worked, because he whirled around and I had to swallow the grapefruit-sized lump of fear in my throat. From the feral fury on the thing's face, I'd succeeded a little too well. He sped at me.

Then he split himself in half, from head to groin, and flung both sides of himself to the ground where they bounced and raised a little dust.

At least, that's what it looked like. When Rani Cross stepped forward she had her sword raised in a salute. 'You see, Anton,' she said as she marched past the demi-Rogues on the ground, 'ghosts *are* dangerous.'

I swallowed. 'Rogue!'

She spun around, blindingly fast, but the pieces'o'Rogue had already righted themselves and were well on the way to stitching together.

I weaved around Rani and, before the Rogue could attack, ploughed into him with my hands outstretched.

I gasped at the greasy cotton-wool feel as my hands sunk into his substance, and he screeched. I'd enjoyed the evening breakfast of toast and orange marmalade I'd had before setting out, but not so much that I wanted to taste it again, coming up this time. I swallowed hard while I hung on.

He was big, as I'd said, and my hands were wrist-deep in his chest, something that was bound to annoy anyone, alive or dead. He twisted and hissed, and his fists thumped on my back. I kept my head down as he spun around and around crazily, with my chin tucked in so he couldn't get at my throat or face. That meant I had my nose against his clammy substance. He smelled vile, sour and sickening, like whatever the heck that months-old thing was you found right up the back of the fridge.

Rani flashed into sight. She had her sword raised. 'No!' I squawked as the Rogue swung me past her. 'Don't! I've got this!'

And, the next second, I had. I squeezed, twisted and the ghost dissolved.

Centrifugal force didn't, though. I was flung through the air and would have kept going for forty or fifty metres, easily, if a tree hadn't intervened.

Trunk. Much trunk. So ow.

I didn't have that convenient blackout, though, so I felt every bruise and every scrape as I lay there on top of twigs and little rocks and other nature stuff that's specially designed to be uncomfortable.

Rani knelt beside me. 'Are you all right?'

'I'm fine,' I gasped. 'Nothing that major surgery and a lengthy convalescence won't fix.'

She produced a light and shone it in my eyes. 'I'll get you to a hospital.'

I tried sitting up, and it taught me how to use stupid exclamations instead of punctuation. 'Don't worry *ack* It's fine *owowow* Just give me a hand *nggg* Not there *aiee!*'

Then I was sitting upright and everything was okay, if a little wobbly. Rani was steadying me with a hand on my shoulder.

'You've never seen a Rogue before, have you?' I asked her.

'Rogue?'

'Thought so. Otherwise you wouldn't have stopped chopping.'

'Oh. I thought ...'

'Yeah. With most ghosts, that sort of vertical bisection would be more than enough to destroy their integrity. Rogues are a bit tougher than that.'

Her mouth turned down. 'My sword is useless against those things?'

'Nope. If you'd kept slicing, that would have done the trick. Itty bitty pieces. No coming back from that.'

'But you stopped me.'

'Ah, yeah, I did that.'

'Why? I could have handled it.'

'I'm sure. You're a whiz with that blade. I reckon you could whip up a truckload of sushi with it, stat.'

'But you didn't want me to destroy the thing, even though it was going to hurt you.'

'Oh, geez. Help me up, will you?'

Getting walking was a whole new adventure in pain, but it showed me that nothing was really serious. Hurty, but not serious.

I stumbled and Rani caught me. 'You work out, right?' I asked.

'You know the phrase "None of your business"?'

'Right. Sorry. But seriously, you ever think of writing a book, *Sword Fighting Your Way to Fitness*?'

She stepped away and poked me in the chest. 'You're babbling. Pull yourself together.'

'Will do. Apologies. Out of line, there.' I slapped at my jeans and coat. 'You want to tell me how you turned up here?'

'I followed you from your home.'

'And arrived just in time to stop me taking care of things?'

'Taking care of things? You were making a right cock-up of the situation. I'll bet you hadn't even reconnoitred the terrain.'

'Look, I don't want to seem ungrateful ...'

'Hah! You should be down on your knees thanking me!'

'That's a bit rich.'

'All right. A bow and some forelock tugging will do.'

'None of your outdated class distinctions here. This is Australia.'

'Killed by a ghost in Australia is the same as killed by a ghost anywhere else, I imagine.'

'You've got a point there.' I stuck my hands in the pockets of my coat. 'On another point, why were you lurking outside my home?'

'Others lurk. I remain unseen.'

'What for? Why did you want to follow me? Looking for a few pointers?'

'Let's just say I'm curious about your approach.' She walked off a little. 'Not that I'm questioning the way of the Company of the Righteous, you understand?'

'Really?' I unslung my backpack and fumbled for the GPS. I logged the coordinates of our encounter. 'I think everyone should question just about anything. Thoughtless obedience is the way to dangerous territory. If you question it, then agree, that's another matter.'

'And that's almost serious.'

'Hey, I can do serious. Given enough time and a good run-up.' I wrapped my coat around me and blew on my hands to warm them. 'I did a bit of research about your social club. It's been mighty effective.'

'We are strong.'

'Say it loud and say it proud. Cutting down ghosts wherever you find them.'

Bam. The world exploded. Bells rang inside my skull. Little lights danced in front of my eyes. I stared at her. 'You hit me!'

'I slapped you, and you deserved it. Open hand, side of the head.'

'What for?'

'I'd had enough of your rubbish, that's what for. The Company keeps people safe.'

'I don't doubt that. But at what cost?'

She narrowed her eyes and nearly became frost-covered. I took a step back. 'I've seen too many friends' names added to our honour boards not to know about cost,' she said.

'Oh.'

'The Company fallen are never forgotten.'

'Sounds like a quality organisation.'

She prodded me in the chest with a finger, again. 'At least it teaches us not to put ourselves in unnecessary danger. At least it teaches us to wield appropriate weapons. At least it teaches us that loyalty means having someone to watch your back.'

I rubbed my bruised sternum. 'So what are you doing out here in Australia all alone?'

'I asked for this assignment. It's a chance to make a name for myself. If I can manage this place effectively, I can look for a more challenging assignment in the future.'

'Uh huh. So how's it going for you?'

'I can't say, just yet. I'm still not sure about some of the people I've met. They could be a help or they could be a hindrance.'

Okay. 'Look, sorry. I didn't mean to insult the Company, you know, before.'

'Before I slapped you?'

'Yeah, then.' I rubbed my ear. 'I maybe went a bit too far.'

'You did.'

'So promise me you won't hit me again?'

'Promise me you won't say or do anything stupid again?'

'Fair point. Want a cup of coffee?'

CHAPTER 7

Rani liked coffee, but she also liked tea. It takes all types, I guess.

We'd found a bar in Clifton Hill that was open. Rani had something called rooibos, that sounded as if it was totally made up. I had a short black coffee because I really needed a pick-me-up.

We found a corner booth. The music was low and old, just right for talking. The decor was a mixture of retro and tacky, with old record covers stuck to the walls and ceiling, and posters advertising dances at the San Remo Ballroom.

Rani held up her cup of tea. 'My view of the world of ghosts and ghost hunting comes from my training.'

'Well, in a way, that's the same for me.'

'My tutors were very firm, though, in letting us know that the Company way was the only way.'

'You had tutors? I just had my family.'

'Early on, I had to go to Saturday morning classes. Evenings, as well, as I got older, and then it was full-time at the academy.'

'They sound like they're organised.'

'We have to be, with the threat we're facing.'

'I know about the threat.'

'The way you go about things? I doubt it. Otherwise you'd be more efficient.'

'Efficient? Is that what you call your approach?'

'We dispatch ghosts cleanly, with minimal impact on the civilian world.'

'You're merciless.'

'You're sloppy.'

We stared – glared? – at each other for a while. 'And we're now calling each other names.' I took a sip of my coffee. Espresso, nice and strong.

She sat back in her chair. 'So it would seem.'

'Look, I'm sorry. It's just that I'm not used to having other ghost hunters around. All I've had, lately, has been my dad, and he's not one of us.'

'Oh?'

'He knows a lot about ghosts. He just can't see them.'

'That's sad. And there's no one else?'

'No one I'd trust.'

'There's no shortage of ghost hunters around Company headquarters.'

'Lots of competition?'

'We're supposed to be supportive and collegial.' She shrugged. 'But people are people. We have rivalries, tension, jockeying for plum assignments.'

'This is a plum assignment?'

'Hardly. I'm afraid that the Company views this part of the world as a quiet and peaceful backwater.'

I snorted at that. 'It must have sent you here for a reason, though.'

That got me a sharp look. 'It didn't send me. I volunteered. I see it as a chance to gain experience those at home won't have.'

'Battling away out here by yourself will look good on your CV?'

A small smile. 'Something like that.'

I toyed with my coffee spoon. I don't take sugar, but I like playing around with a spoon. 'So you're going to be around for a while.'

'My posting is an indefinite one.'

I fumble-tapped the spoon on the saucer. 'And after tonight, you still want to learn about the Marin approach to ghosts?'

'I'm thinking of writing a paper on the Marin approach.'

'Another CV winner?'

'No one back at headquarters will be able to produce anything like it.'

'You sound ambitious.'

'If something's worth doing, it's worth doing well.'

'You are ambitious.'

'I am. And I'm using you to further my ambitions. And your father, and all the Marins. In a businesslike way, of course. Think of me as an Attenborough, curious about a new species in an exotic location.'

'Okay. Glad you're up front about it.'

'Don't be like that. I don't see any harm in being direct.'

'I'm just trying to work out if I'm offended at being used like this.'

'If one knows that one is being used and one agrees, then what's the harm?'

'You're on such shaky ethical ground there, I'm surprised you're still standing.' I shrugged. 'Okay, what do I get out of this?'

'The respect of a fellow ghost hunter? No? What about having someone to talk to who knows what you're going through?'

'The challenges of ghost hunting?'

'That and the challenges of being part of a centuries-old tradition that is often utterly terrifying and sometimes incredibly frustrating.'

That sounded mighty appealing. Dad and Bec were good, but there was no way they could know what it was like to come face to face with a ghost and then ease its passage. 'Deal.'

'Excellent. So let's continue our association, as long as we can be professional about it.'

'Agreed. No more name calling.'

'Disagreements, certainly, but no name calling.' She finished her tea. 'Unless it's warranted.'

'First thing is you should talk to my dad. He's the expert on ghost hunting from a Marin family point of view.'

'Your father would do that?'

'Get him started and you won't be able to shut him up.'

CHAPTER 8

Rani was in the secret room when I hurried into the bookshop. She and Dad were hunched over the little desk and a great big book that overhung it. 'Family,' I said, pointing at her. 'You didn't tell me anything about your family.'

Dad looked up from the great big book. 'Hello, Anton. Would you like to go outside and try coming back in again, less rudely this time?'

'Oh. Right.'

I turned on my heel, went out the door, waited ten seconds and re-entered.

I bowed, deeply, ignoring the aches and pains from last night's adventure, and straightened. 'Good morrow, Father, I hope you are well. My, that is a sprightly tartan waistcoat you're wearing. Can I fetch you something to soothe your ancient bones? And Rani, it is a pleasure to see you on this delightful day. I trust that all is splendid with you?'

Dad shook his head. 'From one extreme to the other, as always.'

Rani nodded, guardedly. 'Hello, Anton.'

'Rani has been asking about our family history.' Dad grinned, and I was pleased.

You see, Dad was in a bad way after Mum left. I was only ten, and it hit me hard too. I mean, she just disappeared. Here one day, not here the next. I know that ten-year-olds aren't the most perceptive when it comes to grown-ups, but I remember how she cried a lot after Carl died, and how some days she wouldn't even get out of bed and that's when I cried for her. When she went she left a hole in my heart the size of my fist. I'd papered it over, but it was still there.

So seeing Dad all perky like this was great. If sharing some Marin ghost-hunting tales made his day, I wasn't going to complain.

'I bought you some tea, Rani.' I fumbled in my pack. 'You like Earl Grey?'

'Thank you, Anton, but Leon already went out for some.'

'I don't know why we don't have any,' Dad said. 'Was it because you threw it all out, Anton?'

Mum was a tea drinker, but I didn't want to think about that right now.

'Must've been a tea thief,' I said. 'Too many of them around here.'

Dad looked at me, then glanced at Rani. 'I think I might have a useful book on the history of societies that have split from your Company of the Righteous, Rani. Let me get it.'

As soon as Dad left, Rani folded her arms. 'I can't remember a thing about them.'

'I'm sorry?'

'You wanted to know about my family. My parents died. I was adopted after they were killed.'

'Oh. And you can't remember them because you were little when they died?'

'It's more than that. I was only seven when it happened, but when you join the Company of the Righteous, you undergo an initiation ceremony that confers extra strength and speed.'

'Cool magic. So?'

'The magic comes at a cost. You give up part of your memory. Everything I ever knew about my parents is gone.'

I rocked back, even though she said it calmly, without a hint of anger. Okay, so the Company of the Righteous was all military toughness, but that was cruel. Magic speed and strength were pretty handy, but at that price?

Everything we've done, everything we've encountered, the people we've loved and the people we've hated, they all combine to shape us into what we are today. If you lose a chunk of your memory, you lose a chunk of who you are.

That's some price to pay.

'You know they were killed, though,' I said carefully.

'I've been told about them, tiny snippets, and I've pieced together more.' She sighed. 'When I was about twelve, a few years after I realised that not everyone could see ghosts and learned to keep quiet about them, a scary woman knocked on our door in London. She had a briefcase full of documents. She laid it all out for my parents. Foster parents. She had what she called my lineage right there on the page. My real parents she called the Honoured Fallen.'

'How'd your foster parents take it?'

'They were shocked. Upset. Angry. What you'd expect when a shadowy stranger comes with a hocus-pocus story like that. Then the Company woman told them about the money.'

'She offered your foster parents money if the Company could have you?'

'Not have me, not entirely. I'd live at home, have a normal life, but I'd be trained by Company tutors and instructors until I was old enough to enter the academy. I'd be inducted into the ranks of the Company to battle the ghost scourge and receive a stipend as well. And in return, the Company would take care of them. Find them jobs and they'd get a fat monthly payment.'

'And they took it.'

'They did, but only because the alternative horrified them.'

'Oh. This was an ultimatum, not an offer?'

'If my foster parents didn't agree, the Company would kidnap me and they'd never see me again.'

'Way to go with the positive recruitment talk.'

Her eyes were bleak. 'So I joined and gave up everything I ever knew about my parents.'

'Wow.'

Rani had clasped her hands, and she was squeezing so tightly the knuckles were white. 'Have you ever been so angry and so sad all at the same time and you had to keep it inside because you knew that talking to anyone about it would be a bad idea?'

I had half a notion, but this wasn't about me. I shook my head.

'The trouble was that I knew that memories of my parents were missing, but I didn't know what those memories were,' she said.

'It would have been kinder if they'd covered up that hole or something.'

'I don't know if they couldn't or they didn't think it was important.'

'That whole "You have no past once you join this organisation" is so Foreign Legion.'

'Some of my colleagues took it as a badge of honour. They belonged to the Company, body and soul.'

'And you?'

'I threw myself into my studies, and, every opportunity I got, I took my anger out on my tutors and sparring partners.'

'This was a bad thing?' I ventured.

'Good and bad. I quickly gained a reputation for my combat skills. Bad because I set high standards for myself and anyone who didn't match them felt my scorn.'

'That doesn't sound like a happy time, or a happy place.'

'I didn't have many friends.' She weighed up her next words for some time before continuing. 'I'll tell you this now. The Company isn't perfect. It has flaws. It could be improved. But I've come to accept that it suits me and it suits my talents. I want to be the best and bit by bit I've channelled my anger and used it to drive me on.'

'Again, wow.' I rubbed my chin. 'And requesting this Melbourne assignment is part of your plan to get to the top?'

She winced a little as she unclasped her hands. 'I never said that career planning was my strength.'

'So you're totally on board as a sword-wielding fanatic?'

'I think you'll find it's rather more complicated than that.'

'That should be my life motto: "I think you'll find it's more complicated than that." I might get it put on a T-shirt. Backwards, so I can read it in the mirror.'

'I'd appreciate one, as well, while you're at it.'

'Did you tell Dad about last night?' I asked.

'He wanted to know all about it, but we didn't get far.'

'He'll be keen to get my take on it. Who do you report to?'

'Report? No one. Oh, I have contacts for anything that goes utterly pear-shaped, but Company field agents are pretty much solo operatives. We meet once a year, but that's usually for a pep talk, a state-of-play sort of thing. Even trainees attend.'

'What, you rally at the old clubhouse, swap stories about the ghosts you've slaughtered?'

'There's some of that,' she admitted. 'We have a lot of older men in the Company. They seem to find me a novelty. Sometimes they even let me talk.'

I could see them clustering around, trying to impress her with their deeds, letting her get a word in now and then as they tried to outdo each other.

Males. Sometimes I feel embarrassed at being on the same team.

'Dad keeps meticulous records of our encounters,' I told her. 'They add to the family archive.'

'So you've got a database of Melbourne ghost encounters going back how far?'

'Just after the Second World War. Late forties. And we've got family stuff that goes back further.'

'Brilliant.'

'But calling it a database would be a bit of a stretch.'

'Can I see it?'

'Commercial in confidence.'

'What?'

'You're a competitor, aren't you? A rival firm?' I crossed my arms. 'Sorry, that sort of stuff is valuable intellectual property. The Coke people wouldn't just let the Pepsi people see their factory workings, would they?'

'They would if they were combining forces.'

Dad came back then, and I wasn't sure if it was good timing or bad. 'Dad, Rani wants me to let her come ghost hunting with me. Can I? Can I, please? I promise to be good.'

'I apologise,' Dad said to Rani. 'He gets like this sometimes.'

'I've noticed, Mr Marin,' she replied.

'Leon.'

'He is useful, though, Leon,' she said.

'Useful,' I said to no one in particular. 'Such praise. All my life I dreamed of being useful, and I've finally got there. It looks like I can retire now.'

'He can be,' Dad said to Rani. 'When he's at his best.'

'I'm hoping he can show me the Marin way of dealing with ghosts,' Rani said. 'I'm interested in alternatives to the way the Company taught me.'

'We can help each other, Dad,' I pointed out. 'I can show her the Marin approach, and she can teach me swording, maybe.'

'I think I need to teach you something more important than that,' Rani said evenly.

'Not swording? What about knife work? I can see myself as a dagger kinda guy.'

'Combat preparation. Tactics. Reconnaissance. How to approach an enemy. Patrol formations. Deployment of forces.'

I opened and closed my mouth a few times. 'Seriously?'

'If I'm going to patrol with someone, I prefer that they can manage themselves well. Judging by your last encounter, you have much to learn. Even if you work alone, a more systematic technique would help.'

I looked at Dad. 'She's right, Anton,' he said. 'We Marins have often been slipshod in this area.'

Rani tapped the table, drawing my attention. 'In the Company, we learn how to position ourselves, the best ways to scope out potential sites, and how to use natural obstacles to our advantage.' She raised an eyebrow. 'Instead of using them as tripping hazards.'

I thought it over. 'Could be helpful, I suppose.'

'It's all about being efficient. A little preparation goes a long way.'

'Anton,' Dad said. 'It's a generous offer.'

'Okay,' I said. 'Okay, okay, okay. We've got a deal.'

Rani held out a hand. We shook.

'Excellent,' Dad said. He took up his pen and notepad again. 'Now, would you care to report about the Rogue? Rani didn't have time to tell me the details.'

We described the events of last night. It was a pretty good double-handed rundown, if I say so myself.

Dad kept scribbling for a while after we'd finished. I didn't say anything, I didn't want to distract him, and Rani picked up the cue and waited patiently as well.

Finally, Dad looked up. 'My father only encountered two Rogues in his entire time as a ghost hunter. Your Aunt Tanja, only one. Both hunters were mature, experienced, when they ran into them – and they barely survived.'

'Teamwork beats solo performance here,' I said. 'Rani and I managed all right.'

'I'm sure I could have handled it alone,' Rani said.

'True, by the Rani MultiSlice approach, approved by the Company of the Lifeless.'

'While the Anton Warm and Cuddly approach would have resulted in you being torn to pieces.'

I looked at her solemnly. 'Together, we are much stronger than the sum of our parts.'

She rolled her eyes. 'Don't be so daft.'

Dad scratched his chin with his pen. 'And you had no rush of memories when the Rogue was discorporated?'

Dad loves a fancy word now and then. Rani and I looked at each other. 'No,' we both said at once.

'I didn't expect so. The available literature suggests that Rogues have abandoned their origins so completely that they have none left when they depart.'

'Rogues,' I said in my best voiceover voice. 'So much more than just a ghost.'

'Rani,' Dad said, 'if you truly wish to understand another way to deal with ghosts, I'd be happy for you to go with Anton. And not just because you would protect him. Sorry, Anton.'

'Hey, I'm confident in my masculinity. I don't mind if I'm protected by a girl. Not torn to pieces beats torn to pieces, any day.'

'Anton said you have records of ghost encounters,' Rani said. 'May I look at them? I might be able to remember some of my own to add to yours. Cross-correlation could be useful.'

Dad's eyes lit up. 'By all means!'

So much for protecting family secrets.

The shop bell rang. 'I'll get it.' I hurried to the front room to find Bec there, red-faced from riding her bike through the chilly day.

'Right,' she said when she saw me. 'Try this on for size. What's the only bone in the human body that's not attached to another bone?'

'You've got me.'

'The hyoid bone. It's in your neck.'

'Fascinating, but that's not what you've come here for.'

'I've come to see your dad about digitising,' she said brightly.

CHAPTER 9

Later that day, partly dazed by Bec's explanation of the benefits of digitising, Dad gave me Grender's number. 'Get him around here,' he said. 'I want to find out if he knew he was sending you to a Rogue.'

Dad should have accepted early on that he was outmatched, but he kept on arguing with Bec before he surrendered. It was a brave but doomed effort. Throughout the morning, I dropped in to see them finger pointing, sketching diagrams on butcher's paper, examining the drawers of file cards, discussing tagging systems and metadata, and I quickly dropped out again to work on my nice, simple inventory spreadsheet.

Wisely, Rani spent most of her time browsing Dad's ghost-hunting library.

Just before lunchtime, I sidled into the secret room. Bec waved to me. 'This is going to take time. Books, reports, newspaper and magazine cuttings, personal papers, journals ... So much to organise. I could really use some help from someone who's an expert in information management.'

Dad shook his head. 'I don't like the idea of letting anyone else know about our work. I'm having enough trouble as it is with you three.'

'You'd have to surgically remove his secrecy gland,' I said. 'He's breaking a lifetime habit just sharing this much.'

'Okay.' Bec tapped her eye, which made Rani jump. 'Anyway, I can make a start on cataloguing the books and arranging them properly. Then you'll be able to search for contents. You'll need to help, Leon, with tagging the actual contents.'

'I can do that.'

'Good,' Bec said. 'As for the reports, it's going to take ages to key them all in.'

'Quicker would be to scan in all the cards,' I said, 'tagging them as we go. If we all do this in shifts, we could get it done before the end of the universe.'

'Why don't we run multiple scanners?' Rani suggested. 'That'd save time.'

Bec stared, open-mouthed. 'I should have thought of that.'

Dad chuckled. 'A fine – what do you call it, Rebecca? – process improvement?'

'Still,' Bec said. 'It'd be good to have someone dedicated to scanning one hundred per cent.'

'Take card, put card on scanner, scan, next,' I said. 'A monkey could do that.'

'A trained monkey,' Bec said.

'Why's everyone looking at me?' I said. 'And why do I feel like eating a banana?'

'No,' Dad said, 'we can share duties. Rebecca, can you buy the equipment? Let me know and I'll give you my credit card.'

'It's carved out of a block of stone,' I mock-whispered.

Dad rolled his eyes like a teenager. What a guy. 'Enough,' he said. 'I'm agreeing, no? As long as you don't hurt any of the existing records, you can go ahead and digitise the records.'

Bec and Rani high-fived.

'You won't regret this, Leon,' Rani said. 'And it might throw up some interesting data.'

'Data,' Dad said. 'My beautiful records have become data.'

'They were always data, Leon,' Bec said gently, 'you just didn't know it.'

'Ah, Anton, save me from this technological hell! Tell me, when is Grender coming in?'

'He didn't answer. I left a message.'

'Strange. He's usually asleep until noon. He would have woken when the telephone rang, surely?'

I'd explained a million times to Dad about turning phones off, but he still thought all phones were landlines. I bet he imagined Grender had one of those old black candlestick phones with the earpiece on the end of a wire.

'I'll try him again,' I said, but the phone actually rang as I was reaching for it.

It was Grender, but it took me a while to realise it. His voice was a screech. 'Anton? Good God, help me! You've gotta help me! A Rogue, it's trying to get in. I'm holding it off, but—'

The line went dead.

'A Rogue?' Rani was on her feet. 'In the middle of the day?'

'It's not unknown,' Dad said, 'but it's not a good sign. Lock up the shop, Anton, let's go.'

I shook my head. 'Stay with Bec. Fill her in on Rogues and daylight manifestations.'

Bec looked at all of us, one by one. 'Shouldn't we call the police?'

'Grender'll be all right,' I said. 'He won't mess around with a Rogue. He'll run if he has to.'

'One of the first rules of ghost hunting, Rebecca,' Dad said, 'is not to involve the ordinary authorities.'

'It never ends well.' I grabbed my pack. 'If there's a real manifestation, civilians panic, and people get hurt. And, usually, it's the ghost hunter who gets dragged in and has to try to explain things.'

'In the past,' Dad said, 'we have had many ghost hunters charged or, worse, committed to psychiatric institutions.'

'So, police are the last resort.' I made for the door. 'Rani? You're coming?'

'Of course.'

'Anton—' Dad looked pained.

'Rani will protect me, remember?'

'We'll be all right, Leon,' Rani said. 'Really.'

I stepped onto High Street and looked for a taxi to flag down. Rani grabbed my arm. 'I have a car.'

Yes, she had a car. It was sleek, grey, low, deadly and

extremely expensive, at a guess. 'Aston Martin?' I said when I read the badge. 'Exactly how much is your stipend?'

'The Company equips its people well. We catch more ghosts that way.' She got in while I stared at the machine. It was so slick I wasn't game to lean on it as I'd probably slide off into the gutter. She turned it on, ignited it, began the launch sequence, whatever the heck they do with these things, and the engine rumbled like a lazy leopard. 'Get in.'

The seats were probably made of unicorn leather, and mine moulded itself to my body in a way that would have been illegal in some countries.

'The Company is hundreds of years old,' Rani said as she pulled out into traffic. She tapped a panel overhead and it whirred open. A pair of sunglasses was lowered down on a spiderwork metal arm. She snapped them up, snapped them on, and pulled around a dithering Camry. 'And it's built up extensive property interests over that time. It hasn't squandered its holdings.'

'Nggggg,' I said calmly as she cut through traffic like a hawk through a flock of pigeons. She didn't do anything illegal, as far as I could tell. She simply made the most of every gap, every shortcut, every opportunity to advance.

The tyres didn't squeal once in the thirty-minute drive, but whether that was due to some super rubber science stuff or Rani's superb driving, I have no idea.

Grender lived in one of the shadier parts of East St Kilda. Not trees shady, but on-the-edges-of-the-law shady. It had the characteristic of many of the ghost spotters' houses I had been to – plenty of exits.

It was one of those 1930s brick Art Deco blocks of flats, two storeys, with three sets of stairs – handy exits, you see. A laneway ran alongside it and along the back for more of that 'easy to slip out of when nasties come banging on the front door' ambience that never features on real estate signs, but is much valued by people like Grender. All the windows, even on the second floor, had bars on them. The bars were serious, too, not decorative.

The front door opened onto a foyer and it was meant to be one of those secure buzz-up arrangements, but the kayak propping it open put an end to that. I scanned the names above the buttons. 'First floor.'

Rani took the stairs two at a time, and I was close behind.

I should have guessed that Grender's flat would be the rearmost. The brick balcony looked over the vacant car park.

The door was shut and, if I knew Grender's ways, locked tight.

'Let me kick it in,' Rani breathed. 'It'll put anyone inside onto the back foot. You follow right behind but keep low. Look to the sides while I take point position.'

I stared. The door looked solid enough to keep Grender feeling secure, and he set a *really* high bar in the personal security stakes.

'How superhuman *are* you?' I whispered back.

'Not a lot,' she said and shrugged again. 'It's hard to measure.'

I'd been joking. She hadn't been. She stepped up and banged a fist on the door.

Nothing.

I tried to ignore how much my palms were sweating. 'Well, that's all okay then. He probably stepped out for a bite to eat, or to buy some shoe polish or something.'

'And he rang, terrified about a Rogue, just before that?'

'Life moves on.' I caught the sceptical look on her face. I'm no fool when it comes to expression catching. I won 'Best Expression Catcher' at my local club, three years in a row, and we were in a semi-pro league and all. 'I can use my pendant to open it.'

'Wait,' she said. 'Is there a back door?'

We followed the balcony. As we rounded the corner we ran into a completely different scene. Rubbish bins outside the door were knocked over and crap was strewn everywhere. The small window next to the door was broken.

My pendant started buzzing. Forget a trapped moth inside, this felt like a swarm of wasps doing a Zumba class.

'This could be a normal mess,' I said. 'A fun party, a few friends, stuff happens.'

Rani took three quick paces, knelt, frowned, straightened and drew her sword. 'And the blood?'

Then I heard it. A thin, high wail that the Marin family records describe as 'keening'.

Rani heard it too. 'We really do have a presence here, in the middle of the day.' She cocked her sword and advanced, glancing at me first. 'When we're done here, I want to compare notes on Rogues.'

'When we're done here, I hope I'm in a state to do some comparing.'

Rani stopped and knelt again. Just over the threshold was a line of sand, blackened and melted in patches. 'Barrier sand. Your Grender knew a thing or two about keeping ghosts away.'

I stared. 'Never heard of it.'

'It's hard to come by, and unreliable, but it has its uses. It looks as if the Rogue eventually forced a way through it, though.'

Rani stepped over the sand. I swallowed and let her get ahead, to avoid any backswing from her sword.

We edged through the tiny laundry, then along a hallway, getting closer to the eerie noise.

'Stop it,' Rani whispered.

'Stop what?'

'You're whistling again.'

'Sorry.' I stopped.

The living room was a disaster zone. Furniture was tipped over, the carpet ripped up, the venetian blinds torn from the walls, the light-fittings dangling. A bookshelf had toppled, scattering books all over the floor. I had time to notice a scatter of documents, but then all my attention went to where Grender's corpse was laid out in the middle of the room, while a Rogue hovered over it.

One part of me was cool and analytical, wondering why the Rogue hadn't gone in the half hour it took us to get here. Most of me, though, was questioning my gap year commitment and pointing out the stupidity of continuing with it.

I'd never say I was best buddies with Grender, but he was a real person I'd known and talked to and now there he was, his throat neatly slit and a look of horror on his face. It made my knees want to give up and admit this load-bearing was just too much work. My stomach wasn't in good shape, either.

The Rogue was female, and modern. She had dark hair and wore a dark skirt and jacket over a white blouse – generic business wear. She looked as if she had been in her late thirties, early forties.

Eyes aren't meant to move like that, though, and mouths aren't meant to do that sort of writhing. It was upsetting to look at her, upsetting at a really deep level, the place inside that shouts, 'It's WRONG!'

The Rogue giggled, a sound that was muffled, as if it came to us from inside a plastic bag, then she spun, twirling like an ice-skater, arms outstretched so we could see that one of her nails, left hand, was dripping red.

'I guess that when a Rogue goes Froot Loops,' I said to Rani out of the corner of my mouth, 'it *really* goes Froot Loops.'

From deeper in the apartment, a woman – a living, breathing woman – stepped into the living room and I nearly lost it. She had an armful of manila folders, but that was about the only sane thing about her. She was wearing a pale yellow dressing-gown, unbuttoned, over a flower-print nightie with a torn and muddy hem. She had one green slipper. The other foot was scratched and bleeding from dozens of places. At least one toenail was missing. Her hair was dark and tangled, with a half-tied blue ribbon draped over one shoulder. She stared at us, with eyes that were wide and red-rimmed and unblinking.

She made the Rogue look like she'd won the Ms Normal of the Year Competition.

She let loose a wild cry and flung the folders from her. 'Get them!' she shrieked, pointing at us, and that explained why the Rogue was still here. Guard duty.

Immediately, the Rogue snapped out of her dainty twirl and launched at us.

I threw myself to one side, but Rani didn't. She just leaned a little and went snicker-snack with her blade and one of the Rogue's hands fell off. The Rogue howled and thumped me with the other.

My shoulder went cold and my arm wouldn't work properly. I nearly went to pieces, then. I scrambled away, on my back, on all threes, moaning, and collided with a kitchen chair.

The Rogue had bounced off the wall hard enough to leave cracks, and was advancing on Rani again. The crumbling plaster and the dust was evidence enough, if we needed any more, of the substantial nature of this ghost. She was here, she was plenty solid, she was crazy and she was angry.

Rani had her back to the wall. Her face was calm, almost serene, as she held her sword vertically, hands at waist level. The Rogue was advancing slowly. She was solid, but she looked as if she was having trouble remaining so, that (tiny) analytical part of my brain noted. She flitted erratically between opaque and translucent, everywhere apart from the arms, hands and teeth.

The ghost feinted right, then darted left, but Rani wasn't fooled. She was ready for it, and all her weight went to her right foot.

Which tangled in the phone cord that had been yanked out of the wall.

In close-quarters hand-to-hand stuff, split seconds can result in split people. The Rogue came at Rani while she was off balance, slashing at her with her one remaining hand, and Rani went down.

I grabbed the kitchen chair, rose and swung it with my one good hand.

The chair was old, and made of the sort of wood that previous centuries would have built warships out of. And I'm tall, remember? My exceedingly wide arm span meant that the heavy chair picked up a fair bit of momentum on its journey, so that when it crashed into the Rogue, the impact was really, really satisfying.

The ghost wailed, which is an upmarket keen, I guess. Then she rounded on me. I was prepared for that – as much as anyone could be – and swung the chair back and forth between us. 'Come on, ugly! You haven't got a chance against the Chairmaster! Or Furniture Man, if you prefer!'

She snarled and lifted her claw. She swatted at the chair, which splintered. I swallowed and imagined writing a short paper for Dad and calling it 'The Use and Misuse of Taunting When Facing a Rogue Ghost' because if I was writing such a thing it would mean that I'd made it through this sticky little encounter.

The nice aspect of working as a duo, though, is that your partner can come through for you.

Rani did. She rose behind the Rogue and with the nicest double-action razoring I'd seen for ages, bisected the ghost at waist level, backhand, then came back again with a deadly diagonal shoulder downwards cut that left the ghost in pieces, writhing on the floor.

Rani didn't stop this time. She used her feet to flick the ghost pieces up in the air, one by one, where she slashed them into tiny, tiny bits that fell to the floor like dog-food kibble. They soon evaporated like rain on a hot road.

I watched, trying to feel my numb arm, and being extremely impressed. This was movie-magic style sword work I was seeing, right in front of me. Rani moved smoothly, mostly using her wrists. Her face was calm, with just a single frown line on her forehead indicating how hard she was concentrating on whirling that blade around.

When she finished, Rani nodded, not panting at all. 'Anton, there's a body here with a cut throat and I'm standing here with a sword. We need to leave.'

I blinked. She was right. 'The woman?'

'She's gone.'

'Wait. Wait a minute.'

'Not sure that's a brilliant idea.'

'I might have a job to do.' My pendant was still humming away on my chest. In all the commotion I hadn't noticed. 'Oh.'

Rani came and put a hand on my shoulder. 'Anton.'

'Do you feel it?'

She touched the bracelet at her wrist, then cast her gaze around the room. 'Where?'

'There, in the corner.'

It was a Weeper, hunched by the tipped-over philodendron, hiding behind the glossy leaves. It was sobbing soundlessly, knees drawn up with arms around them, head down.

It was Grender's ghost.

Grender had been killed, violently. No wonder a ghost had been spawned. It wept, and its bald head and stocky frame were unmistakeably those of Grender.

This was the first ever ghost I'd seen that had been spawned by someone I knew. Those old traitor knees nearly let me down again, and the room went all wobbly for a few seconds. I took a few deep breaths and steadied myself.

I had to keep reminding myself that this ghost wasn't Grender. It looked like him, but it was a result of his death, not a continuation of his life.

Rani had her sword half-drawn, took a step towards the ghost, then with an effort, stopped and thrust the sword back into its sheath. 'Anton?'

'I've got it.'

I didn't care about dignity. I dropped to the floor and crawled – my shoulder where the Rogue had thumped me was working again, painfully – skirting the body and the blood, until I came close to the Weeper. 'Hey there,' I said. 'Easy, now.'

The Weeper shuddered, but didn't raise his head.

I moved forward a little, and then nearly yelped as my hand came down on something sharp. Grender's phone, or the remains of it, crunched to pieces.

I picked some plastic bits out of my palm. 'It's all right,' I said, the all-purpose words that didn't mean what they said, but packed a bucketload of comfort. 'It's all right.'

I rocked back on my knees. I closed my eyes. I took a deep breath, let it out slowly and sought for calm inside me. Then I opened my eyes and reached for the ghost.

My hands sank into him, I wrenched and felt as if I were being pelted with tiny balls of ice as I was assaulted by impressions, shards of memory.

All of them were recent.

Now, maybe I'm a newbie at this whole ghost interaction business, but in my experience the memories that rush out of a ghost at this moment of transition always start with the earliest. There's something about early childhood memories that means they're precious or important – and ghosts seem to harvest them best.

But this ghost's moment of transition was different. I was nearly knocked over by a series of static images, a sort of spiritual PowerPoint presentation that went wham, wham wham, a sequence of punches to the head.

It was Grender's last moments.

I saw him on the phone, I saw the door of his flat opening and the Rogue pushing in and stopped by the barrier sand. I saw and felt Grender's terror as the Rogue eventually breached the sand and came for him, and I saw the fateful slash. And, behind the ghost, outside the door against the concrete balcony, I saw the wild-eyed woman who'd sicked the Rogue on us.

Now, Rogues are twisted with all sorts of nasty emotions, but this woman made them look like happy little Vegemites. Nausea and hatred and flat-out mind-warping fury all battled for facial real estate, and the total effect was inhuman.

Grender fell, holding his throat with both hands. His last images were the ceiling, soiled with cigarette smoke and cracked near the shabby light-fitting, and the Rogue circling overhead.

Rani had to shake my shoulder a couple of times before I came out of it.

'It's gone,' she said softly. 'You helped it on.'

She gave me a hand and I struggled to my feet. 'That Weeper was in pain. A bad death.'

'And doesn't that open up a discussion topic about good deaths versus bad deaths?' she said. 'But I think we need to get out of here rather than start waxing philosophical.'

'We're in big trouble.'

'So it would seem. We can't faff around and let the police catch us here.'

'It's not that. Not just that. We've got a person who can control Rogue ghosts.'

I used my pendant to lock the back door, but before we could leave, Rani stopped me. 'Stay alert,' she said, and she bent to scoop the rubbish outside the door back into the bin, which she tipped upright again after she'd finished.

'Do we have time for that?' I was bouncing from foot to foot, keen to get going.

'It's important. Broken windows, mess like that, will attract attention.' She had a large piece of cardboard she'd ripped from an empty box in the living-room mess, and a roll of sticky tape. She taped the cardboard over the broken window. 'Good enough,' she said. 'Quick. Out the back way.'

Ten minutes later, on Punt Road, my breathing and heart rate were starting to feel normal. Rani's hands were steady on the steering wheel as we slid through the traffic.

'How long were we at Grender's flat?' I said aloud.

'Ten minutes.' Rani accelerated a little to get across the Bridge Road intersection before the lights changed, then she shuddered. 'That woman. Do you think she had anything to do with the Rogue we saw last night?'

'At Yarra Bend? I'd say so. I've never heard of anyone ordering Rogues around like that before, but two Rogues appearing like that in two days? Too much of a coincidence to think that they have nothing to do with each other.'

'Since she certainly had something against that Grender fellow, could it be that she thought he'd be at Yarra Bend instead of you?'

'Possibly. Grender wouldn't tell anyone he was on-selling a tip to us. He kept his business practices close to his chest.' I made a face. 'But what exactly did she have against him?'

We punched north, over Victoria Street, heading Clifton Hill-wards. 'I have a Company of the Righteous help number,' Rani said. 'They should be able to send in a cleaner.'

My heart was still beating hard. '*Pulp Fiction*? Samuel L Jackson? Someone to come in and make a crime scene look as if nothing had ever happened?'

'He was in *Pulp Fiction* but he wasn't a cleaner in it. That was Harvey Keitel.'

'I've never seen it.'

'Never seen *Pulp Fiction*? Anton, you're sorely deprived.' She shook her head. 'I'll have to think about it.'

'What's to think about? Sometime, someone will go into the flat. All it'll take is one look at that carpet and the police will come running. And we probably left plenty of forensic traces around all over the place.'

'I know.' Rani's grip on the steering wheel had gone white-knuckled.

'So can we call on the Company of the Righteous Cleaning Services or not?'

'I don't want to. Not yet.'

I could have asked an annoying clarifying question of someone who clearly didn't want to talk about it, or I could take a stab in the dark.

I went all stabby. 'You don't want to call on them because it'll make them think you can't handle this position.'

'Perhaps.' She nodded, slowly. 'But if we sort things out and I can have some useful information ready to hand them, *then* I could give them a call.'

'They'd be grateful rather than the other way around. Nice.'

'So, why don't we quickly find this person, the one who's ordering a Rogue around, and then I can compile a careful report for the Company, full of insightful detail about this phenomenon, while adding a request for some top-class forensic cleaning?'

'That shows a devious and underhand mind. I like it.'

Rani slipped into the left-hand lane in time to turn into High Street. Rucker's Hill never looked so inviting. 'I've never seen a body like that before,' she said.

'Dad and I saw a motorbike hit a tram once. The motorbike rider was dead, and didn't look like he had a scratch on him.'

'The tram driver, was he all right?'

'She. Badly shaken. Couldn't stand up.'

More silence, more time alone with our thoughts as we drove towards the bookshop. 'I know ghosts can kill,' Rani said, 'but we spent most time on the pernicious death, the slow draining, the leaching. We covered Rogues, but it was almost as if they were a mythological beast, like a dragon.'

'I knew about it, but it's one thing knowing in theory …' I rubbed my face with both hands. 'This sort of changes my outlook on the whole spook enterprise.'

'Quite.'

'Hey, you're not thinking of giving up, are you? I mean, your whole life has been dedicated to ghost hunting.'

'Giving up? Hardly. What about you? I don't suppose you can walk out of the family business very easily.'

I flinched. 'Ah. And that's a touchy subject.'

'What do you mean?'

'You know what a gap year is? Sorry, of course you do. Dad and I have an agreement about what I'm doing in mine.'

And that's how I told Rani Cross, rival ghost hunter, about my gap year in ghost town.

Chapter 10

We all have an embarrassing habit we're not conscious of until someone else points it out. With me it's whistling when nervous or stressed or feeling awkward. It was Bec who did the pointing out. Of course.

So I know that I can start whistling at inappropriate times, like in Grender's flat. I know it but I can't help it.

Bec was also the one who told me that my attempted smart-guy comebacks were probably a cover-up for a feeling of insecurity, and then she claimed that this insecurity all went back to when my little brother Carl died. But since I was eight when that happened and I'd been coming up with smart comebacks since I was in nappies, I told her that her theory was about as convincing as the latest celebrity diet cookbook.

And she said that the lameness of *that* comeback was pretty much proof positive of her theory.

Bec does smug pretty well when she puts her mind to it.

Maybe. But just because she could have been right didn't mean I had to think about it.

Carl was three when he died. He didn't get caught in some arcane battle between our family and a fanatical element of the ghost-hunting community, or savaged by an out-of-control Rogue or anything like that. It was one of those ordinary tragedies, the ones you read about or hear about, that make you feel glum for a second or two before you move on.

It was so stupidly ordinary. Carl was out in the veggie garden, helping Mum in the way little kids help parents who have a job to do. Mum was tying up tomato plants, doing some weeding, that sort of thing. Carl had a little trowel, a kids' version of Mum's, and he was bumbling around picking up stuff and digging little holes where he shouldn't.

He was a good kid, Carl. I was five when he arrived, so I was old enough to know what was going on. I was all set to do the big-brother thing and excited at the idea of having someone to play with. When I saw him at the hospital, though, I remembered thinking that it'd be a while before we'd be kicking the footy together or anything like that.

He was so small.

Dad had to reassure me that all babies were tiny, but it took me some time to reset my plans, brother-wise.

He was a quiet baby, in a good way. He slept, that meant, and I can remember Mum and Dad both congratulating themselves on having a good sleeper this time, a remark that usually went with a sideways glance at five-year-old me. So I was a night owl, even as an infant. Good preparation for now, I say.

I got to feed baby Carl, which I thought was a lot of fun. He had a cool trick where anything he hated, he'd take spoonful after spoonful of without swallowing. He'd hold it all in his mouth until he'd had enough and then he'd give it the old high-powered spray-gun ejection.

And then he'd cackle that high-pitched baby laugh that always cracked me up.

I was inside when Carl was helping Mum in the garden. I can't remember what I was doing when she screamed. I galloped out in time to have her run past me with a limp Carl clutched to her chest. She went straight through the house and out the front door.

She ran all the way to the Children's Hospital down the road, but they couldn't save him.

I was left at home, by myself, terrified and not knowing what to do. I stayed like that until Dad appeared. He took me in his arms, held me for a long time and he told me that Carl had seen something in the garden and bent down to pick it up. A bamboo garden stake had gone right into his eye and killed him.

The next few days, as far as I can remember them, were a jumble of people coming and going. Mum and Dad were zombies, pretty much, as you'd expect. There was a funeral, and what upset me about that more than the fact that Carl was dead was the way the grown-ups were taking it. Their grief frightened me and made me feel worse.

Looking back, I don't know if Carl's death tore my mum and dad apart. Nothing happened straight away, anyway, not that eight-year-old Anton noticed. Mum left when I was ten, and if it was Carl's death that was the issue she would have gone straight away, right? Or maybe not. Maybe it was the start of a long, drawn-out falling apart, or another thing added to a whole heap of other issues that I had no idea about.

I was sad, at the time, and I still am when I think about him. He was a good kid, and getting better. Three-year-old Carl and eight-year-old Anton played together. Little kid stuff, but it was still fun, especially when he cackled that laugh, which he never grew out of.

And so was Bec right when she said that who I am now is a result of what happened then, and that smartarse Anton is covering up the pain of this loss? On the one hand, der. We're all who we are now because of what happened to us in the past. What we do, what we experience shapes us as much as the gene lottery. But is it a one-to-one thing, where X causes Y? I think it might be a bit more complicated than that. People are always a whole lot more complicated that we think. We might like tidy answers and neat equations but humanity isn't like that. We're messy, we're muddled, we're all over the place, and that's fine with me because it makes us more than just machines that have been programmed by our past.

I still miss Carl. He was so little and I wasn't there and I couldn't help him and I hope he wasn't scared.

Messy, muddled, all over the place.

Dad greeted us with, 'Rogues are incredibly bad news.'

Which was a bit of a downer.

'I helped find some useful stuff,' Bec said. 'And it's made me more determined to digitise the collection. What a mess!'

'Rebecca has an organised mind.' Dad studied me. 'Are you all right, Anton? What happened?'

'Grender's dead. Killed by a Rogue.'

Dad went pale. 'Grender? Another Rogue? No.'

'Yes. Really, definitely, unarguably dead.' I took a deep breath. 'I think we need a cup of coffee and a sit-down.'

In the kitchen, we gathered at the round table. Dad fussed around getting coffee for Rani and me and, for Bec, tea. Bec was finding it hard to keep still, and resorted to ordering and reordering the pile of books and article photocopies she had in front of her. Rani hung her coat on the hook near the door. She looked strained, but calm, and started stretching exercises while she sat there.

Dad put a plate of Scotch Finger biscuits on the table. Not my favourite, but Bec and Rani fell on them like wolves on the fold.

I took a sip from the espresso Dad handed me. It was strong, black and tasted like coffee. No sugar, no milk, nothing to dilute that coffee taste. Heaven.

The real world was coming back into focus – I'd been in a nightmare land for too long. 'You want our report first, or do you want to tell us what you've found out about Rogues?'

Dad had settled himself next to Bec. 'Report.'

I kept the speculation out of it, so the report was reasonably brief. We told Dad and Bec about the flat, about the Rogue, about the wild-eyed woman and about Grender's ghost. I tried to explain how the Weeper had felt, too. Then I described Rani's part, she described mine. 'If it wasn't for Rani, I don't think I'd be here now.'

'And if it wasn't for Anton, I'm sure I'd be in pieces,' she said.

'There's that teamwork again,' I said. 'We'll be signing up for volleyball next.'

'Ahem,' Dad said. That's right, he didn't clear his throat, he actually said 'ahem'. 'Can we move on? Especially since we possibly have some extraordinarily malevolent magic on the loose?'

Now *that* made my head jerk around. Dad rarely used the M word. His explanations, the entire Marin approach to the ghost business, was down-to-earth. We didn't concern ourselves much with metaphysics and we kept away from airy-fairy explanations. It was a job. An important, worthwhile job, but a job. Anything like my pendant was in the Magic basket so we didn't talk about it much. We accepted it.

Two things Mum was into, apparently, were tea and magic. Not at the same time, I think, but you never know. A few times Dad said stuff that made me think this had caused tension between them. Mum's family had a ghost-hunting tradition too, but it came from a different base from the Marin family. Not a contradictory base, just another slightly different take on the best way to conduct the final moments a ghost spends here. Dad never hid this from me, but he never really talked about it. 'It's in the archives, help yourself,' was his usual reply.

For him to mention magic now meant that something big was up.

'It's the two Rogues in two days thing, isn't it?' I guessed.

Dad looked at me sharply, but I wasn't expecting Bec to chip in. 'There's that, and then there's this daylight Rogue manifestation. That's almost unheard of.'

Rani looked amused as she nibbled on another Scotch Finger. I had to work my mouth a few times before I could form an adequate response. 'And who made you the Great Ghost Authority?'

Bec threw a pencil at me. I ducked. Without spilling the coffee she was sipping, Rani leaned over and snapped it out of the air.

'I've just collated some information that Leon pointed me towards,' Bec said.

'She's exceptional,' Dad said.

'I know that,' I said, 'and now she's Director of Ghost Operations, Marin Branch? After years of sticking in the mud, things are sure moving fast around here.'

Bec rapped the books in front of her. 'Someone needs to bring you guys into the twenty-first century. It's lucky you've got me. Just wait until I have everything humming along digitally. You won't know yourself.'

'And while I'm afraid of that,' Dad said, 'I'm also strangely looking forward to it.'

'So on top of a murder, what are we up against?' I asked. 'Some sort of magical outbreak? An intrusion from a dark dimension? A few lame card tricks?'

Dad clasped his hands and put them together on the table in front of him. 'I'll need to do some more research, but it looks like phasmaturgy.'

Whoa. It's hard to roll out a snappy answer when someone tells you you're dealing with genuine ghost magic.

'What's phasmaturgy?' Bec asked.

We all looked at Dad. 'It is a perverted form of magic, Rebecca, where depraved individuals seek to use the moment of transition from life to death to gain power.' He rubbed his forehead. 'They either enslave the dead to do their bidding, or they simply wring information from them. It is as evil and self-seeking a practice as there is.'

'Ghost magic,' Rani added. 'Summoning, controlling, and generally using ghosts for one's own ends. It's not healthy, in any way. We must root it out and destroy it.'

'That sounds like a quote,' I said. 'That's the Company line?'

She nodded. 'The Company hates phasmaturgy even more than it hates ghosts. Those who would work with spirits are corrupted and cannot be saved.'

'It's all black and white with Company true believers, isn't it?' I said. 'It must be nice to live a life that's that certain.'

'Enough, Anton,' Dad said.

Rani stood. 'I have to report it. Phasmaturgy cannot be allowed to stand.'

Another quote, I guessed. Those Company of the Righteous types had a way with a dull slogan all right. 'I don't think we're talking about letting phasmaturgy stand, are we, Dad?'

'Certainly not. But I do think that we need more information before any action is taken. This is a Marin matter, not a Company of the Righteous one.'

Hm. Was Dad being territorial?

Bec frowned. 'But it looks like now that Rani knows, she has a duty to inform her superiors.'

'That's right,' Rani said. 'We're good at taking action in these cases.'

Dad was looking decidedly firm. Rani was on her way out the door. Bec was punching something into her phone. 'Wait, Rani,' I said. 'This works out perfectly with your plans to get a cleaner in.'

That sidetracked into an explanation for Dad, and a promise from Bec to find *Pulp Fiction* for us.

'So,' Rani said when we were finally back on track. 'We sort this out and then I can get in touch with my Company contacts with plenty of useful information.'

'Cool,' I said. 'They'll love you for it and send a cleaner around pronto.'

'They already love me,' she said absently. 'They're not fools.' She tapped her foot for a moment. 'All right. Let's do it.'

'Yay!' Bec said. She had her phone in her hand. 'We're now a supernatural investigative team!'

'If you suggest that we all bump fists, I'm leaving,' I said. 'Who were you texting?'

'I wasn't,' she said. 'I was checking to see if there's been any media reports about Grender's death.'

Dad leaned forward. 'And?'

'Nothing.'

'Looks like we have some time, then,' Rani said.

'How much time?' Bec asked.

'Who knows?' I said. 'How fast can we track down this phasmaturgist woman?'

'Quickly, I hope,' Dad said. 'That woman you saw is out there manipulating Rogues.'

Bec was a little green around the gills. 'And there's a dead body lying around in a St Kilda flat, too. Gotta get that taken care of soon.'

I went back to what Dad had been saying. 'But why did this woman want Grender dead? I know he was offensive, in lots of ways, but calling up a dangerous ghost to cut his throat is going a bit far.'

Dad crossed his arms. 'It's unlikely to be for any noble reason. Phasmaturgy is ultimately a selfish craft.'

'You think? Releasing slavering, insane ghost dudes on the city is a selfish thing?'

'You should give up sarcasm,' Bec said. 'People could get the wrong idea about you.'

'Yeah, right.'

'Rebecca,' Dad said, 'how busy are you at the moment?'

'Well, my course is pretty full-on, and I want to do some flat hunting.'

'I was wondering if you'd like to take on a formal, paid, research assistant job.'

'Here?'

'That's what I was hoping. Getting the archives in shape will be a major part of what you do, but we need to find this phasmaturgist. I think your skills might be of great assistance.'

'Done.'

She was happy, and I was happy for her. Marin and Son Ghost Hunters had grown from a two-man operation to a three and a half, just like that, counting Rani as a point-five.

My face nearly cracked with a yawn of titanic proportions.

'I have to get some sleep,' I might have mumbled. 'Sleepy sleep sleep.'

'We must have the same sort of schedule,' Rani said. 'I'm exhausted.'

'I bet you have beepy time reminders and stuff like that though,' I said. 'Company policy.'

'Something like that.' She stood. 'Time for me to vanish like the wind.'

'To your Fortress of Solitude? The Emerald City?'

'Hawthorn,' she said. 'It seems to be a pleasant area.'

'Can you get back here tonight before you go out patrolling?' Dad asked. 'Rebecca and I should be able to find something to help you look for this phasmaturgist woman.'

'Come on, Anton,' Rani said. 'I'll give you a lift home.'

CHAPTER 11

'What's your name?' I asked to her as we drew up at the lights near the Westgarth Cinema.

Rani glanced at me. 'The art of conversation isn't your strong suit, is it?'

'What?'

'Starting off with a blunt question like that would get you killed in some cultures.' People streamed across the road in front of us. On the way to catch a movie? 'Besides, you know my name.'

'Full name, I mean. In all, we really haven't had a chance to do the proper introductions. I've been trying to read your name upside-down on your schoolbooks, but I keep getting distracted by your ponytail, braces and giggling friends.'

'Rani Barsha Cross. Pleased to meet you, Anton Marin.' The lights greened and we surged off, the G force pressing me back into the lush seat. 'Marin. Is that French?'

'Slovenian. My great-grandfather anglicised it when he came here after the war.'

Rani's face took on the faraway look that people do when they're calculating. 'The Second World War?'

'That's the one. Yeah, and he anglicised it pretty badly. He could have stuck a T in it, for a start. No one would have been any the wiser, and Martin is a pretty standard Aussie surname.'

'I think it works,' she said.

'And Cross …'

'Go on, say it: "You don't look like a Cross." '

'Don't you? What's a Cross meant to look like?'

'I told you I'm adopted.' She shifted gears suddenly and sent us scooting past a tip truck that was struggling up the hill towards the cemetery. The engine whined. 'My real dad was Assamese, my real Mum was Chinese Malaysian.'

She turned and looked at me, which freaked me out because we were curving around the cemetery and about to launch into that long complicated roundabout near the university colleges and she WASN'T LOOKING AT THE ROAD. 'I'd really like to be able to remember them.'

She turned back to the front, and sent the car wriggling through a gap that hadn't been there a second ago. Pro-level driving made look easy.

A few seconds later and we were in the quiet back streets of Parkville and I started breathing again. Sweet, sweet air, how I love you.

'Just so you understand,' she said when we pulled up in front of my house, 'we're sharing now.'

'Okay.' I shifted uneasily in my seat.

'Which means it's your turn. That's how sharing works.'

'Uh huh. Anything in particular you're interested in?'

'No.'

'No?'

'It's not question and answer time. You have to volunteer if it's going to be meaningful.'

Family. She opened up about her family. 'I suppose I could tell you about my Aunt Tanja.'

'Not if you don't want to.'

'What? I thought we were sharing.'

'If it's going to be a bore for you, I'd rather we didn't.'

'Bore?'

'Your tone of voice.'

'Look, I'm not responsible for my tone of voice.' I stopped short. 'Did I sound bored? Honestly, I didn't mean it.'

'Tone of voice and body language were consistent with each other.'

'Maybe I was uncomfortable,' I said, more to myself than to her.

'You don't always have to be comfortable. Discomfort can mean something.'

'Maybe.'

'That's not very helpful.'

'I'm lost here. Just tell me what you want me to say, okay?'

'Don't you dare try to make your feelings my responsibility.' She studied me for a while and just as I was getting uneasy all over again, she turned on the engine. 'I think we'd better leave well enough alone. Goodnight, Anton.'

'Wait. I've got a lot to share. I just missed the moment, that's all. Whistle it back and I'll jump aboard.'

'Another time. Perhaps.'

She left me standing by the front gate, kicking myself stupid.

CHAPTER 12

After sleeping hard, showering, picking a jacket (royal blue, with big lapels, hard to miss) and eating, I rode my bike to the shop. I felt like I needed a bit of exercise to clear my head because it was obviously thick as a couple of dozen short planks.

I can overanalyse as well as anyone – no I can't. Well, possibly, in some circumstances. Or can I? – but I accepted that, yesterday, I'd been insensitive, unaware and generally thick as.

Sometime over my slow and soggy breakfast, I'd realised that yesterday Rani had been reaching out to me. I hate the phrase – no one gets in touch anymore, they reach out, and it makes everything sound like a drowning swimmer grabbing at a life preserver – but it described what she'd been up to. She'd started to tell me about herself and how it felt to be ripped away from parents she couldn't remember, and I'd sat there like a stone.

Insensitive, unaware and thick as. I think it's in the job description for an eighteen-year-old male, but I hate it when I fall into a stereotype like that.

And so the bike. I had to get to the bookshop but I wanted to make a detour to the all-night florist on Bell Street in Preston.

Then the weakness in my plan became obvious. Have you ever tried to carry two bunches of flowers while riding a bike?

I tried holding them under one arm, catching them between the handlebars, and clamping them in my teeth like a matador, but eventually I shoved them into my backpack so they stuck out over my helmet as if I was carrying a bunch of floral spears. With the flashing lights and my hi-vis vest, I was hard to miss. I accepted the humiliation and the wild car hoots along the way. I deserved them for being such a fool the night before.

The lights were on in the shop as I pulled up – good – and Rani's car was parked out the back – also good. I locked my bike to a downpipe, held the irises behind me and pushed the door open.

Dad wasn't there, but I could hear him rattling away in the front of the shop. Bec and Rani were sitting at the table, which was heaped with newspapers, books, maps and documents. Rani was in purple and dark blue, a top and jeans. Bec was wearing a T-shirt: *Cosplay – Dress Ups for Grown Ups*.

'Hello, Anton,' Rani said. 'Bec has been explaining all about her eye.'

'Really?'

'She asked,' Bec said. 'Which is the best way, by far. Then we got onto board games. You know that she's heavily into them?'

'We used to play Pandemic all the time while we were in training,' Rani said. 'It was relaxing.'

Bec stared. 'What have you got behind your back, Anton?'

This was the moment for a suave and urbane move. Instead, I fumbled around, nearly dislodged my helmet and got caught up in the straps of my pack before I was able to work the flowers free. 'This is for you, Rani,' I panted, and I presented her with one of the bunches of flowers.

I didn't wait for her reaction. Quickly, I turned – hiding my blush – and gave the other bunch to Bec. 'And for you, Bec.'

This was my masterstroke. The flowers could mean whatever you wanted them to mean. Yes, it was an apology to Rani, but by giving them to Bec, too, it took some of the pressure off, made it less of a possibly romantic statement than a generally chummy one, team-oriented, solidarity, stuff like that. 'Irises,' Dad said as he walked in. He was wearing a black turtleneck under his vest. 'And what's this for, Anton?'

'I was just going to ask that,' Rani said. If pressed I would have said she looked wary. The optimistic take would have been 'overwhelmed and hesitant'. The pessimistic would have been 'embarrassed and looking for a way to leave unseen'.

I can read a whole trilogy's worth of meaning into a simple facial expression. I didn't need a reminder, but just in case this let me know that flowers, while nice, were no substitute for genuine openness, something that glib Anton sometimes had trouble with.

Bec poked at the flowers then pointed at my helmet. 'You've left your lights on.'

'Anton?' Dad said as I nearly dislocated my arm until I found the switch and cut the helmet light off. Saving batteries is important. 'Reason?'

'Ah,' I said, 'does one need a reason to give flowers?'

'Possibly not,' Dad said. 'And possibly one would like the reason to stay personal?'

'I'll get a vase,' I said. As an attempt to shut down that avenue of inquiry, it was an inspired one. Relevant, pithy, helpful, and provided a chance to hide my face as I ratted away under the sink.

There followed the business of undoing the bunches and arranging them, while chatting inconsequentially. Did Rani and I size each other up? Who's to say?

She smiled as she arranged and chatted. It wasn't a brittle smile, or a wistful smile, or a frozen smile. It genuinely looked genuine. Pleased. Relaxed. Amused even.

I figured I'd made amends. I'd make two mends if given the chance. I really liked her.

Flowers arranged, mess cleared away, we were set for business.

I sat next to Rani and put my hands on the table. She touched the back of one of them. 'Thank you,' she murmured.

Bec leaned over. 'You've still got your hi-vis vest on.'

'It might look like a hi-vis vest, but it's actually an original fashion jacket from Milan, the summer collection.'

'You're wearing another jacket underneath it.'

'And that's the layered look, direct from Paris.'

'You're full of it.'

'Yes. Yes I am.'

'And you still owe me an interesting question.'

'I'm working on it.'

Dad tapped the table. 'Rebecca and I have made some progress. Rebecca?'

Bec was immediately all business. 'It looks like this woman, this phasmaturgist, the one at Grender's death site, is the key to what's going on.'

'I have a few questions I'd like to put to her,' I said. '"Crazy, much?" would be the first.'

'We need to find her.' Rani drummed her fingers on the table. 'How?'

'Come on, Bec,' I said. 'You got something?'

She gave me a look. 'Sure, Anton. I'll just use facial reconstruction software to work up an image based on the description you gave us, then I'll hack into the police database and run a matching algorithm. While I'm at it I'll look for correlation patterns based on Grender's known activities over the last few months. I'm sure I can enhance some fuzzy images, too.'

I put my fingertips on either side of my head as I squinted. 'Fry Face. Not sure if Bec is serious or not.'

'Not,' Bec said.

'But geez, Bec, that's what happens in the movies! You get all digital and hacky and find out all sorts of stuff! Are you telling me that the movies aren't a realio trulio guide to life?'

'I hate to disappoint you.'

'No you don't. You love to disappoint me. You were the one who told me the truth about the Tooth Fairy.'

'And the Easter Bunny.'

I slumped. 'I'm still not over that.'

'Never mind,' she said. 'Leon has something.'

Dad looked up from his notepad. 'Rebecca has been doing some fine computer work,' he said, 'or so I understand. While she's been at it, I've been operating in a more old-fashioned way. I've been making phone calls.'

Dad's informants were a rag-tag bunch. Some were other ghost hunters we got on well enough with. Independent operatives. Small enterprises or family businesses like ours. Add to that lots of loners, misfits and shady customers, all with at least a touch of ghost sight. Oh, some were dedicated upright citizens, but there's something about the interactions between ghosts and humans that seems to put these people out on the fringe of society.

Wait, what am I saying?

'Did they have anything useful, Leon?' Rani asked.

'It has been ... interesting.'

I sat forward. 'Interesting' was one of Dad's code words. In that tone of voice it could mean anything from 'mildly diverting' to 'earth-shattering, world-changing stuff'. Whatever, it was worth listening to.

'All of them – *all* of them, even Sightless Sally – reported seeing frightening stuff. Lurkers and Ragers in many places, but four of my informants thought they'd seen Rogues.'

'This place is going to hell in a handbasket,' I observed. 'And don't ask me how you can fit the whole infernal region in a basket, unless it's a junior-grade Tardis.'

Dad underlined something and looked up. 'One of my informants has left the country,' his partner said. 'Others are lying low, not interested in scouting, not for any monetary inducements I could offer.'

Rani raised an eyebrow. 'This is the city I've landed in? Brilliant.'

'I switched tack,' Dad went on. 'I started asking about Grender. It took some time.' He shook his head. 'The fear that is out there, I haven't seen its like before. Finally, though, Bao was willing to talk.'

Bao was good. She'd given us some of the most reliable leads in the west of the city – Footscray, Spotswood way. She was also one of the few ghost people who didn't mind technology. She ran a sort of coded Twitter account where she noted sightings, for the benefit of those in the know.

Bao was genuinely concerned for the welfare of ghosts, too. She took money, but never as much as Dad was willing to give her.

'She said she'd seen Grender three times in the last fortnight,' Dad continued. 'And he'd been with a woman – an older woman. Bao said that this woman wasn't well.'

'If it's the same woman Anton and I saw, I'll endorse that,' Rani said. 'She was in a bad way.'

'Dealing with this sort of magic can stretch a person's sanity,' Dad said.

'So we just have to find this woman,' Bec said. 'Should be easy. Half this city is women.'

'We need some more details,' I said. 'Did Bao have anything else?'

Dad flipped the pages of his notepad. 'Bao told me the three locations she'd seen Grender and this woman. And a fourth, but she was hesitant about this one.'

'Why?'

'She was coming back from a trip up north, driving home along the Hume Highway. At night, just after the Seymour turn-off, she thought she saw Grender and this woman standing on the side of the road.'

Grender? Out of the city? Unheard of. 'But she wasn't sure.'

'At night, driving a hundred and ten clicks? No, she wasn't sure, but she noted GPS coordinates.'

'Why do I get the feeling that this unlikely one is the important one?' I asked the ceiling.

Stupid ceiling. Didn't have an answer.

'Don't tell me you have a feeling about it,' Rani said.

'Not a feeling.' I put a hand to my forehead and tried to look mystical. 'Just a touch of foresight, which is one better than—'

'Threesight,' she finished for me. 'I'm sure.'

'So now it's the Marin Ghost Hunter Detective Agency?' Bec said.

'And Associates,' Rani put in. She and Bec bumped fists. I groaned.

'So it would seem,' Dad said. 'It's all we have.'

'Something must be done,' Rani said.

'And we're the ones to do it,' Bec said.

'Oh, geez,' I said, 'I can feel a musketeer moment coming on.'

Rani stood. She had her car keys in her hand. 'Leon, do you have the addresses of those locations?'

Dad tore a sheet from his notepad and went to hand it to Rani.

She studied it for a moment, then handed it back. 'Humour me, please, Leon. Add the Hume Highway location too.'

I made a noise that some could interpret as sceptical.

'Think about it,' Rani said. 'The choice location, the meaningful one, the right one, is going to turn out to be the last one on our list. They always are. I'm suggesting we should start with the last one and save time.'

'Hume Highway?' I said.

'Let's Go North.'

We left Bec trying to explain metadata to Dad. Hunting ghosts and avoiding Rogues was easy compared to that.

I wanted to go up through Whittlesea and cut across to join the highway at Wallan. Rani favoured Plenty Road to the Ring Road then joining the Hume Highway because that's what the car's GPS said. We compromised by taking Plenty Road to the Ring Road and then joining the Hume Highway.

You have to choose your battles.

With my backpack at my feet, I drummed away on the dashboard for a while, both hands, my version of a contemporary take on African rhythms, more or less.

Rani tolerated it.

'Rani and Anton,' I said after a really excellent thumping flourish, 'riding around in a car, just shooting the breeze.'

'Always struck me as a naff phrase,' she responded, '"shooting the breeze".'

'It'd either be really easy or really hard, depending on the way you look at it.'

'Uh huh. On another matter, you don't mind being in the passenger seat?'

'I accept that I'm not likely to get my licence anytime soon, and I don't take it as a moral failing.'

'So what would you see as a moral failing?'

A snappy answer rose to my lips, but, for a change, I forced it back down again. 'Letting people down.'

'That happens. We can't be perfect all the time.'

'No, I didn't mean that.' I thought hard. 'It's when you make a commitment, when you say you'll do something but, in the end, you don't.'

'So, not when you try hard and fail?'

'No, that's different. If you promise, and then you do your best – really do your best, not faking it – then that's okay. Disappointing, but okay.'

'I can see that,' Rani said and we drove on for some time in silence.

'Right,' she said suddenly, just north of Craigieburn. 'Let's try again.'

'Sorry?'

'Sharing. Let's try again.'

I was determined not to bungle things this time. 'Okay,' I said. 'Janez.'

'I beg your pardon?'

'Janez. My middle name. You told me yours, now I'm telling you mine.'

'That's a good start. I appreciate it. Anything else?'

'My Aunt Tanja showed me most of the practical aspects of ghost hunting because Dad couldn't.'

I looked around. Where did *that* come from? If it wasn't a blurt, it was the next best thing – and I *never* blurt.

'Ah. That explains quite a deal,' she said. 'It hurts him, doesn't it?'

'And has forever, I think. He covers it up by dedicating himself to the job in a different way.'

'Through you.'

'That's okay. Mostly.'

'You're sure?'

'Sure? Me? I'm never sure about anything. I live in a state of constant uncertainty.'

'And Leon's not the only one who's covering up, is he?'

'Don't know what you're talking about. Hey, is that an emu?'

'It's a bush.'

'Nice work, Sherlock.'

'Here's a test, then,' she said, a little later. 'Who's your favourite Holmes?'

'Mycroft,' I said. 'Who's yours? Cumberbatch or Downey?'
She didn't answer.

'Oh, don't tell me you like Miller?'

'What if I do? It takes all types. I might prefer Jeremy Brett for all you know.'

'You know the thing that puzzles me about fandom?' I mused. 'It's the way the object of your obsession is the best, better than anything else, and anyone who fancies anything else is strange or mad.'

'You make it sound like religion.'

'I do?' I considered this. 'I mean, that's my point, in a profound and original way.'

'I thought so. I'm looking forward to the groundbreaking blog post: "Religion and Fandom: Same Thing, More or Less".'

'Maybe they'll make a movie out of it. I'd like that.'

We overtook a truck, one of those big B-doubles. 'You understand, of course,' Rani said when we were back in the left-hand lane, 'that you are a champion deflector.'

'It's better than being a champion defector. What?'

'There you go again. It's mostly automatic, I'd say.'

I thought carefully before I answered. 'We all have ways of managing ourselves.'

'True. Snappy answers are a fine way of deflecting, diverting attention. Covering up, in other words.'

And didn't *that* give me something to chew on.

I'm not sure how long the silence lasted before Rani broke it, because I was doing some deep thinking of a sort that I wasn't used to.

'You began telling me about your Aunt Tanja,' she said.

I nodded, and when I started talking about family in a way I never had before, it was easier than I expected.

'Aunt Tanja hunted ghosts with a fury. On top of that, she was a fiend for ghost-hunting lore and family history. Dad says that, in some ways, she cared more for ghosts than real people, which sounds like code for "difficult person".'

'We have many of that type in the Company,' Rani responded. 'Single-minded.'

'That's it. Single-minded. And her mind was first-class, apparently. She was always scouring the Marin archives, and she was in correspondence with ghost hunters all around the world.'

'Bec showed me some of her work,' Rani said. '"Apparently first-class"? Sounds as if you didn't know her well.'

'I was fourteen when she disappeared. She kept to herself when she wasn't instructing me, so I didn't see this ghost expert side of her. Dad did, and told me about it later.'

'She sounds remarkable.'

I shrugged. 'According to Dad, she wanted to come up with better ways to find ghosts, better ways to ease their passage. And she wanted to know more about their origins, about what they mean for humanity.'

'There's too little of that about,' Rani said softly.

'She was good to me when I needed it,' I added, equally softly. 'I miss her.'

As we drew closer, I used my GPS unit to zero us in on the location. As Dad had said, it was just south of one of the Seymour turn-offs.

When we pulled off the road, Rani didn't open the door. She wound down the window. 'We're at a memorial site.'

'You see anything?'

'You mean apart from the flowers and the crosses and the grief?'

'I'll take that as a no.'

The shrine was in the median, that strip that divides the highway. About eighty, a hundred metres across? Lots of trees, scrubby scrub, stuff like that. Knee-height wire barriers to step over. A wasteland, really; it wouldn't see many visitors.

Before we got out of the car, Rani pointed. 'I'll head to the north, and circle around the back of that tree that looks as if it's the centrepiece. You angle across to the south and we'll meet up. Keep an eye on that stand of trees to your left.'

'This is your combat background talking?'

'Learning to read the landscape quickly could save your life.'

When I got out of the car I already had my torch in hand because I might need to see some colour instead of relying on the silver-greys of my dark sight. The night was cold, but still. No clouds, and out here the half-moon was bright enough to turn everything sheeny. I wished I'd brought my greatcoat, and a scarf, some good gloves and one of those furry Russian hats, but you can't have everything so I just wrapped my jacket around myself and plodded over to the huge river red gum that was the centre of all the mourning.

Just like most people, I'd seen these roadside shrines up and down the highways of this great nation of ours, and

I'd always felt sad as I zipped past. Someone had driven off the road, been killed, and the friends, family and relations had pilgrimaged to the site and marked it. Sometimes they were maintained for years: the flowers renewed, the crosses straightened after falling. Mostly, though, the initial anguish faded, the flowers withered, the crosses blew over, the heartfelt messages painted on the offending tree faded back into the ordinary roadside scenery, and those passing didn't see it at all.

This one was fresh. Lots of wreaths and floral arrangements. A photo in a frame, nailed to the tree, just over a horrible gash that was still raw.

I realised that I was whistling softly through my teeth, and I cut it out.

Rani stood with her hands in her pockets. 'Where do they go?' she said suddenly.

I was crouching, just about to flip on the torch so I could study the photograph better. Rani's question was so unexpected that I stood, pocketing the torch. 'Who?'

'Ghosts. I know what the Company says, but my doubts about the Company's dogma are now growing, thanks to you Marins.'

There was no heat in that remark – it was more thoughtful than spiteful. I rubbed my hands together for some warmth as Rani studied the tributes. She was tall and straight in the moonlight. 'That's a boggy metaphysical swamp to fall into,' I said. 'What happens when we die? What exactly are ghosts? Why do ghosts appear at some deaths and not others?'

'The Company has answers for all of those questions. First, we go to an afterlife that is appropriate to the life we've lived and the belief system we followed. Second, ghosts are impressions left on this world by deaths that are traumatic – an echo, if you like. Third, see Answer Two.'

'But you're not convinced?'

She shook her head sharply. 'For some time I've thought that the official stance on ghosts was too straightforward. The more I read, the more it seemed as if the Company was wilfully ignoring the complexities that others were concerned about.' She took her hands from her pockets and rubbed them together slowly. 'So, where do you think ghosts go after you release them?'

'Okay, there's the official Marin family line and then there's the Anton line.'

'So where do ghosts go according to the Marin family?'

'We don't know.'

'I see. So how about according to Anton?'

'I don't know either, but I'm not as certain about that as the family is.'

'That's not very helpful.'

'Sorry.'

'Anton, the Company doesn't encourage us to think too deeply about ghosts.'

'Well, if you're set on destroying something, it's better to think that it isn't really very important. Or very human. Lessons of history.'

'Lessons of history?'

146

'The way it's easier for soldiers to butcher an enemy if they're convinced the enemy is less than human? Something like that.'

'And what if ghosts are *part* of something? What if they've been left behind and the original can't pass on without being complete? What if your work not only allows a ghost a chance at peace but allows a lost soul a chance of reunification and peace? And what if all my crusading work destroying ghosts has denied some this chance?'

Her voice broke at this. She put a hand to her face and sobbed.

I took a deep breath and went to give her a hug, but she backed away.

Okay, so that was clear. I couldn't do anything for Rani in her distress, or not the right thing anyway, and I wanted to. My hands were suddenly useless objects on the ends of my arms. I straightened my jacket, brushed my sleeves, rubbed my hands together, and studied the sky as my blush flared and slowly receded.

After some time, I said, as if nothing had happened, 'You know, you've put your finger on questions that have been much discussed in the Marin family for a long, long time.'

'I have?' Her voice was muffled, but then she took her hands away from her face. She found a tissue and used it. 'I thought you said the Marin family didn't know the answer to any of this.'

'That doesn't mean it hasn't been argued over. No conclusions reached, but my Aunt Tanja thought that helping was better than destroying, if at all possible, and I trust her opinion.'

'If you mention this to any of the Company of the Righteous, I'll deny it.'

'Of course. No tears, no doubts, no nothing.'

'Exactly. So what have you found here?'

'An interesting photograph.'

A happy family. I shone the torch on it so we could see it in full colour. Mum, Dad, three kids, for sure. The kids were all primary-school young. 'Sad. A whole family wiped out, by the looks of it. Judging by the flowers and tributes, it must have hit a community hard.'

Rani touched it with a finger, and rubbed away a speck of dirt. 'No doubt, but I don't think the whole family was wiped out.'

'No? Why not?'

'The mother. That's the woman we saw in Grender's flat.'

CHAPTER 13

As we churned down the highway, I was in one of those click-click-click modes where a whole lot of pieces move into place. This meant much reading between the lines, but I could do that, especially if there was plenty of room between the lines so I could fit my stuff in.

I'd used my phone to take a photo of the photo on the tree. It was a lousy copy, but at least I'd have something to show Bec and Dad. After studying it for a while, and the tributes all around the site, I thought I was able to put some names to the faces.

The crash victims had apparently been the Evans family. I had names for the kids, and the father, and each match I made hurt. It was hard, looking at faces of people who were once alive but now weren't. Georgia, Charlotte and Jack, and their dad, Scott.

Part of the issue we have with death and afterlife is the horror of coming to an end. Life being full of so much, the thought of it crashing to a complete close is shuddersome. Deep down, we'd love to know that we go on, somehow, somewhere.

Tributes for the Evans family were there from the local netball club, the footy club, two different schools, a youth orchestra and a radio-controlled plane club, all of them now with diminished membership.

While I was taking photos, Rani said she'd patrol the area for Rogues, just in case, but I noticed how, as much as possible, she avoided looking at the tributes closely, keeping her distance from the notes and the photographs in particular.

Me? I pushed on through the blurry vision.

Those kids. It was easy to tag Jack, but was Georgia the one with the curls? Was Charlotte the smilier one? Jack had to be older than the one in stripes, so he was second born, I was sure of that. A crease ran across the photo, right over Scott's shoe. I could probably fix it with Photoshop. Or Bec could. It'd be good to do that.

Those kids. They were so small, so little.

And then there was the mother. Mrs Stacey Evans.

In the photo, she was attractive. Dark curly hair, sunglasses, a hat that she was holding on with one hand. She had an arm around her husband, Scott. The kids were blends of Scott and her. Her wide and unforced smile made me think she was laughing when the photo was taken.

She survived the crash.

After being puzzled by seeing her in the photo and her name on the floral tributes and cards after seeing her in the flesh at Grender's flat, I figured it out. The cards on the flowers and wreaths often used phrases like 'So sorry for your loss, Stacey' or 'Thinking of you, Stacey, in your grief'.

She survived and now she was now into some heavy phasmaturgy.

So now we knew who'd killed Grender, and, roughly, how. It was the why that was baffling. She'd survived a car crash that wiped out the family she loved, and not long after (six months or so, according to the dates someone had carved into the tree) she was working dark ghost magic and using it to kill a fringe dweller in the shadow world a country accountant should have no idea about.

What was she thinking? Had grief driven her mad? Loss and survivor guilt could be a powerful package for change, and not in a good way.

She murdered Grender, and probably set a Rogue on me, but I felt so, so sorry for her.

'You're crying,' Rani said.

'Sad things do that to me,' I muttered, and I wiped my eyes with the back of my hand. Be professional, Anton. 'Look. I think we need more info about Stacey Evans if we're going to get anywhere.'

'Bec might be useful here. We have some names now, and the photo of the photo. She might be able to track down more information.'

I made a noise of agreement, and the headlights carved their way through the night. We hit the gentle ups and downs that mark the dribbly end of the Great Dividing Range, bypassing

Kilmore. In my mind, it always marks inland Victoria from the south.

A kilometre or so further on, Rani spoke up again. 'I'd been having some doubts about the Company before I left London, you know.'

'Uh huh. Its antiquated dress sense, something like that?'

'The attitude to ghosts, among other matters. I'm now wondering if they're deliberately keeping information from us, or if they simply refuse to believe that there is more to know.'

We were coming through Kalkallo. Lots of trucks.

'That's a sort of scary attitude to have, especially for such an old and rich organisation.' I frowned. 'By the way, just how rich is the Company of the Righteous?'

'Very,' Rani said. 'As a novice operative, I'm entitled to eighty thousand of your dollars per year, plus the back-up and facilities of the Company.'

'Booyah.' My head spun. 'And you're, like, a junior employee?'

'Something like that.'

'You're telling me that there's that much money in the ghost-hunting business?'

She glanced at me sidelong. 'Property investments. Long-time members of the Company are very well off, financially. The chief operative in Tasmania has two private jets, apparently.'

'It wouldn't be recruiting, would it?'

'Not that I know of.'

'I've only met one, a semi-retired fellow, but he mentioned others.'

'Wow. I had no idea.'

'We move in mysterious ways.'

'Apparently. You do, that's for sure. Are you sure you don't dance?'

'I've never learned.'

'I bet you're a natural.'

'Maybe you'll find out, one day.'

'Where's my diary? I'll make an appointment now.'

'I'd rather be spontaneous.'

'That's okay, I can schedule spontaneity.'

'I'm quite sure you can.'

'So, new to Melbourne then.'

'A month or so. It's a lovely place.'

'Apart from the supernatural murders and the Rogue ghosts, it's the most liveable city in the world.'

'Really?'

'That's what they say, whoever they are.'

'And you've lived here all your life?'

'I'm a Melburnian, all right. And pro tip, it's "Melburnian", not "Melbournite". It's an amateur mistake.'

'Noted.' She tapped her fingers on the steering wheel for a while. 'Along those lines, if I'm going to fit in here and do my job properly, it could help if I had someone to introduce me to the city.'

'You want a Melbourne guide?'

'If you're not too busy deciding whether you want to hunt ghosts or not.'

'Me? Well, sure, I'm happ[y]
around and all. Born here as a[

'That's a yes?'

'Yes.'

So that's how we ended [
Yeah, I know that there wa[s
magician type on the loose a[
but sometimes sidetracks pr[
can't help taking them.

We didn't use the Ring R[
suburban Sydney Road rou[
Campbellfield and Fawkner. [
of the night, we made it to C[
and much cooler. We curved a[
fields. That got me started on[
Melbourne.

'You need a footy team,' [
Street, looking over the ovals[
zoo in the distance.

'I need a footy team,' she [

'Australian football is t[he
Melbourne, and sometimes[
revolves around it. Most peo[ple
in it.'

'Oh.' She considered this. [
if I have a team.'

'You bet. It gives people s[
on trains, over coffee.'

'So [
'Sup[
'"Ba[
'"Wh[
to-know[
in an Au[
'So, [
'Melb[
'Melb[
'Most[
The Mel[
'I'm w[
'Unde[
lately. Yo[
'That[
'You n[
Later, [
on foot, w[
I preferre[
and lit up [
the books[
And if[
know wha[

'Your firm makes the Marin family business look small time,' I said. 'Hold on a second, we *are* small time, but I keep hearing politicians say that small business is the backbone of our economy.'

'So you're not only keeping society safe from the scourge of ghosts, you're helping the Gross National Product?'

'We would if anyone paid us for taking care of ghosts.' Something had been nagging at me. 'You said you've just moved here to Melbourne.'

'The posting opened up and I saw it as an opportunity.' She snapped the indicator on and surged around a slow-moving Lada. 'Once I was appointed, the Company found Mum and Dad places at the university, but they had no real say in the relocation.'

'Ouch. Were they upset?'

'They were, but who were they going to complain to?'

'Like that, was it?'

'Very much like that. Anyway, I liked London, but I didn't have so many friends that it was a wrench. Besides, Australia!'

'You lucky devil,' I said. 'But I can't help wondering – and that's something I'm doing a lot of lately – why the posting opened up here. Do they need you here, or did they need you out of London?'

She frowned. 'Nothing was ever said, not outright, but I got the impression that there was some need here. I was adding to the ranks.'

'There are other Company ninjas here?'

'I've only met one, a semi-retired fellow, but he mentioned others.'

'Wow. I had no idea.'

'We move in mysterious ways.'

'Apparently. You do, that's for sure. Are you sure you don't dance?'

'I've never learned.'

'I bet you're a natural.'

'Maybe you'll find out, one day.'

'Where's my diary? I'll make an appointment now.'

'I'd rather be spontaneous.'

'That's okay, I can schedule spontaneity.'

'I'm quite sure you can.'

'So, new to Melbourne then.'

'A month or so. It's a lovely place.'

'Apart from the supernatural murders and the Rogue ghosts, it's the most liveable city in the world.'

'Really?'

'That's what they say, whoever they are.'

'And you've lived here all your life?'

'I'm a Melburnian, all right. And pro tip, it's "Melburnian", not "Melbournite". It's an amateur mistake.'

'Noted.' She tapped her fingers on the steering wheel for a while. 'Along those lines, if I'm going to fit in here and do my job properly, it could help if I had someone to introduce me to the city.'

'You want a Melbourne guide?'

'If you're not too busy deciding whether you want to hunt ghosts or not.'

'Me? Well, sure, I'm happy to. I mean, I know my way around and all. Born here as a little kid, mostly.'

'That's a yes?'

'Yes.'

So that's how we ended up taking the long way home. Yeah, I know that there was a deadly ghost-commanding magician type on the loose and we really needed to stop her, but sometimes sidetracks present themselves and you just can't help taking them.

We didn't use the Ring Road, but instead took the long, suburban Sydney Road route right through Craigieburn, Campbellfield and Fawkner. Then, in the quiet of the middle of the night, we made it to Coburg and Brunswick, closer in and much cooler. We curved around Royal Park and the playing fields. That got me started on the great sporting obsessions of Melbourne.

'You need a footy team,' I said. We'd stopped off Park Street, looking over the ovals towards the golf course and the zoo in the distance.

'I need a footy team,' she agreed. 'Why?'

'Australian football is the game that's grown up in Melbourne, and sometimes it seems like the whole city revolves around it. Most people have at least some interest in it.'

'Oh.' She considered this. 'And you think it'd help me fit in if I have a team.'

'You bet. It gives people something to talk about on trams, on trains, over coffee.'

'So who do you support?'

'Support is good. "Barrack" is better.'

'"Barrack"?'

'"Who do you barrack for?" is a standard Melbourne getting-to-know-you question. It means "Who do you support?" but in an Australian way.'

'So, who do you barrack for?'

'Melbourne.'

'Melbourne? You barrack for the city?'

'Most of the original clubs grew out of Melbourne suburbs. The Melbourne Football Club is the oldest.'

'I'm with you, then.'

'Understand, though, that we haven't been very successful lately. You could be in for a world of pain.'

'That's if I take it seriously.'

'You never know.'

Later, after exploring the Parkville and University precincts on foot, we rolled up High Street past the Bizz Buzz hammer – I preferred it in the old days when it was on the hardware shop and lit up in neon glory every night – and pulled up in front of the bookshop at around seven in the morning.

And if that wasn't a mixed night-time excursion I don't know what is.

CHAPTER 14

When Dad came into the shop, I was behind the counter, doing a bit of googling. I'd already done the dishes from yesterday, the ones he'd stacked in the sink after he and Bec must have had a hundred cups of tea and/or coffee between them. I'd also made some headway on the inventory by knocking 'Sports, Non-ball related' on the head. I figured we could lose about half of that stock and no one would know any different. Oh, I'd also done some of the scanning that was a constant background activity these days, since I didn't want anyone accusing me of slacking.

'Anton,' he said as he took off his hat and coat. His current hat was a nice flat cap in a herringbone tweed. Very snappy. 'You have something to report? Let me get my notepad.'

I have a dream, a vision, that one day I am going to convert him to using a digital recorder. This, I believe.

He came back with the notepad and a sheaf of sticky notes. I groaned. It was going to be a nightmare getting them unstuck and into some sort of order. 'Phone messages,' he said, and he shook them as if they were some sort of weapon. 'The last few days, they've been piling up because you haven't been on your regular rounds. My people are worried.'

I'd thought this might be coming. 'Things have been a bit unusual, Dad. You know that.'

He dragged a stool out from behind the counter and sat opposite me. It was a low stool, and I was on a high one near the cash register, so he had to look up to me. I'm not going to say that it was a visual metaphor about the changing-over of the business from one generation to the next, but someone else might, especially after I pointed it out to them.

'I know, I know. These Rogues, the Company of the Righteous, and Rani.' He eyed me carefully. 'Do I need to give you the special father-son talk, Anton?'

'I'll wait for the movie,' I said, 'but thanks anyway.'

'Huh. I seem to remember giving it to you a long time ago, anyway.'

'You should. How could you forget the most embarrassing three minutes of my life?'

'Besides, the way things are in the world—'

'If you're going to say anything like "Young people today" I'll disown you. Immediately.'

'Huh. Children disowning parents. That never used to happen in my day.'

'You're on thin ice, Leon.'

'Huh. You had coffee?'

'Not enough of it.'

'Is there ever enough? I'll get you one from Umberto's, a treat.'

Umberto's coffee shop just up the road is Dad's favourite, with good reason. The espresso machine was one of the first brought to Melbourne from Italy in the 1950s. It's about the size of an industrial refrigerator, and it's probably been repaired more times than a Collins class submarine, but it pumps out coffee that tastes like coffee, which is just how it should.

I went through the sticky notes while he was away. When he came back, I reported – but it was a strange report. No ghost encounters in it, for a start, and it was full of speculation. He kept jotting as I spoke, and I wondered where it would end up in his archiving system.

When I finished, he tapped his pen on his chin for a while. 'So, the Company of the Righteous thinks that something is going on in Melbourne? Interesting.'

'Or else something is about to go on. Hasn't started yet.'

'Hm.' Dad frowned. 'Anton, this woman, this phasmaturgist. I've been thinking.'

'Stacey Evans.'

'Maybe in this uncertain time, we should think about going to the police and letting them handle this.'

'Say what?'

'I know we don't involve the civil authorities, but this is different. This is murder.'

'Sure, but what would we say? "This woman who wrangles ghosts to do her dirty work has killed a guy who spies on ghosts for a living. Oh, and we know this because we see ghosts and stuff."'

'Rebecca is right. You get sarcastic when you feel edgy.'

'I also get sarcastic at other times, like when I think someone is coming up with a plan that's really, really stupid.'

'I think we should consider it.' He stared at his pen for a while. 'Anton, if involving the police would ensure your safety, I'd do it in a flash.'

'You never promised me that ghost hunting would be danger-free.'

'But this is different. The Rogues ... this is a bad time. I only wish I could ...'

He trailed off, but I knew what he was going to say: 'I only wish I could do the job and spare you, Anton.'

'I can't do it all,' I said. 'I need your help.'

One corner of his mouth twisted up. 'So the old man can do his part, eh? The helpful assistant? The minion?'

'I didn't mean that.'

'I know you didn't. I'm sorry, Anton. This is all very trying.' He stood. 'Let me transcribe these notes. If I think of anything, I'll let you know.'

'When's Bec coming in?'

'She's not. She has a full day at the university. Don't worry – I'll send her an electronic mail message with a copy of this report.'

'Email, Dad. Email.'

'I was going to send her a text message, but she laughed after I sent her the last one.'

'You sent a text message? Hallelujah!' I'd been trying to get Dad to send texts for years.

'I couldn't work the keyboard – too tiny – so I wrote out what I wanted to tell her, then photographed it and sent it to her.'

I kept a straight face. 'And she laughed at you? Bizarre.'

I was a bit disappointed Bec wasn't around. Her level-headedness could be useful. I wanted to see her reaction to the Holmes-like conclusions I'd drawn from the visit to the roadside tribute.

Instead, I inventoried my little fingers to the bone, scanned and snuck in some more internet research.

When it was time for me to go, I'd nailed down 'Religions, Animist' and 'Inorganic Cooking', and a stack of old newspaper clippings now had a new life as digital files.

That night, Rani and I checked out a bunch of the tip-offs from Dad's informants. Along the way, I kept my city guide hat on.

We went to the Victoria Market, which is like Ghost Central for Melbourne. I'd cornered four ghosts there in my short time, and Dad's archives have dozens of records of encounters. I thought I felt the trace of a Whisperer, but after spending half an hour poking around the rubbish skips, Rani said she didn't feel anything so I logged the GPS coordinates and we moved on.

I took her down Chapel Street, just to hear her try to pronounce Prahran. It was a crack-up. She did better than the car's GPS, but that's not saying much.

Must say, it was great having someone with their own car as part of the team. Made things so much easier.

Later, we had an awkward time down in Williamstown around what used to be the Naval Dockyard. The security guys must have been trying to impress. No slacking off, no dozing, nothing like that, so Rani and I had to use extreme caution in our sneaking around. The tip proved to be another dud, though. Military bases, or ex-military bases, are often good ghost attractors or ghost-spawning areas, especially if they have a bit of history about them, but even though we roamed right over that site from waterline to run-off tanks to office buildings to slipways: zilch.

None of this was wasted, though. Rani and I swapped city facts. I filled her in with all sorts of stuff about Melbourne and its history, while she did the same for me with London. I actually impressed myself and I realised that I'd absorbed more than I thought I had from Dad's encyclopedic knowledge of the past.

Rani had plenty of London factoids at her fingertips. I had no idea that actual rivers run under some of London's busiest streets, f'rinstance. Rani had been a part of a team hunting ghosts along the Fleet River, right under Fleet Street, central London. Very cool, in a slightly steampunk way.

'So there are tunnels all over the place in London?' I asked her as we headed back out of Williamstown.

'So, so many. Some go back to Roman times, some were put in during the Second World War, some are more modern than that. Ghosts love them.'

'Why, do you reckon?'

'Perhaps those who die underground die in circumstances that spawn more ghosts than usual.' She hit the wipers to get rid of a film of drizzle. 'You're relaxed tonight, Anton.'

'I am?'

'You're not trying so hard.'

I thought about that for a while. 'Trying is good. It means that you want to do something properly.'

'Perhaps the problem is over-trying. Talking too much, not listening enough ...'

I winced. 'That sounds like someone I know, someone who's bordering on clueless and who's lucky not to trip over his own feet.'

'Someone who is starting to realise that there are other ways?'

'Maybe. Oh, he'll probably flub it plenty more times, but later, at least, he'll understand what he did and kick himself over it.'

'Small steps, then.' Rani tapped the GPS. 'Where next?'

'Sunshine Plaza, and step on it.'

'No time to explain?'

'What?'

'Haven't you ever wondered about how often that happens in the movies? Someone jumps into a car and says, "Quick, go here! No time to explain!" It happens all the time.'

'You're right. Why is there no time to explain? They're in a car, probably stuck in traffic. There's plenty of time to explain.'

'The world of movies has rules of its own,' she said, and she downshifted to make the lights ahead.

We found a Moper at the plaza, near Aldi. Before we went in, Rani pointed out the comings and goings of the delivery trucks, and the way goods were shifted into the stock area. With some prompting from her, I was able to plan our movements to maximise local cover from rubbish skips and light posts, and I even nominated a couple of alternative routes of retreat, to be used if necessary. She came up with a twist, though, that showed her experience in these matters – she went in and asked for directions. While she kept the unloaders busy, I homed in on the ghost and did one of the quickest dispatchings I'd ever dispatched, barely taking in the ghost's impressions of machine oil and a pair of canaries before it went.

Mopers are some of the least troublesome ghosts. Like their name says, they mope around, unable to tear themselves away from a location that's important to them. From the looks of this guy, he went back to the 1930s. He wore overalls, boots and a shapeless hat, and was distressed beyond all get-out. Not crying, just resolutely, profoundly upset. I think he must have died back before the plaza was built, when it was a huge industrial area. Why he was manifesting now? I had no idea. Maybe he'd been here all along.

We scampered out, almost laughing. I nearly tripped on the kerbing around a garden bed, and if Rani hadn't caught me by the arm I would have gone sprawling.

Good times.

Later, after a couple of other washouts, we were parked overlooking Blackburn Lake, eating Bruno's Burgers and thickshakes. Bruno's, the best takeaway east of Mont Albert and west of Ringwood. Mmm.

'Ghost Force Prime,' I said, 'that's us.'

'We deserve mission patches.' Rani saw my puzzlement and went on. 'Every NASA space mission gets a special embroidered patch made. It's a literal badge of honour.'

'That is something we should definitely do,' I said, waving my super special burger around. Some lettuce flew off. 'You know what else we should do?'

Rani picked a poppy seed off the dashboard. 'We should find this Mrs Evans.'

'That's it. Start with the basics and work our way up from there.'

'I have an idea, though, that's far from basic.'

'You sound uneasy.'

'What I'm thinking of could take us into uncharted waters.'

'I guess that unusual approaches are needed, since these are unusual times for ghost hunters.'

Rani appeared to choose her words carefully. 'True. And in unusual times, the old rules may not apply.'

Oh ho! 'Go on. I'm all ears.'

'Since Stacey Evans appears to have become deeply enmeshed with the ghost world, why not ask ghosts if they know about her?'

I stared at her. 'You're talking about holding a séance.'

'Some of your Aunt Tanja's work outlines practices like that.'

'You're not talking about hocus-pocus crap, mediums going into a trance and all that, are you?'

'Not at all. Your aunt suggested something much more systematic.'

After I'd got over the shock, I started to warm to Rani's idea. 'It makes sense. Ghosts come and go, they wander around – sometimes – so who's to say they don't talk to each other? Some ghost or other is bound to know something about Stacey Evans.'

'What we're talking about is out there on the edge. Have you ever read anything in the archives about it?'

'Oh, everyone everywhere has written down their favourite way to séance, usually right before "Don't try this at home, kids" warnings. And there's plenty about mediums and stuff. Mostly bad though.' I thought about it. 'Scratch that. All bad. Lots of alarms and alerts and dire prophecies. Nothing to worry about.'

'Nothing to worry about? I'm sorry?'

'Okay, maybe something to worry about. It could be risky.'

'Sometimes we have to risk to gain.'

'I'm always suspicious of anything that sounds as if it could be on one of those motivational posters, with pictures of mountains or windswept sand dunes on it.'

'I'm shocked. Most of my life values come from motivational posters.'

I finished my burger. So good. 'If we can pull this off, we'll need a name for it, something more modern than "séance". What about Ghost Chat?'

'Giving it a cute name isn't making it sound less risky.'

'Spectral Forum.'

'Not working.'

'Spooks Online.'

'Enough.' Rani finished her burger and wiped her hands on a tissue. 'If we're going to try this, we should be on familiar territory. Any suggestions?'

'The shop,' I said without hesitation.

We pulled up out the rear of the shop at just after three. She leaned against the brickwork while I unlocked the back door. 'So, you want me to get anything? Skull? Bell, book and candle?'

I hooked my pendant out from under my shirt. 'I suggest going minimalist. Just these.'

In the kitchen, I made coffee. I wanted to be sharp, and a bit of caffeine wouldn't hurt. 'You?' I asked, gesturing to the machine.

'Thanks. I could murder a coffee.'

So I wasted some time setting up the Gaggia. Not that I was avoiding the issue. Not at all.

Rani put her coffee cup on the bench near the sink. 'Can I see your pendant?'

I held it up. For a second, I was reluctant to give it to her, but I pulled the chain over my neck and handed it over.

'It's old,' I said.

'They all are,' she said as she examined it. She traced some of the metalwork with a finger. 'The best ones, anyway.'

'Your tutors have special classes on ghost-hunting artefacts?'

'It was a small group. I had five classmates to begin with, but it was whittled down to three by the time our training ended.'

'What happened to the other two?'

'I never found out, and they were never mentioned again.' She held up her left hand and pulled back her sleeve. Her gold bracelet, a solid, unmarked hoop, hung on her wrist. 'When we were given our amulets, we had a number of sessions where their uses were explained.'

'Dad went through mine with me.'

'My instructors took me on a field trip because after the theory classes, the only way to get practical was to go out ghost hunting with an experienced hunter.'

'Dad wanted to take me, but he couldn't do what he was telling me to do. He handed me over to Aunt Tanja.'

'That must have been hard.'

'He was patient. He was encouraging. It could have been worse.'

'So these artefacts can detect the presence of ghosts and alert us to them. They can unlock doors. Have you ever wondered why such a range of abilities? How did they become embedded in these things?'

I spread my hands. 'It's another mystery.'

She gave my pendant back and I hung it around my neck again. 'When Dad gave this to me, I did do some poking around, though.'

'So did I, and I spent ages in the Company library. That's when I started having doubts about the organisation I'd become part of.' She rolled her bracelet around her wrist. 'So what did your poking around reveal?'

'Not much. Lots of the "Origins lost in the mists of time" thing, which is why I went the "It's another mystery" route. My Aunt Tanja—'

'You know, I would have liked to meet her.'

'She would have liked you.'

Rani smiled. 'Interesting family, the Marins.'

'And she was one of the most interesting people in it. She thought that those who made the artefacts must have had some help from phasmaturgists, which is why no one wants to talk about it.'

'The forbidden art helping to make the thing that makes our calling possible. If my instructors knew that they'd be so conflicted that their heads would explode.'

'Can't have that,' I said. 'Exploded heads are awful to clean up after.' I took a deep breath. 'And we're really putting things off here, aren't we?'

'I suppose so.' She rinsed her cup. 'But before we move, in a mission like this we need to nominate our roles first.'

'Right. Good idea.' I wiped my suddenly sweaty palms on my jeans. 'I think I should do the séance.'

She straightened. 'Don't you think I can handle it?'

'It's not that. You're the best one to be on guard, just in case something goes wrong and a horde of nasties turns up.' I shrugged. 'I'm clearly admitting I'm not a sword guy here.'

She nodded. 'Do you really think this is a good idea?'

'Who knows? The only way to be sure is in hindsight. In an hour or so I hope we'll be sitting here saying, 'Well, that was a good idea!' and we'll be keen as mustard to share all the good stuff we've found out with Dad and Bec.'

'That sounds like a desirable outcome, in a lovely Enid Blyton way.'

I stood. 'Besides, what's the worst that can happen?'

CHAPTER 15

For secret stuff, the only place to go was the secret room.

When I got there, though, I had to check twice that I was in the right place. Bec had been at work.

Dad has always been what I call semi-neat. He doesn't like mess, but his definition of mess and most people's might be different. He doesn't like dirt, or grime, or anything like that, and he draws a line at stacking work stuff on the actual floor (except in emergencies), but that's about it.

Bec, though, is serious about neatness. The secret room had been transformed. One table was totally clear, another had two neat stacks of books and papers. No coffee cups anywhere. And a spanking new computer was blinking and humming on a new table all of its own. Now, that was a sign of change, something like Robin Hood using a laser sight.

With Rani's help, I moved furniture to the side of the room, against the bookshelves. We were extra careful with the new computer because cables. It looked as if Bec had been doing some networking, among other things. When she did, she preferred hard wires rather than wi-fi for no good reason I could work out.

She'd been doing some sweeping, too, or had got Dad to do it, more likely. The hardwood floor was almost sparkling. 'I could eat my dinner off that,' I marvelled, standing back with my hands on my hips.

'Imagine that,' Rani said. 'Multipurpose flooring – you can stand on it, dance on it, and use it instead of crockery. What'll they think of next?'

She took up a position by the door, removed her coat, and leaned her sword up against the wall. 'You're sure about this?' she asked.

'Certainty is the refuge of small minds,' I said. 'Oscar Wilde.'

'No it wasn't. You just made it up and attributed it to him.'

'Why should I be any different from ninety per cent of the internet? If Ozzie had said half the stuff the net claims he did, he wouldn't have had time to do all the naughty things he got up to.'

I settled, cross-legged, in the middle of the room. I took my pendant off and lay it on the floor in front of me.

'Okay, right. Do I look medium enough to you? And try to resist the obvious pun.'

Rani pursed her lips, denied an opportunity. 'You'll do.'

'Thanks. I love to have such a vote of confidence.'

'I don't want you getting smug.'

'No danger of that,' I muttered. I knew that I was going right out there on a branch that I wasn't really sure was there in the first place, which is a bad way of both climbing trees and handling ghosts.

I touched the pendant with a finger. It was vibrating very slightly. I closed my eyes. 'Hello? Anyone out there?'

For an uncertain amount of time, I cast about, trying to feel for ghosts. I wanted to find some sort of ghost network, some plane that they inhabited, but as much as I strained, all I could feel was a generalised sense of otherness, a faint version of the prickling unease that I felt when I was close to an actual ghost. But if I was responding to that, did it mean ghosts were responding to me? Was it a two-way thing? And if it was, did that extend further out into the ghost world?

While time stretched, I tried and tried to no effect. Then it hit me. What an idiot I'd been! Ghosts weren't social. They were almost the definition of loner. They didn't hang around in groups, didn't go bowling together, didn't buddy up for camping trips or spa weekends.

And – this was one thing that Dad and Aunt Tanja had insisted on – ghosts weren't intelligent or aware in any way that could mean such a thing was possible.

Thirdly (the other reasons were one and two, right?), I was effectively putting myself out there and trying to find ghosts. Or, to put it another way, hunting them. And if ghosts weren't happy about being hunted over the centuries, they mightn't like someone trying it on a less material plane, either.

Three ways that my idea was a bust – and I'd been pretending that it'd be otherwise.

I opened my eyes, ready to confess, and saw that Rani had her sword in her hands.

'I hope that's not because you're mad at me,' I said.

'It's not always about you, Anton.' She was scanning the room intently. 'Something's close. Something bad.'

Then I felt it, a scratchy pressure on my skin, and my pendant started to hum.

Slowly, I got to my feet and did my best to mirror Rani's wariness, while feeling just a little bit sick and more than a little bit responsible.

I mightn't have had any luck finding access to a ghost network, but had someone used my stupid efforts to find access to me?

Something pushed straight through the wall.

Rani had her back to where a Rogue was emerging, a bald-headed guy, huge beard/moustache combo, dark suit – but at my strategic gibbering and pointing, she whirled and then it was all action. As the Rogue came out of the wall, Rani chopped. The thing didn't back off, though – he just kept coming and getting his limbs lopped off slice by slice. Finally he stumbled over the bloodless ghost pieces that were accumulating on the floor in front of him and went sprawling. Rani dispatched him with some extra rapid slashing.

She immediately went back to scanning the room. 'Are you okay?'

I had a book in my hands. It was the most dangerous thing

I was able to grab at short notice. 'I'm fine. Another Rogue. This whole thing has gone big time.'

'What—' Rani gasped, and clamped down on a cry.

Another Rogue had pushed through the door – a female this time, hair piled on top of her head and a long, dark dress, lace-collared – and had *flowed into* Rani's extended sword arm.

Rani backed off, hissing, and her sword clattered to the floor. Her arm hung nervelessly at her side.

Our time sense goes whacko in stress situations. I knew that, but it was still weird the way everything slowed down. Slowly, Rani twisted away from the door and the emerging Rogue. Slowly, the Rogue drifted through the door and turned towards her. Slowly, Rani reached behind her and pulled a long dagger from where it must have been hidden in her belt. Slowly, she backed away, her right arm dangling, trying to avoid being trapped in the corner while shooting me a slow glance and calling my name so slowly that it stretched – 'Antonnnnnnnnnnn'.

The world sped up. Asking for forgiveness from the library gods, I launched the book I held at the Rogue. It hit her right on the back of the neck.

Rani slipped sideways and slashed at the Rogue with her dagger. I darted forward, behind the ghost's back, and scooped up Rani's sword. 'Catch!'

It wasn't a great throw. The sword tumbled, looped a bit, and fell a metre or so short. I thought I'd messed up enough to kill her.

Rani made it look good. She dropped her dagger, slid a

foot forward, bent, and caught the hilt of the sword in her left hand.

She kept the action going, sliding forward and to one side of the groping Rogue, until she was off to the ghost's left instead of being caught in front of it. With two slashes, the Rogue was driven back and now she was the one trapped in the corner of the room.

Rani's right arm was still useless, but the way she wielded the sword made it look as if she was naturally left-handed. The Rogue slavered and tried to attack, but Rani was remorseless. The Rogue was a pile of pieces pronto and I was the one who was left panting. Rani wasn't breathing hard at all.

She reached up and activated the release to the bookshelf door. It swung open. She waited a moment with her sword held at the ready before she stepped through.

Rani stalked through the shop and I nearly felt sorry for any ghosts who might have been waiting for her. The place was quiet, though, and finally we reached the front room.

Standing at the window, with her hands pressed against the glass, was Stacey Evans.

This wasn't the happy mum of the photograph. This was someone who'd been transformed, changed by trauma. She wore a rumpled and creased trench coat, roughly tied around her waist with a mismatched belt. Her hair was tangled and wild.

She shrieked when she saw us, but with fury, not fear. She flung her head back, baring her teeth, and howled like an animal. She pounded once on the glass with a hand, and in that second I saw that all her fingernails were ragged and broken.

Then she staggered away, stiff-legged and awful.

Rani was at the door in an instant, but she swore as soon as she got there. 'Key?'

'Oh. Right.'

We'd come in through the back door. I'd left the front door deadlocked while I was running the busted séance, waiting for opening time.

I plucked the key from the pocket of my jeans, but by the time we had the door open, Stacey Evans was long gone.

The morning was chill, with a breeze that had made High Street its own, but I don't think that was what made me shiver. An early tram rumbled past and whipped up enough grit and dust to make me squint. 'Okay,' I said, 'so we're targets of a possibly insane phasmaturgist who can summon Rogues to do her dirty work.' I blinked. 'You sheathed your sword left-handed. How did you do that?'

Rani ignored my question. She was gazing down the street towards the city, and she was rubbing her right arm. 'And don't forget that she's already murdered one person. She won't feel any qualms about murdering again.'

'Come on. Let's see to your arm.'

I filled the sink in the kitchen with warm water. Rani stripped off her jacket.

'How's it feeling?' I asked while I bathed her arm.

'Like the worst case of pins and needles in the universe.'

'That's good. If you can wiggle your fingers that means there's some feeling there, at least.'

She glared at me. 'Don't tell me what I already know, Anton. I've had battle training.' Her fingers moved minutely. 'I couldn't do that a few minutes ago.'

'That's a relief.'

'The way she flowed into me. I've never heard of that sort of thing happening before.'

'Nor me, but that's about the fourth "I've never heard of that before" that's hit us on the head in the last few days.'

Offering what first aid I could like this, it struck me that this was what I was in, right up to my neck. Supernatural encounters, dangerous – possibly lethal – confrontations, night after night with not much reward. Just to make the outlook even less inviting, I was learning that there were a whole lot of others around the place who appeared to know much more about the business than I did – and they were definitely much better suited to it.

'We need to know more,' Rani said, nursing her arm. 'Otherwise we're going to continue to be taken by surprise.'

'That makes good sense.' I stared at the ceiling. 'And I think I know who can help us there.'

Dad arrived just after nine, and he was really, really upset by what had happened. Part of it was my stupidity at trying a séance – or 'dangerous mumbo jumbo' as he called it – but most of it was about the Rogue attack. He was distressed, too, at Rani's injury, even though she'd regained most of the movement in her arm by the time he walked in. It ached badly, though, even after she'd dosed up on Panadol.

'Tanja knew more about this sort of thing,' Dad said as he gently probed Rani's arm. They were sitting at the kitchen table while I wandered helplessly, having reached the end of my input when I got Rani a glass of water to wash down the painkillers.

She winced as his fingers explored the site the ghost had injured. A patch between her elbow and wrist was mottled with dark bruising, as if she'd been struck by a couple of hundred ball bearings. 'Tanja was going to write a treatise on it before she disappeared,' Dad added.

I know, another woman vanished from the Marin environs. What's that say about us, right? With Aunt Tanja, though, it had been the result of an experiment in ghost interaction. After the way Mum left, a while after Carl died, it was the third blow that hit Dad hard.

He still hasn't recovered.

'Did she tell you anything about this?' Rani gritted her teeth.

'Not really,' Dad said, 'except that ghosts recoil from passing through living flesh. It causes them great pain.'

'It didn't seem to hurt this bugger,' I said. 'I think she did it deliberately, as a tactic.'

'That would be unusual,' Dad said. 'Nothing in my rapid

catching-up on the subject suggests that Rogues use anything like tactics.'

'I think we know where the tactics were coming from.' Rani's words were clipped. 'Stacey Evans.'

Dad finished his probing, then gently patted Rani's shoulder. 'I think you'll recover,' he said. 'I can get you a sling from the chemist's, if you like.'

Rani made a fist, clenched it, and shook her head. 'No need, thanks.'

And that's when the doorbell rang. I jumped, then charged to the front room in time to see Bec hurry in, grinning, wearing a 'Say "NO!" to Phasmaturgy' T-shirt.

'Rani's been hurt,' I said, and all smugness disappeared from Bec's face. 'She's in the kitchen.'

After a fair bit of backwards and forwardsing between Bec and Rani, which seemed to include far too many glances at Dad and me as representatives of something or other that was probably to blame, Bec summoned us over.

'I've found something useful about our Stacey Evans.'

'Our insane murderer Stacey Evans,' I added.

'Our wretched grieving Stacey Evans,' Bec corrected. 'I went back over newspapers, court proceedings, and I found that she has a Facebook page, full of tributes. You know, she only suffered minor injuries in the car crash that wiped out the rest of her family, but she hurt a number of people who were first on the scene.'

'What? How?'

'She didn't want to be taken away from the wreck.

She struggled, lashed out, broke a police officer's nose, even.'

'Grief, pain, loss,' Rani said. 'It can undo anyone.'

'She was in hospital for some time, under sedation,' Bec said, 'but she went to pieces again at the funeral. She was confined after that and only got herself together for the inquest.'

'How did the car crash?' Dad asked. 'Was she driving?'

Bec shook her head. 'Her husband was driving. At the inquest, some witnesses thought that a truck clipped the car and sent it off the road, but in the court case that followed, the truck driver was cleared.'

'Having no one to blame for a tragedy is a hard thing,' Dad said.

'Oh, she found someone to blame,' Bec said. 'She made a real scene in the court, pointing the finger at the barrister, the police, the truck driver, even the judge. She had to be restrained and sedated all over again.'

'What a mess,' I said.

'She went back into hospital,' Bec said, 'but she disappeared two weeks later. That was a month ago.'

I did some figuring. I kept my hands below the table so no one would notice me counting on my fingers, but I think Rani saw. 'We have a gap between then and Grender's death. I guess that gave her time to get the hang of this phasmaturgy.'

'It looks so,' Dad said. 'Although I can't imagine where she would have learned such a thing.'

'Come on, Dad, Grender was a mercenary. He would

have known enough to get her started, at least, and he could probably have pointed her in the right direction, put her in touch with people...' I stopped. 'That's why he was murdered, so he couldn't identify her.'

'Huh,' Dad said. 'Grender was no good, but no one deserves that sort of end.'

Rani pointed at me. 'And you were nearly killed by that Rogue at Yarra Bend because she thought he'd be there, checking out that tip. But what's she after?'

Bec tapped her eye with a fingernail. The clicking noise was her guaranteed attention-getter. 'Revenge.' She took some sheets from her pack and spread them on the table in front of us. Newspaper articles, complete with pics. 'Last week – that's before Grender was killed, kiddies – a barrister was attacked in his home by – get this – "an unseen assailant".'

'Not "an unknown assailant"?' Dad asked.

'Nope. "Unseen".'

'Now,' I said, 'I'm guessing that this barrister was the same one who represented the truck driver?'

'You got it in one,' Bec said.

'But he survived,' Rani said. 'How?'

'It's hard to tell from the articles, but it looks like he ran away.'

'The *Holy Grail* method,' I murmured.

'That only works with rabbits,' Rani murmured back.

Dad made an impatient gesture, a sort of air karate chop. 'Let Rebecca finish.'

'Thanks, Leon. This barrister guy is a serious runner. He'd

been out for a late jog when this "assailant" apparently nearly tore off his ear. The barrister guy just turned and ran.'

'And there's something else?' Rani asked.

'You bet. Police are looking for a potential witness, a tall, curly-haired woman who the barrister saw just outside his flat.'

'Tall and curly-haired, just like our photo of Stacey Evans,' Rani said.

'Close enough for us to get suspicious,' Bec said.

'Okay,' I said, 'look at the date. This has to be early, maybe her first attempt? Maybe she didn't have the knack yet. Maybe she couldn't spring a trap. Maybe she couldn't control Rogues very well at this rookie stage of her career.'

Rani sat back in her chair. 'You know that this means we aren't really her targets.'

'We're just getting in the way,' I said.

'So it would seem,' Dad said. 'But that doesn't make her any less dangerous.'

'This could give us an idea of her plans, though,' Rani said. 'Bec, who else did you say she blamed?'

'Whiteboard time,' I suggested.

That's how the 'Specials' whiteboard from the bookshop became an Investigation Whiteboard. I wheeled it back to the kitchen and soon I was standing in front of it after having written 'Judge', 'Police', 'Barrister' and 'Truck Driver'.

'Add "witnesses",' Rani suggested, and I did.

'Can you find out more about these people?' Dad asked Bec.

'A bit,' Bec said. She shrugged. 'I'll do what I can.'

'Can you get the address of the barrister, the one who got attacked?' I asked her.

'I can get the street, at least.'

'That's a start. We could have a look around later, see if we can sniff out anything.'

Rani raised an eyebrow. 'We?'

'Your arm is better, I hope?'

She lifted her arm and flexed it. 'Good as new.'

'Sleep will help,' I said. 'Then we can chase up this barrister.'

'I was just about to suggest that.'

Dad and Bec had been watching this carefully. Bec with amusement, Dad with some puzzlement. 'We'll leave you two, then,' he said. 'We'll plough ahead with this information revolution. You'll mind the shop until midday, Anton?'

'I'll let you know before I head off.'

Dad and Bec left for the secret room, arguing about Rogues as they went.

Rani toyed with her empty mug. 'I suppose I should go. I'll pop in and remind Mum and Dad who I am.'

'They're at home?'

'If they're not, I'll leave a note.'

'You don't have to go. I mean, if you don't want to. You're welcome to hang around here.'

'There's plenty to read, at least.'

'Help yourself. Be my guest. Take whatever you want.'

'That's kind.' She stretched and yawned. 'But I really think I should visit home.'

'Do you think you'll be safe?'

She raised an eyebrow again. 'Without you, are you saying?'

'I was talking in the most general and sincere way.'

'Think of it the other way around. Are you safe here without me?'

'Good point. You'd better stay.'

She laughed. 'Text me if you need me.'

As soon as she left, I realised I wasn't joking. I did feel less safe without her.

CHAPTER 16

I camped out in the front of the shop, yawning and trying to make sense of some of Aunt Tanja's notes that Bec had just found. Just before midday, a woman opened the door and came straight to the counter, which was unusual. Usually people browse first, then front up. Bookshop, after all.

I took one look at her and I knew she was famous – even if I didn't know who she was. I'd seen her face somewhere public – billboard, TV, Twitter, Facebook, maybe. Whatever, she had style, from the way her orange scarf was arranged around her neck to the way she pushed her sunglasses up and they stayed there without messing up her hair. Famous style. Celebrity style. Look-at-me style.

'Nineteen-forties film stars,' she said.

I handled this query with so much cool. 'Nineteen-forties stilm fars?'

'Film stars,' she repeated slowly.

'Of the nineteen-forties, got it,' I said. 'A terrific decade. One of my favourites, all ten years of it. As long as you overlook the war, which was bad. Really bad. Inspired a few good films, though.'

She waited and when I didn't add anything else, she sighed. 'And do you have any books about the stars of the forties?'

'Books? Yeah. Hah, hah! We're a bookshop!'

Things went downhill after that.

She did end up buying three books she found without my help, so it wasn't total loss. She eyed me warily when she came to pay, and I was able to stop her bolting out by the simple but effective means of not saying anything at all and conducting the sale via mime.

Later, my chin was heading deskwards when my phone rang. I gave a yelp like a frightened hyena – the worst kind – before I realised what was going on and dug it out of my pocket.

I always keep my phone in my left pocket. That's so I hold it up with my left hand and I have my right hand free to write down anything. Planning.

'Anton? Can you come to my home?'

'Rani?' I glanced at my watch. It was really time for me to be heading home for some shut-eye myself, but Rani. 'Sure. Thing. Sure thing.'

'I need you to talk to someone.'

'I can do that. Talk. I can talk.'

She gave me the address. 'I'll be there in half of an hour,' I said. 'Roughly.'

'Hurry.'

I let Dad and Bec know I was off.

Tram, train, walk, and I got to Rani's tree-lined Hawthorn street in forty minutes, which is half an hour if you look at it sideways and squint. A nice house, it was. Double-storey, lots of windows, balcony, a column or two, big iron fence and gates and maybe three million bucks, at least.

This selling out to the Company of the Righteous looked pretty lucrative.

I buzzed the gate intercom. No one answered, but it clicked open. I walked on the lawn alongside the red brick path just because. When I rebel against the man, I do it in small, sneaky ways.

I did, however, use the time to drag my fingers through my hair, and use my mirror app to understand how pointless it was.

Rani opened the door just as I got there. She was wearing a red stripy dress, mid-calf, halter neck, with red cardigan. Her feet were bare.

'We have a visitor. She's from the Company of the Righteous.'

'Oh.'

Rani grabbed me by the arm and dragged me inside. I was dumbfounded. I mean, if she'd said that Merlin himself had turned up for a cup of coffee I probably would have felt about the same.

'How's your arm?' I asked.

'It's fine, but it's not something I want to repeat. It was creepy.'

Rani led me through an expensive hall over expensive

carpet into an expensive sitting room. Three people were in it. Two stood, a woman and a man. They weren't a couple. I could see that because it was so freaking obvious. The woman who was sitting on the sofa, pale-faced, with a handkerchief in her hands, was the partner of the man who had stood. The woman on her feet was the representative of the Company of the Righteous.

She was striking. I mean really striking. She was short and sort of squarish, but there wasn't a skerrick of fat on her. Dark brown eyes, dark brown skin. She had a long grey braid that nearly reached her waist. She flipped it back over her shoulder, but didn't take her eyes off me. She was wearing black leather trousers and some sort of leather tunic that extended just below her waist. It wasn't sexy leather, either. It was workaday, protective, hard and crusty leather. Black leather boots, too, of course. She had no weapon that I could see but I had the feeling that about a dozen would appear if I as much as thought an aggressive thought.

'Anton,' Rani was saying. 'This is Commander Gatehouse of the Company of the Righteous.'

Bingo.

Okay, so I'm a flippant, run-off-at-the-mouth kinda guy because I find it helps me get my brain in order and it sometimes buys me time when I need it. While the tough guy is wondering what the heck I just said I'm already running away, usually.

But I'm not stupid. Facing this deadly serious woman I had no desire at all to make a joke. And not just because I thought she might gut me as I stood there, but because it probably wouldn't help Rani if I was too much of a wise guy.

I crossed the room and held out my hand. 'Commander Gatehouse.'

I was prepared for a crusher handshake, and I was ready to fold my hand inwards when she did – the cunning counter ploy – but she had no need for such crude tactics. Her handshake was firm, her hand warm and callused. 'So this is the Marin boy,' she said in a way that let me know they'd been discussing me, and also hinted that she'd known about my family for some time.

'Anton,' Rani said, pivoting me by the elbow before I could have a crack at Commander Obvious, 'this is my mother, Olivia, and my father, Kristoff.'

Rani's dad had grey hair and a close beard, and he was tall – nearly as tall as me – and skinny, mostly made up of elbows and wrists. He nodded at me instead of going the handshake. He wore a tweed jacket and a shirt, open at the neck. He didn't look happy, but he wasn't as upset as Rani's mum. She was in gym clothes, and her blonde hair was pulled back with a cheery yellow Alice band. She was red-eyed from crying and glared at me as if I was every mother's nightmare.

So, Meet the Folks plus One was off to a flying start.

'Sit, Anton,' Commander Gatehouse said in a voice that was northern North American, with a touch of the Caribbean, maybe? Her tone showed she was used to snapping out orders, and that she was in charge of this little get-together, not Mr or Mrs Cross. 'How is your father?'

I'd been trying to catch Rani's eye to get a reading of which way to go, but this question from CapCom caught me off guard. 'Sorry?'

'Leon, your father. I haven't seen him for some time. How is he?'

She knew my dad? 'This is a social visit, then?'

'Not exactly. This visit is about as serious as it gets for a member of the Company.'

'He's fine, then,' I said. 'Sends you his love.'

She had a twinkle in her eye. 'He might, as well, if he knew I was in this country.'

Information, too much of. I tried to absorb it but it got stuck in my brain, sideways, and gave me a headache.

Rani's dad cleared his throat. 'Commander Gatehouse is here because you have led our daughter astray.'

I rocked back for a second. 'Geez, Kristoff, what is this? The eighteenth century? Next you'll be saying that I sullied her reputation. I haven't even kissed her yet.'

Slippery stuff, language. It gets away from you sometimes. Like, how did that 'yet' get tacked onto the end of that sentence? And how did that sentence tag onto the other sentences?

Rani sent me a look full of daggers. Her mum groaned. Commander Gatehouse smiled grimly – she was a master of grim, I could tell that already – while poor old Kristoff just looked around blankly. 'I was talking about your leading her away from her duties as a member of the Company of the Righteous.'

'Oh, that,' I said.

'Enough,' Commander Gatehouse growled. That twinkle that I thought I'd seen in her eye was actually a shard of ice. 'Rani has committed to us. She has shown promise. You must have nothing more to do with her.'

'Well, she—'

'I'll speak for myself, Anton,' Rani snapped. She drew herself up. 'I'm not a baby, Commander, and I'd appreciate not being treated as one. It's my future at stake, after all.'

Gatehouse regarded Rani in silence. Rani gave as good as she got and regarded her right back. The air between them crackled and hummed. Almost.

Gatehouse broke first and I wanted to cheer. Go Rani! 'You are correct. You have a vested interest in this, of course. Choose your words carefully, though.'

'I always do,' Rani responded. 'And that's why I want to know what Anton is doing here.'

I cleared my throat. It was a little stagey, but it worked. 'I'm in the witness box, I guess.'

Kristoff sat, all saggily, as if his bones had turned to noodles. 'Commander Gatehouse. Sort this out, please. Tell this young man that he must leave us alone.'

Okay. 'With respect,' I said, 'I'm hearing plenty of assumptions here. For instance, you people are overlooking the fact that it's Rani who asked to hang out with me, not the other way around.'

'That is neither here nor there.' Kristoff scratched his beard. 'She should not be associating with people like you.

Commander, I hope that you will understand that Rani is not to blame. You will take her back?'

Rani hissed. 'Take me back? Why doesn't anyone believe me when I say I haven't left?'

'Wait,' I said. 'What? Leaving? Taking back? What's going on?'

Rani rubbed her forehead. 'I wish I knew.'

Gatehouse clapped her hands together. It wasn't loud, but we all looked her way. Neat trick. 'When our operatives are sent into the field,' she said, 'they represent an investment of years and much, much money. If they fall from the path we don't throw them away. We bring them in and we help them understand their wrongs.'

'You bring them in?' Rani asked woodenly. 'What does that mean?'

'It depends. For you, Rani, it will be Kuala Lumpur, one of our regional training schools. A few years should be enough.' She glanced at the Crosses. 'You will continue to be paid her subsidy.'

Mrs Cross spoke for the first time. 'The money isn't important.' She addressed Rani. 'What is it you want, Rani?'

'I want to do the right thing,' Rani said simply.

Gatehouse grunted. 'I think we need to discuss this alone. Kristoff, Olivia, can you leave us?'

He went to object. 'But—'

'It is best,' Gatehouse said.

Olivia helped her husband out of the room, her arm around his shoulders. After they closed the door behind them,

Gatehouse gestured for us to sit. To make some sort of a point, I sat next to Rani on the sofa.

Solidarity.

Gatehouse said to Rani, 'So you want to do the right thing?'

'I do,' she declared. 'But I'm still deciding what the right thing is.'

Gatehouse's gaze locked on me. 'You've led her astray with your Marin heresy. You've tainted her.'

Rani shot me a look then went back to her boss. 'No one has tainted me, Commander. Not now, not ever.'

I flicked my gaze from Rani to Commander Gatehouse and back again. I wasn't needed here. This was between Rani and her commander. Rani had experience dealing with her and I could only put my foot in it. Since sneaking out was not exactly an option, I vowed I'd make myself as unobtrusive as possible. This situation needed less Anton, not more.

'This is ridiculous!' Rani was saying. 'You're making accusations with no evidence at all! Why on earth would you think that I'm considering abandoning the Company?'

Commander Gatehouse flicked a finger in my direction. I bit my tongue so hard. 'You've been consorting with the Marins. This is your first solo assignment. You're young. You're likely to be easily influenced.'

Rani rubbed her hands together, slowly. 'I think that one person's taint is another person's knowledge, and knowledge is never a bad thing.'

The hint of a shadow of a touch of a smile hovered on

Gatehouse's lips for a microsplitsecond. 'That is a topic for another day.'

'I haven't renounced our cause,' Rani said. 'Just because I've been observing other ways doesn't mean I'm defecting.'

'Other ways,' Gatehouse snorted. Grunting and snorting. She was good. She eyed me again. 'You know, I'd like to see your family archive. To get a defector's perspective.'

I winced, but simply nodded and waved a hand in a non-committal way. I guess she saw my lack of verbal response as a challenge. The ice in her eye swapped for the twinkle again. 'And I would like to see anything about your Aunt Tanja.'

I broke my self-promise and spoke. Somewhere, a fairy dropped down dead. 'You knew my aunt?'

'Your Aunt Tanja and I were a couple, when we were younger. We had a falling-out that I regret.'

Zap. Powie. Blammo. 'I'm sorry. I thought you just said that you and my aunt were an item.'

'And a hot item we were, too,' she said, and I came over all faint. I mean, there are things that you really don't want to imagine your older relatives doing.

'All right,' I said, covering my eyes with a hand. 'I'm just going to sit here for a while and whimper.'

'You do that,' Rani said, not unkindly. 'Commander, let's get this straight. I am questioning the Company's teaching, and I'm not inclined to mindless obedience.'

'Obedience is the highest duty of each member of the Company,' Gatehouse said.

Rani shook her head. 'Surely a modern organisation has learned that unthinking obedience is limiting? What about initiative? Innovation?'

'Obedience is the highest duty of each member of the Company,' Gatehouse repeated, 'but it is accepted that the higher duty is to listen to one's conscience.'

'So that's higher than the highest,' Rani mused. 'What does it mean, though, in practical terms?'

'In practical terms it means that I might be prepared to listen to why you shouldn't come with me for re-training, if you can be persuasive.'

Rani didn't miss a beat. 'I need to deal with an insane phasmaturgist.'

In an instant, and by only moving a few millimetres, Gatehouse went from grim to formidably alert. 'What is this?' she snapped. 'You never said anything about a phasmaturgist, Rani.'

'I thought it might make things worse if I mentioned it.'

'You need to explain,' Gatehouse said.

Rani explained while I sat there, still shell-shocked by Commander Grumpy's revelation about Aunt Tanja and her. I mean, they were so *old*!

When they finished, Gatehouse drummed her fingers on the arm of the chair she had taken while Rani shared our story. 'This is not good, this happening now on top of everything else.'

'That sounds ominous,' Rani said.

'I was on my way to Melbourne already when the news came of your problem, Rani. I had been sent because troubles seem to be circling this city. It seems there is movement among the darkest of those who hunt ghosts.'

'Trespassers?' Rani said. 'Who? The Burnt Hand? Paltrino's Brood? The Ragged Sisters?'

'We are not sure. Perhaps all of them.'

Rani put both hands to her mouth.

I'd only known her for a few days, but I'd learned enough to know that anything that scared Rani Cross was definitely worth getting worried about.

Yikes.

'What does this mean for me?' She nodded in my direction. 'For us?'

'It means that you are not simply facing danger from ghosts, but from people with aims that are less noble than yours. If you get in their way, they will not hesitate to do you harm.'

'I can deal with them,' Rani said. 'But not if I'm taken away for re-training.'

'They will be dealt with by your replacement,' Gatehouse snapped. 'The protocols of the Company of the Righteous will be followed. Rani Cross, in one week you *will* be taken in for re-training. Ready yourself.' She pointed a finger at me. 'And don't have anything to do with him.'

Rani took a deep breath before answering. 'I won't, Commander, but I need to tie up some loose ends here. Can the Company help with neutralising a crime scene?'

'One that could incriminate you? We can.'

'Thank you, Commander.'

Gatehouse studied Rani for a moment, then she studied me, and left without saying another word.

Rani stood when she heard the front door slam. 'Now she's gone, we should get on with things.'

I stared. 'You heard. Don't have anything to do with me.'

'Yes, well, there is that.' She shook her head. 'I know her – once it gets to a certain point, the quickest way to get the argy-bargy over and done with is to agree with her.'

'You what?'

'I lied.'

CHAPTER 17

After Gatehouse left, Rani had a mini-scene with her parents. Short on the shouting, long on the strained silences.

I waited in the kitchen and tried to stop myself falling asleep. Nice place, that kitchen. It had a white marble and black surface design going. The twin fridge-freezer arrangement was neat, but I thought the downlights could have been better spaced.

I kept myself awake by checking the stream of texts that Bec had been sending. Mostly updates on the search for info about Stacey Evans, our phasmaturgist on the loose, but also about the reorganisation of the Marin family archives. She was still optimistic and I still shook my head, wondering if she really knew what she was getting into.

Then again, if everyone really knew what they were getting into before they started something, not much would get done, I expect.

A couple of texts were reporting progress on a special sideline project I'd asked Bec to look into, one that had me thinking, very deeply, about ghosts. Her findings were promising.

Rani found me after sixty-four minutes or so, but who was counting?

I was on my feet immediately. 'All sorted?'

'They don't want me to have anything to do with you, either.'

'I've been banned? I'm the bad guy from the other side of the tracks? Hey, who would have thought?'

Rani went all brisk, as if this was some sort of business meeting. 'I told them I needed to continue working with you if I was to finalise things here before my re-training.' She took her phone out of a pocket but put it back without looking at it. 'Just about everything in that statement made them unhappy.'

'You know, I have a feeling that Commander G didn't like me, either.'

'I wouldn't say that.'

'On the other hand, she didn't kill me on the spot, and I reckon she could have done that.'

'As easily as peeling a banana.'

'Do I detect some respect there for Commander Icy Stare?'

Rani took her time before answering. 'It's more than respect, I think. She was the only one who truly, reliably took my side all the way through my training.'

'Took your side by being incredibly harsh and disciplinarian?'

'That's part of it.'

'I was joking.'

'I wasn't. She was harsh, tough and uncompromising, and I believe it will stand me in good stead.'

'She also played a part in wiping out your memory of your real parents.'

Rani shook her head sharply. 'That wasn't her. That was the Initiation Department. Afterwards, Gatehouse sought me out and talked to me about it.'

'They have an Initiation Department? What next? Birthdays and Anniversaries Department? Wait – Leather Britches sympathised with you after they blotted out the memories of your parents? She went all soft and cuddly?'

'She let me know that she understood what I was going through, and that she didn't like it.'

'Ah. Sharing something personal?'

'That's what it sounded like. And after that, she was always the one who advised me to keep an open mind on all matters concerning ghosts, but counselled me to have patience, as well.'

'I'm hearing a mess of contradictions here. Hard and scary on the one hand, and thoughtful and understanding on the other.'

'Sometimes, I think she's playing a long game. That's why I think that if we can get to the bottom of this Rogue issue, she'll be prepared to accept that I'm capable of staying here.'

'And you won't need to be shipped off for re-education?'

'Re-training. No.'

'She won't be angry that you lied to her?'

'I'm not saying that, but she'll understand. Later. Necessities of the situation and all that.'

'So where do her loyalties lie, then?'

'With the Company. There's no doubt about that. But that doesn't necessarily mean loyalty to the current board of the Company and its direction. I think her view of the Company is larger than that.'

'I love it when something complicated becomes even more complicated.' I took a right-angle turn, conversationally. 'I'm guessing, though, that your parents aren't totally over the moon about your independent stance.'

'Not totally, but they've acceded to it.'

'I guess they have to, otherwise it's goodbye river of gold.'

Rani's hands turned into fists really, really quickly. 'It's not like that. They're good people. They're just worried about me.'

I held up my hands, not as fists, but palm upwards in a placating gesture that worked on dogs and small, rabid children. 'Okay, sorry, I withdraw that slur. They've got your best interests at heart and no one's good enough for their girl.'

'Like just about every parent ever.' She unclenched her fists. 'People think it's hard being adopted, but I don't know any different. I do know that it's hard being an adoptive parent. So many doubts, so much wondering about where love comes from and where it goes.'

'Same goes for step-parents,' I said, thinking about Judith.

I get on well enough with Judith, and Dad has been a whole lot brighter since they hooked up three years ago. She spends a lot of time away at conferences – medical – too, which could be a good thing, could be a bad thing. She's a neurologist, smart, kind enough, had been some help with my studies (especially chemistry), but hadn't really had an impact on my life – except in the way she made Dad happy. I have to like her for that.

Their marriage had lasted this far, and that was evidence of something, right?

'I think it's the same for people. Full stop.' She yawned, covering her mouth. 'It's late. Early. Whatever. I need some sleep.'

'Good idea. We can leave Bec and Dad working away and hope they'll come up with something while we get some rest.'

Rani looked away. 'You can stay here, if you like.'

Okay, so I'll explain in detail how I felt at that. It was as if a gremlin had secretly planted a whole lot of high explosive charges throughout my body, and then tied invisible ropes to my wrists and ankles with the other ends attached to high-speed winding devices. Winches. Capstans. Whatever. I'm imagining this as I go along, right?

When Rani made her tentative offer, all the explosives went off at once and all the high-speed winders went into action simultaneously. So I was jolted by dozens of conflicting impulses and torn in many directions, all at once.

I might have been reading too much into Rani's overture, but that's what it felt like.

'I beg your pardon?' I managed to say.

'There's lots of spare bedrooms.' She caught sight of my face, and she rolled her eyes. 'Not in a month of Sundays, you plonker.'

I blushed, tried to backtrack and babbled unconvincingly about how I hadn't been thinking what I'd obviously been thinking until she turned me around and propelled me towards the gate. 'Go.'

I wandered home, pretty dazed, as if I'd run a marathon and then taken part in a casual mixed martial arts bout. I was glad to be in the commuter rush, when no one asked any tourist questions or anything. To tourists, I have an approachable, harmless and knowledgeable face, apparently. I'm always being asked directions, for help with ticket machines, or for opinions about the weather by people who are clearly from elsewhere.

Anton, Friend to Tourists, that's me.

I got home, made some Anzac biscuits, tidied up a little, had a shower, and went to bed.

When I woke at around eleven, Dad was at the kitchen table nursing a cup of coffee. His old Gladstone bag was on the floor at his side.

'I had someone at the shop today,' he said.

'That's good,' I said, yawning and desperate for a coffee myself. 'Business must be looking up.'

'Diane Gatehouse.'

My coffee hunt came to an abrupt end. 'Get a feather and knock me over with it.'

'Surprised that she called in to the shop?' Dad asked.

'That, and that her first name is Diane. What time was this?'

'About three.'

'She must have gone straight to you after leaving Rani's parents' place.'

'She said she'd seen you, but she didn't say where. I think it's time for a report of a rather different kind, don't you?'

I wanted to know about this Commander Diane (Diane!) Gatehouse bookshop drop-in, but Dad could be incredibly stubborn when it came to reports. I gave him the edited low-down about the tense little meeting between Gatehouse, the Crosses, Rani and me. He didn't scribble away, though. He just made a few notes.

'And that's it,' I concluded. 'Your turn.'

'You're not going to take notes?'

I tapped my temple. 'It's all up here.'

'You can imagine my surprise when Diane walked into the shop,' he said. 'Rebecca had just left . . .' He paused. 'I'll wager that Diane had been observing the shop and waited until Rebecca had gone.'

'Rani said she's a pro. She fights the war in a different way from us, though.'

'I recognised her straight away, and after I got over the shock of seeing her I had a fleeting moment when I thought she'd come to eliminate me.'

'Are you saying she's an assassin or something?'

'She's many things. An assassin is only one of them.'

'This Company of the Righteous is one mixed-up enterprise.' I stumbled to the bench. Our coffee grinder is an old manual one. Dad insists it gets the best results, and grinding away with it gave me something to do with my hands. 'So why would she want to kill you?'

'It's a long story,' Dad said.

'I get the feeling that there are a whole lot of long stories that I need to get hold of. They might explain a few things.'

'They might help keep you alive, too.'

'There is that.' I filled the espresso maker with ground coffee, and added water. 'But how about the short version of the story about why she might want to kill you?'

'It's nothing personal.' He frowned for a moment. 'It might have something to do with what my ancestors took with them when they left the Company so abruptly, of course.'

Okay, so more mysteries to follow up. Not now, though, Anton! 'Which means that she might want to kill me too?'

'This is all possible, which is why I was a touch anxious when she came through the door. But eliminating Marins isn't on her agenda, at the moment, anyway. She has other fish to fry.'

'Busy, busy, busy.' I lit the stove top and settled the espresso maker on it. Next, juice. 'But it wasn't just a social call, was it?'

'She wanted to talk about the Trespassers that seem to be descending on Melbourne.'

'Yeah. They seemed to be on her mind.' Pine orange. Good. 'You haven't told me much about these Trespassers, though. What is it? Some sort of collective term for nasty, evil ghost hunter types?'

He rubbed his forehead and I was abruptly taken by how old he looked. How old was he, really? Forty-eight? Forty-nine? Something like that. 'It's been difficult, Anton, with your hesitation about entering the family business. You only agreed to do the job for a year, so I didn't want to burden you too much. Besides, if you're not in this business, there are many things it's better not to know.'

'Ignorance is bliss, right?'

'It's more of a "need to know" situation.' He fiddled with a waistcoat button for a while. 'The ordinary people out there, the ones we protect, they don't know about our doings, and they're better off for it.'

'Mmm ... been meaning to talk about that. It might be the wisdom of the ages, but what about transparency and a right to know rather than a need to know?'

Dad drooped. 'Not now, Anton, please.'

'Let's table it.' But not forget it. 'So Commander Diane was all antsy about some of these guys blowing into town and taking over the joint?'

'Huh. Antsy. I can't imagine Diane ever getting antsy, but she was concerned.'

'It's a dog-eat-dog world out there in ghost-hunting land.'

'You're right, though. "Trespassers" is a name that's used to cover a range of unsavoury ghost hunters. Some of these Trespassers are quasi-military orders, like an evil version of the Company of the Righteous. Others are quasi-religious. Some are small family groups bound together by blood ties. There are even those who are organised as a collective with shared decision-making and responsibility.'

'All shapes and sizes, hey?'

'They all have their own reasons for hunting ghosts. None of them are good.' He drummed his fingers on the table. 'They wouldn't just congregate by coincidence.'

'Trouble at the mill.' Coffee was ready. I poured myself a cup of bliss. 'One of the crossbeams gone askew on the treadle.'

He smiled, catching the reference for once. 'Trouble at the mill, indeed, but just who is the Spanish Inquisition? Them or us?'

'I hope it's us, and I get to wear those stunning red robes.'

'With all this increase in movement among the dark set, Diane wanted to warn me. Warn us. Off the record.'

'Not in her official capacity as Grand Poobah of the Company of the Righteous?' Coffee, juice. Now, I wouldn't mind porridge, but the Weet-Bix were ready-made. I pawed around in the pantry.

'As an old friend.' Something about the way he said that made me look over my shoulder.

Dad was blushing. He rubbed his face with both hands, but he couldn't hide it. It crept up his neck and under his beard.

'No,' I said. 'Tell me it isn't so.'

'It was a long time ago,' he said, but he smiled at the memory.

'I don't want to know,' I said.

'Many, many years past. Before your mother.'

'I'm going to stick my fingers in my ears, I tell you.'

'We were young. Not much older than you.'

'I'm dying a little inside.' I found a bowl and emptied a few slabs of wheaty nourishment into it. 'Wait, was this after Aunt Tanja and her or before?'

His eyes went distant. 'Before. I think. Yes, definitely before.'

Milk from the fridge. 'Speaking of stuff that it's better not to know.'

'That wasn't the point of telling you that, but I'm happy you see the relevance.'

'And otherwise you were telling me just to see me squirm?'

'It's the sort of background detail that might be important one day.'

'That you and your sister dated the same person? Important? Can't see how.'

'It shows that the Marins and the Company of the Righteous haven't always been on the outer with each other.'

'I'll keep it in the back of my mind at all times.' I started in on the Weet-Bix. They didn't taste great. 'So, after her ominous warning, she scarpered?'

'"Scarpered"? Too many nineties British police dramas there, Anton.' He crossed his arms on his chest. 'She didn't leave immediately. We had coffee.'

'Cosy.' I wondered if he'd tell Judith about this. I guessed he would. They were pretty open, Dad and Judith. She knew about the ghost-hunting business, and it's a sign that she really likes him that she didn't flee when he told her.

And, with that, I spent a moment or two contemplating the many and various forms of human relationships in all their glory, as you do, in between shovelling spoonfuls of breakfast cereal into my mouth.

Dad reached into his old Gladstone bag on the floor. He passed me a folder. 'Rebecca said to give this to you. She's found some possibilities.'

I scanned the printouts. Newspapers, some columns of figures, some maps. 'And how's she been going otherwise?'

Dad brought me up to speed on Bec's progress on the archive (outstanding) and on his research into Rogues (slow) before he finally headed off to bed himself.

I love my dad. He's frustrating sometimes, and irritating, and confusing, but I was starting to understand that I may have been all that as well – and he put up with it. His patience was maybe his greatest strength and it meant that after sailing through some stormy seas we looked as if we were reaching calmer waters, where I could appreciate him a bit more than I did when I was younger.

And that's another notch on the maturity belt, I'd say. Excuse me while I buff my fingernails.

So now it was back to business as usual – finding a homicidal phasmaturgist while keeping an eye out for evil ghost hunters with an agenda all of their own who wouldn't blink at snuffing out Rani and me.

Sounded like easy street.

CHAPTER 18

I heard Rani's car coming so I grabbed my backpack, my dark green blazer, my flat cap, my green scarf and my long black wool overcoat. Not the greatcoat. I had a feeling we might need to be nimble.

'What's in the folder?' Rani asked as I jumped into the car. She was in a black night-time-ninja-raid outfit. Black coat over black sweater and black pants. She looked like a panther.

'Stuff from Bec.'

'She's a treasure,' Rani said. 'How long have you known her?'

'All my life, more or less. We've grown up together.'

Rani made a job of adjusting one of the control knobs on the dashboard. 'You seem very close.'

'I hope you're not one of those people who think that men and women can't be close friends without being romantic.' Hold on a second. 'Of course, if a man and a woman would like to be romantic that's okay too, and friendly in a different way.'

Rani got out of the car and extracted her sword from the rack by the car seat. She slipped her phone out of a pocket and studied it, smiling slightly. 'Any leads on the one-eared barrister?'

'Stacey Evans's target?' I flapped a hand. 'Not yet.'

'Bec has discovered that he lives in a Docklands apartment. She's sent me the address.' She held up her phone so I could see.

'You two are collaborating behind my back.'

'We have an understanding.'

'So I see.'

'Anton, Stacey Evans isn't going to let things lie. She tried once and failed, but that won't stop her from trying again.'

I kicked that one around for a second or two. 'How can we know that?'

'Perhaps we can't, but rather than patrolling aimlessly, we should drive by and see if anything is happening.' She opened the car door. 'So, which direction is this Docklands?'

It was an unusual time in Melbourne – we were between festivals. This city, over the years, has grown festivals the same way a beach picnic sprouts seagulls. Comedy festivals, fashion festivals, food and wine festivals, writers' festivals … Melbourne seems to roll from one to the other without a break, so to find ourselves in the middle of the city at night with no festival crowds making merry was a bit strange.

We cut across the top of the city, around the market, and then, following my directions, down Dudley Street and Wurundjeri Way.

All Nite Parking was all night. We parked.

Like most modern car parks, this one was a concrete monster, largely open to the world to save on lighting bills. Rani went to the balcony/retaining wall and scanned the jumble of corporate headquarters, giant hotels, retail outlets and apartment complexes that made up this newish corner of the city. Lots of water around, with Victoria Harbour and, out past that, the Yarra. Once upon a time this was a busy working place, ships berthing from all over the world, cargo being unloaded by sweat and muscle power, nothing fancy at all. Lots of history, though.

Well past midnight made it like a bit of a ghost town (heh), especially with the wind whipping off the water. I wrapped my scarf tightly around my neck, jammed my cap on and made sure my coat was buttoned, wishing that I'd brought gloves.

Rani had. They were black, naturally, leather. She'd also found a hat, round, narrow brim. A toque, like 1920s flappers would wear? Very cool.

We turned a corner. The cold air slapped my face and I pointed. 'There. That's the one.'

The apartment block wasn't far from the cluster of hotels that overlooked the north end of Victoria Harbour. It was another steel and glass slab, with nattily quirky balconies that swooped and curved along the flanks of the building.

'We watch and wait, I suppose.' Rani had gloves, true, but she kept her hands in the pockets of her coat. The wind was that wild.

I followed her lead and rammed my hands further into the pockets of my coat. 'We could use that trained monkey to do that, if we could afford the banana bill.'

Rani scanned the area. 'If only there was a warm bar we could sit in around here, one that overlooked the place we're meant to keep an eye on.'

I risked taking a hand from my pocket so I could slap myself on the forehead. 'Welcome to Melbourne, the city of intimate and characterful bars.'

Rani's smile was appropriately wintry. 'I thought I'd read something about that.'

Near the apartments, we had a choice of three bars. We settled on Wimsey's, which had a 1930s murder-mystery vibe going on, suiting Rani's headwear well enough. I didn't really care, because warm beats freezing to death, especially since just as we found the place, rain began to bucket down.

Rani had a wistful glance at the wine list, but in the end we both ordered coffee, being on duty and all. Maybe Rani could afford it, but I knew that I wanted to be at my sharpest if we were going to have any encounters with anyone or anything this evening.

We didn't have any competition for a window table. A few other couples had found their way to the bar, some of them in pretty authentic 1930s outfits, but they gravitated to the gloomier inner reaches of the place.

Rani and I talked. At first it was all professional. We pawed over the printouts that Bec had provided: info about Stacey Evans's possible revenge targets, and some more stuff about the background of the Evanses that had the effect of making me sorry for a potential serial killer, which was quite an achievement.

What she'd been through.

Rani told some hair-raising tales about her training, and she made it sound like a combination of boot camp and torture chamber. She then revealed an appreciation of London's museums, from the grand halls of the British Museum to the more homely Garden Museum on the other side of the Thames. 'Who did you go museuming with?' I asked her after she lingered describing the Portrait Gallery. 'Company buddies?'

She looked startled. 'Myself. I went by myself.'

'That can be best. No interruptions.'

'I suppose so.'

She faltered then, I told her some more about Dad and his troubles with not having the family gift. I described Mum and what I could remember about her. That, of course, led to telling Rani about Carl. Then I got on to Aunt Tanja again, and Rani was really interested. Not that she was uninterested in the rest of the family stuff, it was just that she now had this connection, knowing Kommander Krazy as she did. She admitted, though, that she couldn't imagine her as young and in love.

'And hot,' I reminded her. 'Hard to imagine that.'

'Oh, I don't know,' Rani said. 'You haven't seen her stripped down and sweating after a fencing session.'

'No. No, that's true. No I haven't. Not planning to, either.'

You hear about soldiers, in wartime, in the trenches and foxholes, sharing intimate details of their lives because death is just around the corner. I don't think it was like that for Rani and me, not totally. We'd been through a lot in a few days, and that broke down barriers.

'I want to be a guardian,' she said solemnly after I told her the joke about the shoemaker and the optometrist. 'A sentinel for humanity against the dangers of the ghost world, and I don't care if it sounds pretentious.'

'Doesn't sound pretentious to me.' I toyed with my coffee spoon. 'It sounds like one of those things worth doing.'

'But I'm over the "don't ask questions, just follow orders" expectation.'

'Okay.'

'And this is where you can help. I want to understand ghosts, not just destroy them.'

'I support that.'

'Where do they come from?' she asked, as if she hadn't heard me. 'What are their motives? Can we truly determine their origins? Oh, there's so much we don't know.'

'Hidden, lost or never discovered. We should be in a better state of understanding than we are.'

She stared into her empty coffee cup for a while. 'Where did you go for your summer holidays?'

I dropped the coffee spoon. It bounced off the saucer and fell in my lap. 'That's a conversational tangent if I ever heard one.'

'I'm curious.'

'The beach. Different beaches, different summers.'

'You remember your brother there?'

'He was only little. He loved seagulls.'

'Tell me more.'

So I told her the story that Dad loved telling me, about the car trip we took to the Sunshine Coast. She laughed so much at the famous breakdown outside Albury that I had to grab napkins from another booth for her tears.

'I want to share something special,' she said after she'd composed herself. She didn't take sugar, but she'd spilled a packet on the dark wood of the table in front of her. She was using her coffee spoon to make trails and hills in it as she talked. 'Something that Commander Gatehouse told me before you arrived yesterday.'

I sat up straight. 'Are you sure?'

She rubbed the side of her nose. 'She told me that it was one of the Trespasser cliques that killed my parents.'

'These same Trespassers who are congregating on Melbourne?'

'She wasn't sure.'

'So it's a possibility that the people responsible for the death of your parents are coming here, right now?'

'The organisation responsible, maybe. The actual killers? I don't know.'

'Let me take a guess – you don't feel terribly kindly towards them?'

'These Trespassers, by and large, are dangerous, blood-thirsty and callous, which is good enough reason to oppose them.'

'But you have an extra reason.'

'I do.'

She flattened out the sugar, erasing all the lines she'd made, and then she drew a spiral in it, starting at the middle and working outwards.

A good sign.

She glanced through the window, then looked harder. 'We have movement.'

'At the station?'

'What?'

'Australian reference. I'll explain later.'

I paid the bill and we hurried out into cold that slashed at us. The row of shops and cafés opened out onto the waterfront so Rani held me up at the corner, a souvenir shop that was having a sale on both opals and pearls. 'This is strange,' she breathed while peering around a concrete pillar. 'Five people, all armed, black coats that nearly touch the ground, flat hats with wide brims.'

'Doesn't sound like Stacey Evans. What are they doing?'

'They're standing with their backs to the water, and they're looking at the same apartment block we're interested in.'

I joined her. The five figures were black and bulky, but the wind that whipped a few stray pieces of paper along the walkways didn't affect their coats at all. It was as if they were carved out of one piece of dull black material.

Water dripped from their hats and their hands and was pooling around their feet, which looked far too narrow and long for such blocky guys. 'You're thinking Trespassers, aren't you?'

'I hope not, but I fear so.'

'They're armed, you say? Guns?'

'Possibly, but from the way they're holding themselves I think it's more likely to be bladed weapons like mine.'

'What is it with you violent ghost-fighting types and swords? What's wrong with a nice handy Uzi?'

'Apart from the dangers to bystanders, you mean?'

'Good point, but bad guys don't usually care about stuff like that.'

'Guns don't work on ghosts. Bullets move too fast to interact with ghostly substance. Something slower, like a good blade, is just right.'

I'd never call Rani's blade action slow, but everything's relative, I guess. 'You learn something every day. So we watch the watchers?'

'Until they move. Now, tell me, where should we position ourselves? Where could their reinforcements come from? What can we use for cover?'

'Um.'

'Too late. They're not watchers anymore.' They'd started to move along the promenade in a bustling, urgent way that reminded me of rats off to spread some bubonic plague. They rolled along, up a side street and stopped at a large roller door. A loading bay? Rubbish bin drop-off? They clustered around it and, within seconds, it was opening. They disappeared inside.

Rani set off after them. I followed, squinting against the wind. Call me the one-man back-up team.

Rani was unbuttoning her coat as she ran, which signalled that things could get a bit slashy in the near future. I caught up with her at the entrance of the apartment building. 'Yes, it's complicated,' she said as she drew her sword. She grabbed my arm with her other hand. 'I know I'm conflicted, I know that I'm being pulled in different directions, and I know that what I do over the next few days could determine the course of my life, but let's not worry about that right now. I'm about to launch into doing something that I've been trained for, that I'm actually very, very good at. For now, that's enough.'

Then she was off and I ran after her.

The loading bay was a cold, flat, concrete holding area lit by some big LEDs that were struggling to illuminate the storage bins, the rubbish skips, the empty shelves and racks. When LEDs struggle, I find that the light goes slightly fuzzy, making everything look soft, including the dripping Trespassers who, as one, swivelled when Rani and I entered.

The Trespassers, with almost identical moon-like faces and swords drawn, had cornered a dark-haired, wild-eyed woman who just happened to be standing behind a tall and frothing Rogue, up on the loading platform, in front of a locked door that must lead into the apartment building proper.

The newcomer bad guys had bumped into Stacey Evans, who was also up to no good, and it was a whacky time in the old town tonight. So embarrassing.

Without a word, two of the Trespassers broke off and confronted Rani. The other three closed on Stacey Evans and her ghostly charge.

That's when it started getting hectic. Rani moved like a cat, and soon the two Trespassers were wondering why they hadn't phoned for reinforcements before they jumped in.

And speaking of reinforcements, even though none of the combatants were shouting, the sound of blade on blade and the painful howling from Stacey Evans's Rogue was bound to get someone calling the police. I figured we had about ten minutes, tops, before the civilian authorities turned up, and that was something I'm sure everyone wanted to avoid.

So, remembering that I should always consider optimal deployment of forces, I sidled up to the recycling bins and starting lobbing bottles at the bad guys.

I don't know much about sword fighting, fencing or hand-to-hand combat in general, but I do have a good arm. I can throw long, hard and accurate. I don't care how committed you are to your Dark Overlord, having a bottle conk you on the forehead is going to ruin your day just a little. I was hoping for distraction, at least, or even disablement. And with the range of ammunition I had, the latter was a possibility. The people who lived here knew a thing about drinking from the top shelf and, let me tell you, a genuine French champagne bottle was heavy enough to do some real damage.

I threw bottles, alternating head shots with body shots, while Rani closed on them.

I couldn't help it. I broke the silence of the battle. 'Booyah! He shoots, he scores!' I crowed when a Taittinger bottle cracked one of Rani's assailants on the side of the head. He staggered, and Rani slid forward and bodychecked him into the concrete wall. He didn't get up.

She rounded on the other guy in time to meet his blade with hers. They grappled long enough for me to find a nice heavy Mumm bottle. I took it by the neck and pinged the guy right in the middle of the back. He grunted and folded. 'It's a sausage roll!' I danced around, punching the air, while Rani thumped him on the back of the head with the hilt of her sword.

Down and out.

Okay, so maybe I'd got carried away. Up on the loading platform, it was like a kids' party. A violent kids' party, maybe, but not much more so than some I've been to. It's that red cordial. Or the weapons, one or the other.

Stacey Evans had disappeared, but the Rogue was still there. He was strikingly tall and thin, with a huge armspan, dressed in funeral black, with hair like a silver skullcap. The three bad guys surrounded him, forcing him to turn in circles, snarling, darting forward only to be driven back by their weapons.

The Rogue wasn't happy about this situation. I mean, I know that Rogues aren't happy about anything, but this clever arrangement by the bad guys was making him wild. He howled and slashed with ragged fingernails, and when he twisted he went around so hard he nearly turned into a corkscrew.

A quick head gesture from one of the bad guys and the other two stepped closer to the Rogue and engaged him twice as hard, blades doing the old snicker-snack, vorpal style. The third bad guy, the head nodder, sheathed his sword and – I swear – pulled a big old hessian bag out from under his coat.

With a well-practised movement, while the Rogue was roaring at the other two guys, he stepped forward, and bagged the ghost.

So it was 'I don't believe what I'm seeing' time, because as soon as the bag went down over the Rogue's head and shoulders, the ghost started to shrink. When the bad guy dragged the bag down to floor level, twisted, and scooped it up, he was holding nothing larger than a small, struggling puppy inside.

Job done, they turned to us. I was hoping for one of them to make an offer, say, 'Our quarrel is not with you', but the bag guy slung the sack over his shoulder like a bizarro Santa while the other two jumped off the platform and menaced us in silence.

That was uncanny, and more than a little bit unsettling. Some boasting, some taunting, some sort of villainous cackling would have been almost comforting, given the circumstances, but this deadly silent attacking was chilling.

These guys must have been keeping an eye on us while they were bagging Mr Rogue. One went for Rani and the other went for me.

Aiee.

Turning and running was a definite option. These long legs, once they get going, can cover the ground – but that would mean leaving Rani.

I sconed my guy with a Jim Beam bottle (a bogan must have been visiting the apartments) and missed the other guy with another Mumm bottle. He was fast, and things were getting serious when a bunch of vehicles squealed to a stop outside and I was trapped in a good news/bad news joke. The good news was that the police would stop the bad guy from chopping me up with a sword, but the bad news was that I'd have involved the civil authorities in a ghost-world matter and, oh, my friend was carrying a really offensive weapon too.

And I'd probably get charged with littering. So much broken glass.

The sword-wielding bad guy stopped about five metres away from me. He didn't lower his weapon, though. He smiled, despite me brandishing a bottle in either hand.

I risked a glance over my shoulder and that's when I knew I wasn't in a good news/bad news story, I was in a bad news/bad news story.

The police hadn't responded fast enough. A couple of dozen more identically clad Trespassers were pouring into the loading bay.

CHAPTER 19

The Trespassers drove tow trucks and vans and were very polite. For kidnappers, that is – kidnappers who went around bagging up dangerous ghosts for who knew what.

Rani and I were tossed in the back of a white van that was towed by one of the trucks. They apologised as they threw us, but it didn't stop them throwing.

'You know more about these guys than I do,' I said to Rani after I tried the doors. Locked. The van smelled of sawdust and grease. 'Who are they?'

'I knew I should have brought my *Spotter's Guide to Trespassers*.' She kicked the wall of the van. 'At a guess, they could be the Keepers of the Mysteries, or the Vitalarians, or any of a dozen others. These fellows do seem a little more organised than most, though, which is unfortunate for us.'

'Mm. The sort of unfortunate that could end up with us in mind-numbing danger, but I suppose you can't have everything.'

They'd taken my backpack and phone, and they examined my pendant for some time before, surprisingly, giving it back. They'd taken Rani's sword, the dagger she kept at the small of her back, and her phone. They let her keep her bracelet, though.

'Did you see what they did to that Rogue?' I asked. Better to talk than to brood. 'What's that about?'

'I saw.' She made a fist and thumped the wall of the van. 'Some of these groups don't want to destroy ghosts. They use them for their own awful purposes.'

'Oh, I don't know,' I said. 'Maybe they're like Japanese whalers, just hunting those pesky ghosts so they can study them. Scientific ghost hunting instead of scientific whale hunting.'

'And you know that most of the whale meat from those scientific tests ends up being eaten in restaurants, don't you?'

I had a vision of these bad guys tucking into a nice plate of ghost stew and I couldn't unthink it fast enough.

We were driven around for a while. Even though I tried to listen, to get some sense of where we were going, all I heard were generic city noises – traffic, clicketty pedestrian-crossing sounds, snatches of music from who knew where.

Just before we pulled up, I did feel us head downwards at quite a slope. The big truck engine shut off, signalling that we had arrived. The doors were flung open.

'Out, out, out,' one of the Trespassers ordered. He had a pistol, which suggested that we comply.

226

'Please,' he added, and then – amazingly – did a quick look around, like a naughty schoolkid hoping that no one had noticed his lack of courtesy.

Rani and I climbed out, and we were surrounded by Trespassers in a standard-issue underground garage, empty apart from the concrete pillars that held up the roof. They stared at us without hostility, and with open curiosity on their bland faces. Gun Boy waggled the pistol. 'This way. The elevator. Please.'

It was clear that English wasn't his first language. He was correct enough, but staccato, as if he had to think each sentence through in his own language before saying it. His accent was North Asianish. Mandarin or Japanese or Korean, maybe, with an extra touch of -ish. Lots of muscles, big shoulders, thick neck. The others were a mix of builds and heights. Even their skin colours were an assortment, ranging from deep brown through dark brown and into a paler mixture of brown and pink.

I stared at the tow trucks that had parked behind the van, all six of them. 'Nice cover, guys. Tow trucks can roar around the city at all hours and no one gives them a second glance. Hey, do you know the Kerrigans?'

Gun Boy frowned. 'Kerrigans? No. Elevator, now, please.'

Rani looked as puzzled as the bad guys. I shook my head. 'Nobody appreciates a classic Aussie comedy reference these days.'

We were crowded into the small lift with Gun Boy and half a dozen of his jolly buddies. They smelled of stale sweat.

'Okay,' I said, and since no one had warned us not to talk yet, I thought I'd get in a few questions while I could. 'Where are we then?'

'Toorak,' Gun Boy said, and I nearly fell over. I expected a surly response, or a snarl, or a pistol whip. Didn't these guys know anything about being kidnappers?

'Nice,' I said. 'If I have to be kidnapped and kept somewhere, I always prefer it to be in one of the better suburbs.'

Gun Boy shrugged. 'Toorak is quiet and close to the city.'

'A top choice, my good man, top choice. And while we're being so friendly, would you mind telling us what you're going to do with us?'

He considered this. 'You will first be presented to the local leader of the Malefactors, then kept in a room and then we will perform a rite on you that will determine your ghost-hunting ability. Any you have will then be extracted to add to the power of our group. This will leave you mindless and like a jelly.'

I caught Rani's eye. 'Oh, they're the *Malefactors*.'

Then it hit me. Brain. Jelly. Mindless. I swallowed hard.

Rani saw. 'Good thing our commando squad is tracking us right now, Anton. I'd be worried if not for them.'

Gun Boy's eyes widened, but he said nothing.

I gave Rani the thumbs-up. Nothing like the non-existent reinforcements bluff to lift the spirits.

CHAPTER 20

The lift opened onto a sort of reception area, designed to impress. Expensive black marble on the floor and walls. Mirrors, potted palms, four doors opening onto other parts of what promised to be an extensive complex. It looked more like a hotel foyer than a home, and that told me something. This place was made for rich people to live in short term.

Gun Boy and his buddies ushered us to the big double doors facing the lift. He was nervous, his gun wobbling as they stood in front of the doors. 'Do not upset our leader, please,' he said.

'Great.' I tipped him a salute. 'Go straight to the top, I say. Messing around with underlings is a waste of time.'

'Do not upset him,' Gun Boy repeated. 'It will go ill for us.'

'I like to see naked self-interest like yours,' Rani said. 'But we can't make any guarantees.'

'It will go ill for you too,' Gun Boy said, almost as an afterthought. 'And we hate disposing of bodies.'

Okay, then.

They opened the doors and escorted us inside.

If the reception area was designed to impress, this was too, but on a bigger scale. The room was at least ten metres long, and about half as wide. The ceilings must have been five or six metres overhead. The floor was that jigsaw wooden stuff. Parquetry. The floor-to-ceiling windows were bare of curtains and they looked out on a quiet, leafy street. The house opposite was a massive three-storey construction with more pillars and columns and balconies than a little kid's Lego idea of a mansion.

This was a room for gatherings, cocktail parties maybe, with the snooty crowd milling around with champagne glasses that were half-full and egos that were overflowing. They'd have to be well rugged-up, though, because it was definitely chilly.

A desk stood at the far end of the room. It was a bit obvious, really, how that made us cross about a kilometre of floor before we reached it, to underline how insignificant we were. Intimidate Your Enemies 101.

Sitting behind the desk was the big boss of these Malefactors, our Trespassers sub-set of the day.

I'd like to say he was an average-looking guy, someone who could be mistaken for an accountant or a public servant. It'd be a commentary on how evil lurks everywhere, blah, blah, blah ... but I'd be lying. This guy was seriously weird.

For a start, he had an almost triangular-shaped head, with the top much wider than his chin. Glossy, black, slicked-down hair, with a hairline alarmingly close to his eyebrows. I never trusted a low hairline. If I had one I would have learned to shave my forehead, let me tell you.

His eyes were small in that bizarre head, small and grey-blue. His mouth was small, too, and so red I wasn't sure if he was wearing lipstick or not. He also had ears, one on either side of his head, which was about the only ordinary thing about him.

The whole effect was like a little kid's drawing of a person, brought to life. That is, if the little kid was having a really off day with sub-standard crayons.

He was wearing a grey silk shirt, unbuttoned at the neck. His hands were resting on the desk in front of him. The desk was totally bare.

'Nice place you've got here,' I said. 'Did you decorate it yourself or did you get someone in?'

The man lifted one hand and batted this aside, as if he was flapping away a bad smell.

I've had worse reactions.

'Who are you?' he said in a voice that could have come from anywhere. It was educated, soft, cultured even, but I couldn't pin down the accent.

Rani stepped forward. 'Did you kill my parents?'

I stared. I hadn't been expecting that.

The man curled his lip. 'I have no idea. One kills so many people, these days, that it's hard to keep track. Tell me – who were they? Where was I supposed to kill them? How?'

Rani's face screwed up, half with pain, half with frustration. 'I don't know. I have no memory of that, and I can't find out.'

The man frowned. 'To whom do you belong?'

'I am a member of the Company of the Righteous. Release us immediately or you will be faced with our might.'

The man raised an eyebrow, and his whole slick puck of hair moved. It made me queasy. 'The Company of the Righteous? What are they doing in this forsaken backwater?'

'Hey,' I said. 'That's my forsaken backwater you're insulting.'

He raised both forefingers from the desk and let them fall again. 'I always insult places that are at the end of the earth.'

'And that's totally a matter of perspective, something you seem to be lacking. Where *you* come from is the end of the earth if you measure it from here.'

He pursed his lips. It wasn't a good look. He resembled an out-of-shape football with a bit of the bladder poking out.

Rani went on. 'This, of course, raises the question of what you Malefactors are doing here, if it's so forsaken.'

'Malefactors,' I said. 'Where do you people get these names from? Is there some sort of Evil Organisation Random Name Generator that I don't know about?'

The big boss looked at me then. I mean, really looked at me. Before, he'd given me the once-over, but now he locked his eyes on mine.

It was like looking into the pit of doom. Those bland eyes were a prop, and as I looked it was as if they were whisked away and I was looking at depravity, at heartless, pitiless malignancy. This man was a walking, breathing tumour.

Talking smart to this guy might be stupid, but show me

anyone who hasn't done anything stupid and I'll show you an alien.

'You must be a hit at Halloween.' I won't say that my voice squeaked at first, but it definitely got stronger as I went on. 'You could hire yourself out. You know: scary times guaranteed or your money back.'

'Be quiet, boy,' he said, 'or I'll have one of your fingers cut off, for a start.'

It was the calm way he said it that was chilling. That and the way Gun Boy and his buddies – who had been standing silently to one side while all this was going on – produced big shiny knives all at the same time like a chorus line of sleight-of-hand artists.

'Okay,' I said. 'So I can either have my brains sucked out with ten fingers or with nine.'

He frowned at that. These big boss bad guys. It's only funny if they say it. I think that's why they cart so many underlings around with them. Guaranteed laughter. 'And why would we...' He saw my pendant. 'Ah. You have the sight too. Good. We will take you as well as the girl.'

Okay, so I dropped myself in it there. On the other hand, I didn't think they were really about to let me walk out of here just because I was underpowered in the ghost-seeing department.

'You thought it was just her?' I said, nodding at Rani. 'We don't all need a sword to show we're in the seeing-ghosts club.'

'We don't often see independent operators,' the big boss said. 'Mostly it's because they don't last long.' He glanced at Rani. 'Or is the Company of the Righteous – pompous name, that, boy, if you're being critical – so desperate that it's recruiting way out here at the ends of the earth?'

'That's two cracks you've had at my city,' I said. 'If you keep it up I won't show you Captain Cook's cottage.'

He frowned at this, and I counted it as a hit. 'By the looks of you,' he said, 'you are unlikely to provide us with much that is useful, but we'll take it nonetheless.' He turned to Rani. 'You should give us more.' He tapped his fingers on the desk again. 'But before that, I'm interested in finding an amateur phasmaturgist who seems to be making mischief hereabouts. She appears to be a dab hand at summoning and controlling Rogues.'

Okay, confirmation that these guys were after Stacey Evans. Way to go.

Rani bristled. 'Why would I share anything with the Malefactors?'

'Quite.' He drummed his fingers on the desk. 'This may be pointless, but – with some hesitation – I will offer you both the traditional offer to join our organisation.'

Bingo. 'Sure thing,' I said. 'When do we start?'

Rani stared at me, open-mouthed.

The big bad boss, though, smiled. Nastily. 'Oh dear, that was far too quick. I detect insincerity.'

Gah. How could I be taken on staff and then work from inside the organisation to help us both escape if I kept up the smartarsery? 'Sorry. I have trouble with sounding sincere. It's a condition.' I held up both hands. 'But I am sick of blundering around in a rundown family organisation with no prospects.'

He didn't move. 'I see.'

I tried a shrug. 'Besides, I'd rather be working for you than dead, if you know what I mean.'

'No, I'm not convinced,' he said. 'Not even by the candid selfishness. I withdraw my offer.'

'Offer?' I scoffed. 'You weren't serious about it for a second.'

'True. I simply like amusing myself, watching how people betray themselves when their lives are at stake.'

I shook my head at Rani, and I hoped the gesture expressed that I hadn't really thought of turning traitor, and that I agreed just so I could possibly find a way out of this. Which is a lot to convey with a headshake, admittedly, and I'm not sure if I pulled it off.

He studied us in a way I didn't like. 'I'm still after this phasmaturgist, and your appearance just as we were about to take her makes me think that you know something.' He clicked his fingers. Gun Boy loped to his side. 'Lock them away while we make preparations to find out what they know.'

Gun Boy nodded. 'And the ritual? Are we still going ahead with it after that?'

'Of course. Their strength may be meagre, but it could be usefully added to ours. Make haste!'

CHAPTER 21

We were locked in a bare room in the middle of a night that hadn't gone in any direction I'd anticipated. It might have been a bedroom, once upon a time, but all the furniture was gone, leaving only the carpet and the built-in wardrobes, mirror-doored, with nothing inside. The windows looked out over a back courtyard, where clever garden lighting showed us red brick, some small box trees that looked as if they badly needed clipping, and a dry fountain. The cherub holding the dolphin looked really irritated at how things had turned out for him.

The window was barred. Seriously barred. It could have kept out an attack by a megashark.

'Sorry,' Rani said.

I whirled. Maybe not ice-dancer perfect, but not bad. 'What for?'

'Back at Docklands. We should have waited, observed, picked them off one at a time.'

'True. I mean, after all your pointers on reconnoitring and sizing up the lines of fire, just ploughing in like that was unexpected.'

'I see. And you've never made a bad decision before?'

'Not with a sword in my hand, that's for sure. There's only one way things can go when you're armed like that, and that's badly.'

'It would have been bad for you if I hadn't been armed.'

'If you hadn't been armed we would have done things differently.'

'And ended up torn to pieces? Lovely.'

'We could have kept our distance.'

'When these people could be those that killed my parents?'

'You don't know that. And, anyway, what about tactics and preparation and all that? You just charged in!'

'You'd rather we skulked about?' She folded her arms and her foot started tapping. 'Hiding and cowering, the classic Marin approach?'

'That's not how we do things,' I snapped.

'You should be proud, really, of the small achievements of your family. Out here, all by yourselves? You've done well, considering.'

I jabbed a finger at her. 'Don't patronise me.' I took a step away. I was breathing hard. 'Sorry.'

Rani looked away. 'Sorry? Isn't that where we started?'

'Yeah. Look, we're in a bad situation. It got to me. I didn't mean it.'

'Neither did I,' she said softly.

I glanced at her. 'We're polite, aren't we? We say we didn't mean it, but it came from somewhere.'

'Your point?'

'My point is that even though I said what I said, and it came from somewhere inside me, I take it back.' I started a slow circuit of the room, inspecting the architraves, the ceiling, the door. 'Besides, you would have demolished them all if their reinforcements hadn't turned up.'

Awkward silence is awkward.

Rani saw my impressive, methodical approach. She began to inspect the wardrobes. '"If he sends reinforcements everywhere, he will everywhere be weak." Sun Tzu.'

Grateful for the bone, I grabbed it. 'Oh come on, are you sure that wasn't Oscar Wilde?' I bent and picked up a piece of fluff. I narrowed my eyes. It could be important. Or it could just be fluff. Hard to tell in these crazy times. I dropped it on the floor, but promised myself that I'd keep an eye on it. 'Besides, the reinforcements didn't have to be everywhere, they just had to be where we were.'

Rani finished her exploration of the wardrobe, didn't find any entrances to Narnia. She went to the door and tested it with a shoulder. 'I can get us through here, but with the Malefactors waiting for us, a distraction could be useful.'

'Distraction. Right.'

I kept pacing and the more I paced, the smaller the room seemed and the further and further away from brilliant I got. In fact, the closer and closer I got to thinking that maybe definitely I wasn't cut out for this, and that got my palms sweating and my stomach flip-flopping at the fate these Trespassers had in mind for us. I had trouble keeping my thoughts straight – they refused to stick and they all scuttled away before I could nail them down. I didn't know what to do with my hands and after flapping them around for a while I stuck them in my pockets just to keep them still.

'Okay,' I said, and I had to clear my throat before I could go on, 'what are we especially good at?'

'Seeing ghosts?'

'True, but it's more than that. We're good at detecting ghosts, interacting with them and, in your case, dispatching them into oblivion. In my case, easing their passage to the great beyond.'

She frowned. 'So?'

'That sort of thing was one of Aunt Tanja's obsessions. I've had Bec looking into her work.'

Noises came through the door. Either the bad guys were having a little sing-along, or an argument was breaking out. I cheered that thought on, because if they all killed each other, the future would be a whole lot brighter for Rani and me. Even if it would leave us locked in a room.

I continued. 'The Marins have had to think about this whole ghost interaction thing a bit differently, you know.'

'I think that's the definition of "heresy" that Commander Gatehouse was using.'

'Right, right. Since we're not as dedicated to chopping up ghosts and assigning them to oblivion as your team is. And I don't know if you realise it, but even though you're re-evaluating the whole thing, your hand has just gone to where your sword hilt usually is.'

'Go on,' she said. 'Carefully.'

'So we've explored all sorts of aspects of this ghost–human interaction thing.'

'And when you say "we" you mean the Marin family.'

'That's right. Apparently Aunt Tanja had an idea that instead of just hunting ghosts, sniffing around for them, maybe she could attract them.'

Rani stared. 'Just in case you can't tell, this is my "Was she bonkers?" expression.'

'I guessed. And she wasn't bonkers, just a deep thinker. Dad pieced all this together later, because one of Tanja's experiments went horribly wrong. So horribly she disappeared.'

'She died?'

'She disappeared. During a séance.'

'And you tried a séance two nights ago knowing your aunt disappeared during one.'

'Well, yeah, sort of. I was careful.'

'You might have just been lucky.' She put both hands to her forehead and massaged it. 'Don't tell me that you want to try again.'

'It's not a case of want to, really, but if it's the choice between what our cheer squad out there is offering and trying a crackpot experiment, I'll go with my aunt. In a manner of speaking.'

'That's not very reassuring.'

'Look, Bec has uncovered some of my aunt's records that have cleared up a few things. I think I know what I did wrong last time, for a start.' I paced about a little. 'Last time, I was trying the séance cliché, trying to stretch out and contact the ghost world, and it didn't work. The notes Bec found suggest that this approach is too active.'

'That would tend to distress ghosts, repelling them rather than bringing them closer.'

'Right, Tanja's theory is that a much more gentle approach is needed. It's like turning yourself into a lighthouse, but one that isn't saying "Keep Away! Dangerous Rocks!", it's saying "Come here! Come here!" and the metaphor has really fallen apart, hasn't it?'

'You're under strain.'

'Yeah. Funny, that. Bad guys just about to pulp our brains does put pressure on. And then there's the possibility that if this scheme goes wrong, ghosts could tear me apart.'

'That's what happened to your aunt?'

I shook my head. 'When Dad broke down the door she was gone. No body left behind, no blood. This coming just a few years after Mum left was another blow. He threw himself into the archives to try to work out what happened and came up with some ideas – that she'd been taken, body and all, into some weird realm by something really nasty, that she'd become so close to ghosts that she became one too – but nothing convinced him. Finally he gave up.'

'He's suffered, but doesn't show it.'

'Not so that people would notice, maybe.' I kicked at the carpet. 'If I try what she tried, something bad could happen to me and I'm not crazy about that possibility. I'm selfish like that.'

'Understandable, but if you could move things along, it'd be appreciated.' Rani took up position by the door. 'I'll guard your back.'

All right. Clearing the mind. In future, I thought, if this sort of thing became important, I might need to practise mind-clearing to get good at it, because it could be difficult and maybe Bec could help because she did some of that mindfulness or meditation or something like that and that loose thread in my sock was really starting to irritate me and—

Okay, so the mind-clearing was getting off to a rocky start.

This time, for sure.

I took the pendant from around my neck and put it on the floor in front of me. I ran my finger over the metal basketwork, and shivered. When Dad gave it to me I spent hours looking at it, but he didn't tell me anything except that it had been in the family 'forever'.

It was metal, silver-grey, but I had no idea if it was steel, nickel, silver or something else. It was about the size of a fifty-cent piece and it looked like a whole bunch of wire that was criss-crossed and woven in on itself, a tight sort of spherical knot, as light as a feather.

I touched it, fingertips of my left hand only. I closed my eyes and sank into myself, concentrating hard, trying to be open to any ghostly presences in the area without actively looking for contact in any way.

Bang. The pendant vibrated and suddenly it was as if the whole world had shifted a millimetre or two to the right, or the left, or up or down. Or like an Instagram filter had been slapped on the whole universe. My awareness of our surroundings uncurled. I could take in, mistily, not just the room we were in, but the building, the neighbourhood and the district in the way that ghosts must perceive the world.

We were in Toorak – thanks for telling me, Gun Boy – a nice old part of the city. Plenty of history, plenty of lives, plenty of time to spawn ghosts. Rich ghosts, probably, for the most part, Toorak being what it is. But I'd already learned that even in the rich areas of Melbourne there are plenty of out-of-the-way locations, back streets and shady alleyways, sites of unhappy and traumatic deaths, home to the insecure and unwanted. I'd be surprised if any big city is different.

I had to welcome all this, passively. I had to let the ghosts see me as they hung on here, the stubborn cast-offs as they hung on here, clinging to a semblance of life.

My pendant was barely stirring. The ghost sensation was horribly fuzzy. I couldn't make out how far away they were, or even how many – apart from the fact that there was more than one. I could tell, however, that they were dormant and had been for some time.

So, carefully, I tried to shine brighter, in a ghosty sense. I was putting myself up as ghost bait.

Ghosts lack a lot of things. A sense of humour is one notable omission in their make-up, and time sense is another. Don't make an appointment with a ghost and expect it to be punctual, is what I'm saying. And as for remembering birthdays, forget about it.

Which is a roundabout way of saying that even if I managed to rouse these ghosts and hold myself up as a tasty ghost titbit, they could take forever to turn up.

Or they could arrive quick smart.

That's when I had a horrible thought. Last time I tried anything like this, Stacey Evans and her Rogue slave homed in and tried to kill Rani and me.

What if they were just waiting for me to pop up on the ghost radar again? What if, really and truly, I was out of my depth here?

I nearly started nervous whistling then, but cut it off sharpish. No time to worry about that. If Stacey and Co turned up, they could run interference for us with the Malefactors. We'd make use of the distraction to escape.

Yeah, that.

A quick intake of breath from Rani and a jerky buzzing from my pendant alerted me that something was happening. The ghostly world receded and I was back in the here and now.

'They're here,' I said, showing a fine appreciation for another early '80s ghost movie. Yeah, I know, but it's one of Dad's faves.

They were showing a classic ghost lack of appreciation for normality in that they were pushing up through the floor, three of them, a man and two women. The man and one of the women were early twentieth century, and well-to-do. She looked as if she was in her fifties, and was wearing a long dress, naturally, and a hat the size of a wagon wheel. He was older and had a top hat, long topcoat and a moustache he must have wrestled off a walrus.

The third ghost was younger – in her thirties, maybe – and more modern. Late 1950s? Early '60s? It was the spectacles that hinted at that – nicely pointed at the corners, the cats-eye style that hipsters would fight over. Her dress was knee-length, long-sleeved and pretty ordinary. She had the dazed and baffled look of so many Lingerers and Mopers.

She drifted over and huddled in the corner, shaking.

The Edwardian duo – I had no sense that they were a couple – eyed us hungrily. Slowly, they raised their arms, hands like claws, and drifted towards us, waves of fear rolling off them like cheap perfume. No-nonsense types, Thugs. See person, latch onto person, make them feel really bad. Even if they were out of practice, they'd be a nightmare for an ordinary member of the public.

I hurried to my feet. We backed away, Rani steering me until we were in the corner with the door. 'So far so good,' I said to her.

'This is good?'

'It's a relative term. It's still bad but it's better than it was.'

'Because?'

'Because – if I can do this right – we have a distraction.' I took a deep breath. The whole concentrating and luring thing had been more exhausting than I expected. 'I'm going to try something fancy, but I can only do one at a time.'

'I can handle either of them.'

'Great. I'll take him, then. On the count of three. One—'

As well as no time sense, ghosts have trouble counting, too. The male lunged at me, shunting the female aside. I may or may not have sworn, but I bounced off the door behind me and that propelled me forward.

Long arms, me. That meant I latched onto him before he latched onto me.

The ghost's eyes went wide as my hands plunged into his chest. He flailed and emitted a high-pitched whine, while shivering like a sick dog.

I automatically went into 'easing' mode, but I clamped down on it. With my hands deep in the ghost's chest, I swung it around in an arc and the ghost was taken by surprise. He didn't weigh anything – ghost, remember – and so he whipped around in a big circle until at the strategic moment I pulled my hands out and he flew backwards through the door.

It was hard to pick the tone of the cries that came from the living room on the other side. Surprise? Delight? Hunger? It didn't matter, because Rani had seen what I was up to. She turned her calm grappling with the female ghost into a straight-arm shove and then a shoulder charge that sent the ghost spinning my way.

'Steady her!' I called as the ghost whirled drunkenly at me.

Rani darted and grabbed one shoulder, enough to jerk the ghost to a stop, but she was more resilient than her buddy. She swung an arm and clubbed Rani aside, then came at my throat with her teeth.

We had no time for this. I tucked my chin to my chest and grabbed for her essence. 'Be at peace,' I whispered, and she dissolved in a flood of memories of the beach, violets and the faraway sound of horses' hooves.

Rani lined up the door with her shoulder. 'Wait,' I said. 'I can't leave her like this.'

The third ghost hadn't moved. I bounded over to where she was huddled in the corner. She had stopped sobbing, and was sitting under the window, clutching her knees. 'It's all right.' I closed on her, arms spread. 'I'm here. Don't worry.'

She looked at me. She looked at me properly, I mean, with something close to focus. It rocked me. In all my, admittedly limited, experience with ghosts, they stared as if they were seeing right through you. This time, though, the sobbing ghost looked at me as I'd look at another human being.

Then she reached out and took my right hand.

I froze, mostly because my hand went numb as the ghost essence sank into mine, but there was more than that.

She'd locked her gaze on mine and was talking to me.

This was unheard of, basically, but I wasn't thinking that calmly. I was thinking, 'A ghost is FREAKING TALKING TO ME, GETITOFF, GETITOFF, GETITOFF!'

I wanted to shake her free, but I couldn't. I wanted to scoot back from my crouch, but I couldn't. I wanted to bolt out of there and hide under my bed, but I couldn't.

And when I say 'talking to me', it wasn't really like that. Nothing in any coherent order. Instead, it was a series of impressions, of feelings, of half-formed wishes, stale aromas, lingering tastes, and partial sentences mixed with fragments that could have been songs. It was a barrage, a wave, a flood of chaotic communication, the incomplete record of a life, splintered and poorly put together.

I could tell, though, that the ghost was astonished by what I'd done. The way I'd called and made myself open to them was part of it, but she was also amazed at how I'd eased the way for the female Thug. That wasn't something she had ever countenanced.

Countenanced. The word came from her, and she wanted me to help her go the same way as the Thug.

She drew back a little. She'd become aware of the nasty situation that Rani and I were in.

Without letting go of my hand, she came upright, her bare feet drifting a few centimetres above the carpet.

She looked at me again. She wanted to save me, so I could then help her.

I struggled to my feet. My right hand, the one the ghost held, was a block of ice. I shook my head. 'Not without my friend.'

Rani was staring, not afraid but undecided. 'Hold my hand,' I croaked.

Rani intertwined her fingers with mine. The ghost approved. She turned slightly and she took us into the ghost world, the silvery, faded realm I'd experienced earlier.

We were no longer in the Toorak mansion. Or, rather, we weren't in the same Toorak mansion. We were in a building that looked just like it, but all the colour had been washed away. The walls, the floors, everything solid was slightly wavering, as if they were made of smoke. The only thing that was more solid than previously was the ghost. She'd become more substantial while still remaining blanched of colour. Her outline trembled less. She was much more difficult to see through.

We were seeing the world as ghosts saw it.

I looked down and then at a startled and wary Rani. We were the ones who were now translucent. I could see the walls, the window, the bars on the outside, right through her. I should have been excited at the effect – X-ray vision! – but all I could feel was a mild interest.

Colour wasn't the only thing washed out of this eerie, insubstantial plane.

Our ghost guide was smiling. She tugged on my hand and we drifted right through the barred window, which meant we were now a good four or five metres above the ground. Normally this would have been cartoon character time, where I'd look down and gravity would start working again and I'd panic, but I couldn't summon up any such strong emotion. With our ghost guide we simply kept walking. Coolly, we ambled along, passing over the portico, the driveway, the fountain, the garden and the fence until we were between the plane trees and the footpath, where we descended as gently as a soap bubble.

Still hand in hand in hand, we came to a halt that traditional few centimetres above the ground. I stole a quick glance at the house. It was a phantom version of the place in which we'd been imprisoned. Near silence surrounded us, a world where the noise of the city had gone and been replaced with a low-level rustling, the sort of sound I'd imagine clouds making when they cruise past each other.

My ghost guide tugged my useless hand until she had my attention. She nodded, dropped it, and we dropped.

The outside world returned and assaulted us. Colour and sound and smell and the whole flood of sensation smashed into me. The drop didn't help, either, tiny though it was, and I staggered, nearly falling, until Rani caught me.

'Quickly,' she said, but her voice was faint and laboured.

'Quickly what?' My own voice rasped. If I was tired earlier, I was exhausted now. My legs were trembling not with fear but with flat-out fatigue.

Rani didn't answer. She nodded instead.

The ghost was still hovering in front of us, translucent once again.

She was smiling, but hesitantly.

I pulled myself together. 'Thank you.' Working hard with my numb right hand, I slipped both inside her torso. 'Go now.' I wrenched. 'Seek your rest.'

The sleekness and purring of a favourite cat, the smell of damp socks and the sharp, peppery taste of an unfamiliar tonic. Ants, a father's love, loss and reunion. The peace that comes at the end of a good day touched me for a moment, and then she vanished like a birthday wish.

Rani and I limped away, arms around each other, looking for a taxi.

CHAPTER 22

'You walked with a ghost?' Dad put some real flabber into being flabbergasted.

'Hand in hand,' I said. 'But, believe me, it's not something I want to repeat soon.'

'No.' Dad's pen was flying as he wrote in his notebook. 'No you wouldn't.'

Rani had both hands around her cup of tea. It was her second in the half-hour since we'd staggered back into the bookshop in the early morning and locked the door behind us. Bec had just arrived, and after pinning me with a cracker of a question about the proper name for the dot on top of the letter 'i' (it's a 'tittle') made some for herself too.

Me? I was so shaken up that I'd had a cup of not-coffee as well. I surprised myself by enjoying it. Black, strong, with a smoky bite to it. Definitely not coffee, but it was something I could get used to.

Which goes to show that I'm a mess of contradictions, but I've learned to live with it.

The ghost encounter had exhausted both of us to the point of passing out. I was worried, too, that it had had other effects – my sight had been blurry for about half an hour after our ghost guide left – but I'd tabled that for worry later. My right hand was still numb, too, but the iciness was receding.

'A full report can wait,' I said to Dad, then I yawned the mother of all yawns. I thought my head was going to crack. I wiped away tears. 'Gotta sneep. Sleep.'

I shut my eyes for a second, then realised this was a bad idea unless I intended to keep them closed for a good long snooze. I dragged them open again to see that Rani had her head on the table next to where she'd put her cup.

'She can have the bed in the crash room,' I said. 'Bec. Help me get her there. Please. Then ring her folks. Leave a message. Tell them she's safe and with us. Also please.'

Dad rolled the camp bed out from the wardrobe in the crash room. I found the blankets and pillows and helped him set it up. While Rani mumbled, 'I'm okay,' Bec and I made sure she was lying down. Dad covered her with the blanket and we left.

'What about you, Anton?' Dad asked. He had his hand on my shoulder, steadying me, and, for a moment I was taken back to when he helped me ride a bike the same way, a long, long time ago.

'Couch. Archaeology, Music, Poetry room.'

I wouldn't have got there without Dad and Bec. The last

thing I remember before sleep finally won was Bec and Dad looking at each other over and Bec asking, 'Do you think we should tell him about the barrister?'

Even a teaser like that wasn't enough to keep me awake. Sleep hit me like a—

I woke from one of those sleeps that was one solid slab of unconsciousness. No half-waking, no dozing, no frustrating tossing and turning, just time out from the universe.

It was just what I needed, even though I woke with gritty eyes and a mouth that felt as if it had been used to road test tyres. 'Coffee,' I croaked. 'For the love of everything that's holy, I need coffee.'

I stared at my right hand. Then I made a fist. It worked well enough. The dead feeling had gone.

It was dark, inside and out. I studied the window for a while before I accepted that this meant it was night. Okay, so I was a bit sluggish.

I rose carefully, and my legs hadn't forgotten how to support me. Good.

On bare feet, I hobbled from the room. Street lights angled through the big front window, while car lights streaked across the shelves and the counter.

I remembered my watch. Ten-thirty-something. I peered at the window again. It was the night-time ten-thirty, not the other one. I could go out for coffee or make some.

I headed for the kitchen.

Dad. Bec. Rani. Dad was wearing jeans and a sombre black waistcoat over a black T-shirt. Bec looked like she was ready for action – combat pants, a many-pocketed camo vest over a black top. Rani was dressed as I'd seen her last night, and the outfit didn't look creased even though she'd slept in it. They were drinking something that smelled like heaven.

'Like some?' Rani said, gesturing with her cup. 'It's moreish.' She had a sword on her hip. I knew that was worth noticing, but wasn't sure why.

I rehearsed the words mentally before I had a go at them. 'Yes, please.'

I sat. Bec was doing something on her laptop. Dad was shuffling a pile of note cards. Rani pointed. 'You know how to use the Gaggia.'

The actions of finding a cup, measuring the coffee and water and heating up the espresso machine started to make my brain turn over a bit better. By the time I had a cup of very strong coffee and had retaken my seat, I think I could have passed as a human being, as long as no one looked closely.

Dad scribbled something on a card then capped his fountain pen. Bec glanced at me, hit a few keys then shut the lid on her laptop. Rani draped an arm over the back of her chair and sipped her coffee. She looked as if she'd been out for a night of clubbing, then had a sound sleep and a brisk morning jog.

'So,' I said after I'd burned my mouth on my first sip of coffee and then immediately had another. 'We were kidnapped by a bunch of nasty ghost hunters who were quite happy to sacrifice us, and we have a grief-maddened phasmaturgist who is murdering her way across the city.'

'It's good to have you back with us, Anton,' Dad said. 'You sum up so well.'

'I didn't go anywhere. Just to sleep.'

'You were on the verge of collapsing.'

'That's just gravity winning out for once.'

'Never mind. Rebecca and I have been researching these Malefactors, as Rani called them.'

'That's their name for themselves. If you ask me, they need a modern makeover. A new name like EvilCo or Da Dark Boyz. They could have a logo, too.'

'Describe their leader.'

Rani spoke first. 'He had a triangular head.'

Dad held up a hand. 'Enough. That's Emil Sabry. He's Egyptian. At least, he was born there three hundred years ago.'

I rolled with it. Shows how many unbelievable things I'd had thrown at me lately. 'Hm. He didn't look a day over two hundred. Good genes, I guess.'

'Magic,' Dad said. 'They hunt ghosts and use them to extend their own lives, among other things.'

I tried to imagine living for three hundred years, and all the stuff you could learn in that time. If you were a bad guy, that's lots of nastiness.

I felt sick.

Dad went on. 'I've been trying to find any mention of incidents like this very close encounter you had with the ghost, but I couldn't find anything. Maybe with some more details.'

Bec kept her head down, but Dad noticed. He has a sixth sense for knowing when someone was hiding something, honed on me over the years.

'Rebecca?' He tapped the table. 'Do you know something about it?'

Bec looked up and shrugged at me. 'Anton asked me to look into your sister's notes. I found something about attracting ghosts.'

'She was experimenting with that when she disappeared,' Dad said softly.

'We were in a dire predicament, Leon,' Rani said. 'The Malefactors were going to kill us.'

Dad slipped on his professional mask, but I saw the brief flash of pain before he did. 'Anton, you must help me take down a detailed account of your approach, your method and anything you can remember about this ghost world you entered.'

'I will.' I sipped some more coffee. 'Any news about our outlaw phasmaturgist?'

I could have called her Stacey Evans, but I didn't. If we were going to hunt her down, I didn't want to get all lovey-dovey and personal. I glanced at Rani's sword. It had to be a replacement – the Malefactors had taken her original. It might have some serious work to do in the near future, though, so I hoped it was up to the job.

'She was busy last night.' Bec swivelled her computer. 'Barrister Found Dead' screamed the newspaper site, and it hit me hard enough to hurt. We weren't fooling around here. We were up against people who killed – and worse.

'His throat was cut,' Bec continued, 'just like Grender. And I'm getting reports through Twitter that someone else was killed last night in a similar way. A judge.'

'The judge who presided over the case where the truck driver was declared innocent?' Rani asked.

Bec nodded. 'She lives ... lived ... in Jolimont. Lots of police action around there right now, news helicopters. Nothing confirmed, but first reports seem to point this way.'

'We have to stop her,' I said.

Rani had her cup on the table. She turned it around in her hands while she stared at it. 'I've already been in touch with the Company of the Righteous,' she said. 'I've sent them the address of the Toorak mansion we were held in last night. I could tell them about Stacey Evans. They'd bring in plenty of resources and would be efficient in hunting her down.'

'I don't like the idea of the Company of the Righteous busybodies taking over Melbourne.' I glanced at Dad and he gave a small, satisfied nod.

'It'd be in service of a good cause,' Rani said.

'A cause they consider good,' I said. 'And along the way, I'm sure they'll step in and do some cleaning up of good ol' Melbourne town's ghosts.'

'They wouldn't be able to help themselves,' Rani said. 'And they'd be convinced they were right.'

I waved my mug. 'Bec?'

'This is our problem,' Bec said. 'We should take care of it.'

'If nothing else,' Dad said, 'we owe Grender.'

'And what does it say if we don't pay the debts we have to sly, scheming, underhand, shifty weasels?' I said. 'If paying debts is good enough for the Lannisters, it's good enough for us.'

Dad and Bec had waited around for much longer than usual, letting us sleep past shop closing hours, but Dad said he really needed to get home for some sleep himself. 'I'm not as young as I used to be,' he said.

'Time works like that,' I said. 'You'll get used to it.'

Dad offered Bec a ride home. 'We can put your bike in the back of the van.'

She grimaced. 'I want to stay, but I think I'd better go. Busy day tomorrow.'

'Study?' I asked, and it sounded like a whole other world.

'Nope. It's cosplay time this weekend. I have to get started on my costume.'

Rani was instantly alert. 'What are you planning?'

'I have this fantastic idea for a Sherlock/Harley Quinn mash-up.' Bec tapped her false eye with a fingernail. 'And I can use the red staring eye I've been saving up.'

'You'll knock 'em out,' I said. 'Go, go.'

Bec picked up her backpack. 'Wait.' She dived in and pulled out two boxes. 'Rani said your phones had been taken by the Malefactors, so I went and organised replacements. Leon paid.'

I tried to remember how to get my contacts down from the cloud, a problem that linked to a whole ordinary world that I once knew. 'New numbers?'

'Afraid so.' She handed them over. 'They're ready to go.'

Bec explained the features to me, then went on to use it to show me some of her cosplay inspirations. It wasn't my thing, but I had to admit that these people took it seriously. The time that must have gone into some of those costumes.

I'd just finished farewelling Bec and promising her that I'd photograph her costume when Rani jabbed at her phone. 'Shit,' she said. 'Shit, shit, shit, shit, shit, shit, shit.'

'It can't be tragic news,' I said, 'not from your tone of voice. But it's not good news, that's for sure. Angry-making news is my guess.'

She growled. I mean, actually growled, before answering. 'Commander Gatehouse has been rerouted back to Melbourne.'

'Ah. The message you sent to the Company with the location of the Malefactors' house kicked this off.'

'She's been tasked to take over my wardenship of the city.' Rani swiped the phone so hard I thought it was going to break, then tossed it on the table. 'I'll be demoted to some sort of junior assistant dogsbody. Or even sent back to headquarters.'

'When's she expected back here? When do you have to report to her?'

She paced the room, looking for something to slice up, I guess. 'Tomorrow. Nine a.m.'

'Wait. Wasn't she on her way back to headquarters? Even if

she got off the plane in Dubai or Singapore, it'd take her a day to get back here.'

'So?'

'But if she's around for you to report to tomorrow, that means she never left.'

She stopped pacing. 'She was always planning to take over.'

'It looks like that. As long as you're suspicious.'

Rani thought this over for some time, tapping the hilt of her sword in a way that would have made any ghost nervous. 'It's a pity I didn't get that message, then, isn't it?' she said eventually.

'What?'

'If I had, I'd probably be duty-bound to stand down, or find a base for her or something menial like that.'

I grinned. 'You know, I've heard that the entire network's been having problems lately. Whole data packets have been dropping out.'

'That would explain it. A shame.' She held out her hand. 'Can you pass me my phone, please?'

I picked it up and the screen sprang to life. 'No lock?'

'Please. I need to delete that message from Commander Gatehouse.'

'Oh. Oh no.'

'What?'

'Don't tell me.'

'Don't tell you what?'

'Does Bec know this?'

'Anton!'

'You're an Erza Scarlet fan.' I flipped through the pics. 'You've had this phone for ten minutes and you've already downloaded dozens of images!'

'I had a back-up gallery on Dropbox.' She snatched the phone from me. 'Of course Bec knows.'

'And she approves?'

'Bec approves of any serious fandom.'

'Yes. Yes she would. And have you, you know ... dressed up?'

Rani deleted Gatehouse's incriminating message. 'I have been known to participate in cosplay.'

'Oh. Wow.'

'Bec and I are going to Supanova.'

'The cosplay thing? In costume?'

It was with pity she looked at me. 'Of course in costume.'

'Can I come?'

She considered me carefully. Her hands were on her hips and one foot went into its tapping routine. 'On one condition. You come in costume.'

You could have tossed three or four ping-pong balls in my mouth before I shut it again. 'Me? Dress up?'

'And properly. None of this male half-cos stuff.'

'Half-cos. Sounds serious.'

'Half-cos. You see it with guys who've agreed to go with their female friends. Their headdress will be fantastic, their facial make-up will be great, their chest and torso will be okay, then they lose interest. Jeans and trainers down below.'

'You want me to go the full-cos, if that's a word.'

'Yes.'

'And then I can go with you?'

'Indeed.'

'Deal.' I stuck out my hand. We shook.

I'd work out the details later. It gave me an extra incentive to sort out a bunch of magical assassins and a homicidal phasmaturgist.

Ghost hunting was never meant to be easy.

CHAPTER 23

Rani was tending to the hilt of her sword with some electrical tape. 'We need to alert the police,' she announced.

'Civil authorities? Not part of the program.'

'Stacey Evans has a list of targets. We can't protect them all. If the police offer them protection, then they might scare our phasmaturgist off. It's not much, but I have to do something.'

'You don't like to see people getting hurt.'

'If I can do something to stop it, I will, especially for those who can't help themselves.'

'I know how you feel.'

Rani snapped off the tape and glanced at me. 'Perhaps you do.'

'I see someone who understands what duty means, but if duty clashes with what she thinks is right ... Well, she'll try to do the right thing regardless.'

'You make it sound easy.'

'Oh, I've seen the struggle, but that's good. Doing the right thing when it's easy is okay. Doing the right thing when the choices aren't clear, when the outcomes are dire either way, when the going is tough … Well, that's the real deal.'

A small rough patch on the hilt of her sword was suddenly intensely absorbing. 'That's an interesting assessment.'

'Um. I hope I wasn't out of line.'

'I'll let you know when you're out of line.'

'Oh, yeah.' I rubbed the side of my head. 'You do, don't you?'

I ran my hands through my hair and looked for a subject changer. 'Hey, is that a new sword?'

'Your father gave it to me.'

I gave it the old double-take. 'We're a bookshop, not an armoury. Where'd he get it?'

'From a locked cupboard, behind a panel in the secret room.' She unsheathed it. It was unornamented, with a simple wire-wound hilt – now complete with contrasting electrical tape – and a brass crosspiece. 'I had to put in some work with a whetstone, but it's sharp enough for now.'

She swung it a few times. 'Is that the Aragorn move or the Legolas?' I asked.

'Aragorn. Viggo is the best.' She sheathed it. *Shnick.* 'Your father said it came from the Company of the Righteous many years ago.'

'From before this split we've heard about, I'm guessing. I'm looking forward to when we sort everything out and I can interrogate him about that, and a few other things.'

'Family secrets,' she said a little sadly.

'Let's put that on the agenda,' I said, 'unravelling a few family secrets of your own.'

She turned away, with her action fairly and squarely leaving that painful matter aside. 'Because of the way you've gone about your business, you haven't needed weapons, have you?'

'I hope you're not suggesting that it's time for me to learn. I haven't changed my mind.'

'Why not? You've seen how useful they are.'

'True.' And with Rogues popping up all over the place, swords could get more useful than ever. 'But it's a mindset thing with me. Remember the hammer problem? I don't want all ghosts to start looking like ghosts that need to be chopped up.'

'What about self-defence?'

'That's where running away comes in. If they can't catch me, I don't need to defend myself.' I looked at my watch. 'Look,' I said, 'I'm not a fan of waiting around until your Commander Gatehouse comes back with her reinforcements.'

'I know what you mean, and I've been thinking. What exactly was Stacey Evans doing at Grender's flat?'

'Apart from killing him, you mean?'

'Grender was dead when we arrived, but Stacey Evans was still there. Remember when we first saw her? She had an armful of folders.'

'Ah. She dropped them when she saw us.'

'That's right. I'm guessing that after she killed Grender, Stacey was looking for something. But what?'

'Nice thinking, Sherlock,' I said. 'You think we should go and have a poke around?'

'I'll drive.'

We had to get to Docklands to pick up her car, but on a night that apparently had hordes of nasty imported ghost hunters scurrying around and Rogue ghosts all over the place, we had a dull trip.

Hooray.

Once we paid the humungous overtime fine, we buzzed through South Melbourne. I started to pick up on my Melbourne Guide responsibilities, but at Rani's nods and murmurs, I changed tack.

'I know nothing about cars,' I said as we edged past the greenery of Albert Park. 'What makes Aston Martins so special?'

'They're the best, that's what.' Rani grinned, touched the accelerator, then eased off. 'How long do you have?'

She lost me after the first few minutes with her talk of eight-speed gearboxes and twin-turbo engines, but I listened hard, mostly to the enthusiasm in her voice.

I like enthusiasm, for just about anything. People who are apathetic about everything are hard going. Enthusiasm beats apathy hands down.

It was after one o'clock when we made it to Grender's place. His street was far enough away from Acland and Fitzroy Streets to be quiet.

'Too quiet?' Rani asked.

'A place can never be too quiet for me. I reckon I'll be

lying in my grave and complaining about the racket from the neighbours.'

We kept to the shadows and slipped around to the back of the property. Some of the flats had lights on.

Rani used her bracelet to get us through the gates that guarded the back stairs and then we were up to Grender's back door and inside, seeing in the dark like cats.

'The cleaners have been in,' Rani whispered. 'The Company of the Righteous is nothing if not efficient.'

'I'll remember that next time I need a murder scene fixed up.'

The place was still sad and shabby, though. The body had gone, and the carpet that had been underneath it, too. The floor was well scrubbed, as far as I could tell, but that was the extent of the crime-scene makeover. The trashed flat was still a trashed flat. Furniture was still overturned. Papers were all over the place. Cupboards had been emptied. Bookshelves heaved over.

I stood staring at the floor for a while, with the barest whisper of a whistle leaving my lips. Grender had been killed there, horribly. I'd eased his ghost and it had gone. I couldn't feel a thing – no presence, no scratchy tickliness.

Did anyone mourn for Grender? His flat didn't remember him – did anyone? Did he have family? Did they even know?

I'd check on that.

As we nosed around, it became pretty obvious that Grender had been a bit of a slob. Surprise, surprise. Loads of dirty dishes in the sink, lots of garbage sitting around the bin in the kitchen, and the bathroom was a horror from the lowest levels of hell. No home-beautiful awards would have gone his way, that was for sure.

The flat smelled bad.

I found the manila folders that Stacey Evans had dropped when we saw her here. I sat cross-legged on the floor and flipped through them. Printouts and newspaper cuttings, lots of highlighting and underlining and annotations – in Grender's writing. All of them concerned people who must be on the Evans hit list. A judge, a barrister, some police officers, others. She'd been working with Grender for a while.

The second bedroom was mostly full of crap – boxes, two exercise bikes and two cross-trainers that were heavy with dust, makeshift racks of clothes, plenty of shoes. It wasn't hoarder heaven, but it was getting close.

The tiny desk in the corner under the window was also groaning under rubbish. Lots of papers, piles of books, an old computer and printer.

Rani found gold inside the printer, in the paper drawer.

'He had to hide it somewhere,' I murmured as Rani handed the little black book over. 'In a messy life, it was his one little oasis of organisation.'

I flipped through it. Dozens of names, many crossed out, all showing the way Grender moved through the murky world of Melbourne's fringes. The book also showed how he didn't trust info like this to a phone. Smart guy, Grender.

'Stacey Evans,' I breathed. 'Two entries.'

'One's in Nagambie,' Rani said.

'That's near Seymour. Where the family lived. Before, you know.' I shook my head. 'It must be Grender compiling background stuff on her.'

'We need to investigate this Kensington address.'

We were a grim pair as we cut through South Melbourne and whipped up CityLink to Kensington. No chit-chat, no friendly Melbourne tourguiding. We were going to a confrontation, one I wasn't looking forward to. Grender's grubby death and the ghost it spawned was really getting to me and making me – all over again – question this shady world I'd signed up for.

I sent a text to Dad and Bec so they'd know what Rani and I were doing. I hoped they'd get it in the morning. By then we'd have everything neatly sewn up and we'd be sipping coffee at the bookshop.

The Kensington address was tucked in behind the busy multiculturalism of Racecourse Road, towards the end of a neat row of terraced cottages. Nine out of ten of them had picket fences. Ten out of ten were as cute as a button.

We drove past, turned and came back again, noting that no lights were on in the place before parking fifty metres or so up the road.

'There'll be a lane at the back,' I said to Rani. 'All these early inner suburbs have them.'

'For nightsoil collectors.'

'You know about nightsoil collectors?'

'I know far more about sewerage, drains and other sanitary arrangements than I really want to.'

'London ghost hunting?'

'London ghost hunting. It isn't all castles and grand houses.'

Rani locked the car and we walked down the lane until we were behind the right house. I counted three times to make sure.

The back fence was newish corrugated iron with a gate of the same material. Rani took care of the lock with her bracelet, drew her sword and stepped inside.

The backyard was tiny, but large enough for a plum tree, bare now, and a small sandpit.

Rani wafted up the three stairs and over the minuscule deck. Two glass doors opened onto it, under a verandah that bent around at right angles and led to another door. Rani stood alongside the glass doors and peered at the darkness inside.

She looked back at me. I'd taken up position by the sandpit, just in case, you know, nasty sand monsters erupted from it.

Rani had the doors open. She beckoned to me and I joined her. I had a hand on my pendant. It was reassuringly still, but that didn't stop me trying to look in all directions, anticipating something appearing at any time, and my hands started to shake. Rani saw this. She put a hand on my upper arm and left it there as we scanned the room that looked out over the backyard. A sofa, two stuffed chairs either side of a door that led to the rest of the house, a TV and an empty bookshelf. I gestured at that. It didn't look like the bookshelf of someone who had been here long – or who was staying long. If it was, I didn't want to meet them. No books, what kind of craziness is that?

The reality of the situation bit. Either we were going to find Stacey all nicely tucked up in bed – unlikely – or she was out in the night pursuing her revenge.

Of course, there was a third option.

My pendant buzzed, that annoying prickly, itchy sensation on my chest, and the light snapped on.

'Oh, visitors! Lovely!'

Stacey Evans stood in the doorway, gaunt, eyes wide, hair all over the place, dressing-gown buttoned up on the wrong holes.

'Come in,' she croaked, 'and we'll have a nice cup of tea.'

CHAPTER 24

I'd spent a lot of time, lately, dealing with things that would freeze the blood of any ordinary hard-working citizen of our great city, but they had nothing on Stacey Evans. It wasn't just the glassy, half-there look in her eyes, or the stuttering jerky way she walked, it was her hair.

Her hair freaking well moved by its freaking self.

At first, I thought a breeze from the open doors was stirring the hair on her head, but I couldn't feel any air movement at all. It creeped me out, her hair curling and uncurling slowly, writhing like some sort of underwater plant, something unwholesome and poisonous.

It was also a lot greyer than it had been in the photos. Almost white, really. White, writhing, unwholesome. Yep, not exactly a candidate for a shampoo commercial.

The glass doors closed. 'Good,' she said. 'Now we won't be disturbed.'

I know, spooky door-closing is a horror movie cliché, but it added a lovely little layer of creepiness to the whole scene. My stomach did a terrified flip-flop.

Rani gripped my upper arm. I swallowed. 'We'd love to,' I said, 'but I just realised what the time is. We have to dash.'

'Tea,' Stacey said, and then she swivelled like a shop mannequin given a good hard spin, and disappeared. A few seconds later the sounds of tea making came from further inside the house.

I stared at the glass doors. 'Rogue,' I whispered to Rani.

This explained the way my pendant was behaving. An extremely unhappy Rogue had closed the glass doors and was standing with his back to them. He was male, bald and wearing ragged robes. Judicial, maybe? His face, though, was – to use an unusual description for a ghost – haunted. His eyes were dark-rimmed, his teeth were bared and his hands were curled into claws, but he wasn't attacking us. His gaze darted from side to side as if he desperately wanted to get out of there.

Rani had her sword raised. 'Don't,' I said. 'Let's watch and see what happens.'

'You're learning,' she replied, 'but pay more attention to your own role than mine. I know what I'm doing.'

'How do you like your tea?'

Stacey Evans was back, carrying a tea tray.

I nearly said, 'As far away from me as possible,' but I caught Rani's hard stare. 'Black,' I said.

'Milk and one sugar,' Rani said and I glanced at her in disbelief. We might be in danger, but it wasn't the time to betray principles.

Stacey put the tray on the table between the chairs and the sofa, which Rani and I took. I was nearest to the doorkeeper Rogue, which made me a tad edgy. Rani laid her sword across her knees. The action drew Stacey's attention but she barely glanced at the weapon, frowning, before turning to pour herself a cup of tea. 'Delicious!' she announced. 'There's nothing like a good cup of tea, don't you agree?'

She poured Rani and me a cup each. I sipped it, keeping an eye on her.

I nearly spat it out. It was stone cold.

I stared at it and then at Rani. She'd seen the expression on my face and had put her cup down before tasting it.

Stacey Evans was beaming at us, eyes glassy and wide, teeth bared. In another person it would have looked like a horrible mixture of hilarity and terror. On her, it looked at home, which made it all the more terrible. 'Now,' she said. 'You're the young people who've been flitting around the fringes of my doings. What brings you here?'

Of all the possibilities, a polite sit-down chat wasn't high on my list. In fact, I think 'asteroid strike' was higher.

I glanced at Rani. 'We wanted to see you,' I said carefully.

'Well, isn't that nice,' Stacey Evans, phasmaturgist, said. 'I haven't spoken to anybody for simply ages.'

'Not since Grender?' Rani ventured.

'Grender?' A brief frown creased her brow, but it was gone in an instant. 'I'm afraid I don't know any Grender.'

'Avocado-shaped guy,' I said. 'With reasonable ghost sight.'

'Doesn't ring a bell.'

'You killed him.'

She jerked as if she'd been struck. Then she chuckled. It was a horrible thing, as if something both spiny and slimy had lodged in her throat. 'I'm afraid I've been killing so many people lately that I can't be expected to keep track of all of them.'

Okay. So the accountant from country Victoria had apparently gone the full Hannibal Lecter.

Stacey Evans, or the person who had been Stacey Evans before she was transformed into this supernatural serial killer, put her hands together on her lap. 'Would you like a biscuit? I have Tim Tams somewhere, I'm sure.'

I hesitated. After all, Tim Tams.

'No? All right then, I have two questions before I dispose of you.' She stirred her stone-cold tea for a moment. 'Why are you here, and why did you disturb my holy place?'

Holy place? Rani and I shared a look, one that told me not to make any stupid quips. 'We're here to help you,' Rani responded.

Stacey's grin went even wider and even more horrible. Something was stuck in her front teeth. I guess dental hygiene hadn't been at the front of her mind these past few days. 'Oh, I don't need your help,' she said. 'I have all the help I need.'

At this, Rani leaned over and, smoothly, took hold of Stacey Evans's hand. The woman's eyes went wide, then she jerked her hand away and was on her feet, snarling and hissing like an angry cat. 'What?' she demanded. 'What is this?'

Rani stood and I scrambled to join her. 'She's possessed,' Rani said to me. 'I could feel the presence of a Rogue inside her.'

So the pendant vibration I'd assumed came from the Rogue also came from poor, benighted Stacey Evans. Possessed? It explained how a grieving mother had so quickly become a powerful phasmaturgist. Forget trying to get even through normal, civilised means like suing those responsible. She'd been so traumatised that she'd been jolted out of the ordinary world into the world of those who dealt with ghosts. To achieve her revenge, she'd made an unholy bargain with a Rogue – one that Grender found? – for power, skipping all those boring steps like committing arcane lore to memory.

Caramba.

My pendant went crazy and the after-midnight tea party exploded into an action scene. The Stacey Evans Experience – the human/Rogue hybrid – backed away, growling from deep in her chest. The hovering Rogue by the door flew towards us. Another Rogue started to take shape as it pushed through the wall on our left.

We wasted no time on words. Rani and I swapped positions. I had to leap over a footstool to get there, and it put my timing off enough so that the Rogue emerging from the wall got a good swing in. She smashed me on the side of the neck and sent me spinning, and I almost fell across an easy chair. When I twisted around to face her, she wrapped me up in her ghostly arms and dragged me closer to her choppers.

With my arms pinned to my sides – this Rogue was pretty substantial already – all I could do was twist, kick and wrench my head from side to side to avoid those horrible, misshapen, snapping teeth.

I yelled, too. I yelled a lot – and jerked and flapped as if I'd been tasered. I hate ghost teeth.

In a blur, Rani was there. She ripped the Rogue apart with three precise cuts, freeing me before she whirled back to her original foe, the door Rogue.

I fell over, coughing and pushing myself away from the Rogue pieces Rani had left behind. They were trying to reunite themselves, squirming in a way that made my stomach heave.

I used the wall and dragged my useless self up in time to see that Rani had lopped off the other ghost's arms. It was doing a fair Black Knight impersonation and was screeching at her, not taking a backwards step. Or backwards drift. Whatever.

I gathered myself. 'I'm going in,' I called. Rani nodded without looking at me, then kept her sword in front of her, wrist movements only, limiting her back and side swing to allow me past.

The footstool, though, succeeded where it had failed the first time. It tripped me a beaut.

Instead of wasting time and energy swearing I went with the flow and dived straight at the Rogue, hands extended. 'Look out!' I shouted desperately. 'It's the Ghost Destroyer!'

The ghost heaved itself aside, and I crashed into the wall. This time, I swore – because it hurt.

I rose just in time to tangle with Rani as she stepped up to confront the Rogue. She stiff-armed me aside with a push to my chest. 'Out of the way.'

I staggered backwards, barely staying upright. The Rogue had seen Rani's sword. It oozed back through the wall as Rani slashed, carving a gash in the plaster.

She glanced at me then, and without a word, she bolted after the ghost.

I followed, swearing some more under my breath.

The Rogue was halfway through the back gate, snarling and frothing at the mouth. Rani was nearly on it but it pushed through the corrugated iron.

Someone screamed.

By the time Rani had the gate open, I was there. In the lane, in the shadows, a slight guy wearing a black beanie stood motionless. The Rogue was confronting him, a towering, gibbering presence distilled from nightmares.

Beanie Guy had time to whisper, 'Oh, God,' and then the Rogue was on him. He started shrieking.

Rani pointed at me. 'Stay back.'

She darted forward and lashed out with a kick that connected with Beanie Guy somewhere meaty. His shrieking turned into a scream of pain.

A metal bar hissed past Rani's head, only missing because she'd jerked back as it came. She drew a long, wicked slice across the ghost's shoulderblades, then kicked again, and Beanie Guy tumbled out of the clutches of the Rogue and sprawled across the bluestone.

The Rogue threw his arms up, screeched and twisted to face Rani, but she had her sword ready. She was fast and ruthless, and she cut the ghost to tiny, tiny pieces while

Beanie Guy sat on the bluestone, wide-eyed, swearing softly and continuously, running one word into the next in a stream of terrified consciousness.

All I did, though, was stand there and get the shakes. I'd messed up, badly, when those Rogues came at us, and now the near miss hit me hard. I grabbed one arm to stop the trembling, and then the other, and I ended up sort of hugging myself – but that couldn't stop my legs and I was as unsteady as anything.

Slowly, Beanie Guy got to his feet. He held his iron bar in front of him.

Rani approached him. 'Are you all right?'

He moaned. 'Don't you come near me.'

He dropped the iron bar, turned and ran.

'A burglar, most likely,' I ventured. Dogs were barking in nearby backyards. 'Explains the iron bar.'

Rani wiped her sword on a piece of cloth she pulled from a pocket. She gave me a look, started to say something, but then pushed past me in silence. She went back through the gate and left me shivering, staring at the shadows. I was already replaying the events of the last few minutes and my part in them was depressing. That guy, in those movies, the one with the small role and is credited as 'Stupid Bystander'. Yeah, that was me.

Rani reappeared. 'Stacey's gone. The other Rogue has, too. We'll have to start over.'

'We?'

'That's usually how I refer to you and me when we're hunting ghosts.'

'Yeah, right.'

She clicked her tongue. 'We've no time for this. Let's get to the car.'

I went with her. I could manage that, at least.

'You're not the first one, you know,' Rani said as we took off.

'First one to what?'

'To go to pieces in a hot situation.'

'You think that's it, do you?'

She drove in silence for a while before answering. 'Ghost hunting can hit people hard. We have a whole medical unit devoted to PTSD.'

'You think that I'm feeling the after-effects of a nasty encounter? Is that it?'

'Easy, Anton. You don't have to shout.'

I looked through the window. I had a sour taste at the back of my throat. I swallowed, hard, and grimaced. 'I'm just being rational about this whole deal.'

'Go on,' she said warily.

'I said I'd give ghost hunting a go – the gap year, remember? The way I stuffed up tonight makes it pretty clear that it's not my bag.' I scrabbled for my pendant and dragged it off. I dropped it in the centre console. 'Let someone else have a go.'

'Don't be an idiot.'

'I'll choose what to be, thanks.'

'Miffed because you cocked things up? I have news for you, chum. If your heart isn't in it, maybe you should throw in the towel.'

'I was useless. Worse than useless. And I let a civilian get involved. He could have been killed because of me!'

She growled. 'Self-pitying and half-hearted. I thought you were better than that.'

I snapped my head around. 'It's easy for you, though, isn't it? Sword and superpowers? Not having to worry about whether you're doing the right thing or not because the Company tells you? Plenty of cash to soothe any conscience you might have?'

'Give up now, Anton, and save us all the trouble of picking up after you.'

We drove in a long, strained silence after that. I kept my mouth shut because who knew what I might say if I got started again?

It was getting close to 6 a.m. when we parked out the back of the shop. Rani spoke to the windscreen, not me. 'The only reason I'm not leaving right now is that Leon deserves a report about tonight's events.'

'Suit yourself.'

I opened the door and turned on the lights and then we busied ourselves doing important things in completely different parts of the shop.

When Dad rolled up at about eight o'clock, Rani and I reported. It took about ten seconds of stiff and awkward recounting before Dad put down his trusty fountain pen. 'Enough. What is wrong here?'

I didn't answer. I looked at Rani and she didn't answer either. She looked at me. Okay, so we were being petty.

'I'm quitting,' I said.

'Quitting. I see. And you don't like this, Rani?'

'It's up to him.'

'If it's up to him, why are you angry about it?'

This time, Rani harpooned me with a look. 'Because giving up is the easy way out.'

'Yeah, right.' I had my arms folded. How had that happened? 'Anyway, you told me I should give up.'

'I said it because you'd lost the plot and needed a kick up the arse.'

'I don't need you to point out that I messed up. I can do that for myself.'

Dad cut in. 'Things didn't go well, then? Can you tell me about it while leaving out the finger pointing?'

Rani nodded sharply, and launched into a cold, objective rundown of what had happened. She paused at times for my input. I delivered it in an equally clinical way, while, all the time, wanting to storm out and slam the door behind me.

'More Rogues,' Dad said when we finished. He shook his head. 'Very bad, this.'

'Awful,' I said. 'Now, about my quitting—'

Dad patted this down. 'We'll get to that. First, though, I'd like to know more. This encounter could go some way to explaining Stacey Evans.'

'How, Leon?' Rani asked.

'The tragedy she suffered.' He shook his head. 'Her grief has consumed her. It has changed her so much that she has been able to assume great power quickly.'

Grief and loss. I couldn't help feeling sorry for Stacey

Evans and, being in the gloomy frame of mind I was, this led me to thinking about Mum and her loss and how grief changes people.

Oh. Moment of Understanding here. I'd felt for Stacey Evans; her situation had affected me so much because she was like Mum. Grief had changed both of them and torn their lives apart.

Wow.

'And that's not the end of it,' Dad was saying. 'What you are reporting might help explain why so much ghost activity has been going on in Melbourne lately.'

That snapped me out of my brooding. 'You think she's responsible? How?'

'Bear with me here. Firstly, if anything in this area can be called unnatural, this blending of human and Rogue ghost can be,' Dad said. 'It's forced, and cannot endure for long.'

'So she's working to a deadline as well,' I murmured.

'Exactly, but more than that, this unnatural union is under strain, under tension.'

'Like two magnetic poles being pushed together?' Rani suggested.

'Not a bad analogy.' Dad was impressed. 'In this case, the tension could be causing ripples that are disturbing dormant ghosts, making them manifest whether they like it or not.'

'Reluctant ghosts,' I said. 'That's all we need.'

'Huh.' Dad rubbed his beard, then spread his hands. 'This is barely charted territory we're in.'

'It makes me wonder if this is the real reason that Commander Gatehouse is so interested in Melbourne,' Rani said.

'She is?' Dad said.

Rani outlined the change of Gatehouse's schedule.

Dad grimaced. 'Typical of the Company of the Righteous soldiers. If they knew about this, or even suspected it, they wouldn't tell anyone about it. They'd declare it Company business and handle it themselves.'

Dad crossed his arms, leaned back in his chair, and looked up at the ceiling for a while. He apparently found the answer he was looking for as he stood up. 'Do you think you could find Stacey Evans again, Anton?'

'I don't see how.'

'Rani?'

'It wouldn't be easy.'

Dad nodded once, sharply, then left the room.

'I thought you were quitting,' Rani said.

'I am. He just hasn't let me get a word in.'

'Really? You looked as if you'd become intensely interested in what's happening.'

'I was just being polite.'

'Oh. And here I was, thinking that you were accidentally showing your true, deep attraction to the complexities of ghosts and ghost hunting.'

'I wasn't.'

'Admit it. You love the thrill of it as much as I do.'

'Thrill?'

'The hunt, the chase, the danger. It gets your blood racing, doesn't it?'

I was groping for a snappy comeback – something about not mistaking terror for excitement – when Dad walked back in, which wasn't unexpected. He walked in carrying a sword, however, which was.

Rani gasped. I groaned. 'Where'd that come from?'

The sword was in a black leather sheath that was scuffed, worn and smelled of age. When Dad drew it, the black steel gleamed dully. He hefted it, feeling its weight. It was nearly a mate of the one that he had lent Rani, but it was more battered, with a sizeable nick near the hilt.

'It's been here for some time.' Dad held up the sword and turned it in his hand, watching the way the light played on the metal.

Rani leaned forward. 'That's a beautiful weapon.'

I shook my head. 'While you're at it, is there anything else you haven't told me about this family? We faked the moon landing? We're secretly in contact with the league of lizard aliens who really control the world? Please tell me we own a castle somewhere.' I pointed at him. 'And don't say "It's a need-to-know basis", because I need to know.'

Dad sheathed the sword and put it on the table in front of him as he sat. 'Discovering that what you thought you knew isn't the entire story is one of the hardest things about being a Marin.'

'Apart from telling people "No, it's Marin, not Martin"?' It was feeble, I admit, but my heart really wasn't in it.

'The challenge is deciding what to tell one's offspring, and when.'

'That's not hard. Just give it to me straight.'

'That's not the Marin way.'

'The Marin way? What, is there a Marin Family User Manual?'

As soon as I said it, I knew the answer, and Dad's chilly smile came a split second later. 'In a way,' he said. 'Did you think a family that has handed down its traditions and practices over hundreds of years and kept records for just as long wouldn't write down something as important as raising children in the family business?'

'Show me.'

'I can't. Not until you have children.'

'I can't wait nine months, which would assume something happening mighty quickly with nothing on the horizon.'

Rani groaned. 'Let's just move on, shall we?'

'You'll have to wait, Anton,' Dad said. 'It's for parents only, and we're sworn to it.'

'You're not going to show me, are you?'

'And you won't find it.'

'Magic?'

'Something like that.'

'Uh huh. So I'm not being told stuff because it says so in a book I can't see.'

'I know it's hard.'

'Like hell you do.'

'Because I went through the same thing.'

This was one of those times I felt the Marin family business as a weight pressing on me, something that was happening more and more lately. Taking up that uni course seemed very, very attractive. Studying, learning stuff, talking about things that didn't involve the possibility of a screaming, painful death, all seemed rosy right now.

'Where did your weapons come from, Leon?' Rani unsheathed her sword and compared it to the one on the table.

'We have assembled them over the years,' Dad said. 'Some souvenirs, but mostly from our days when the Marins belonged to the Company of the Righteous.'

'So the sword you gave me is two hundred years old?'

'It is. And it's apparently good, solid work.'

'Oh, it is that,' Rani said. 'Perfect for the job.'

'Which brings us back to wonder why you're toting one now,' I said to Dad. 'Like me, you're no sword-fighting guy.'

'But unlike you, I'm not a ghost-hunting guy either,' Dad said quietly.

There you go. Family can make you flip from one emotional state to another just like that. In an instant, I'd somersaulted from being angry with him to sympathising with him. 'I'm sorry about that,' I said. 'I know how much it gets to you.'

'I thought I hid it.'

'Well, yeah, let's just say that only someone close to you would know.'

Other things suddenly got really interesting, for both of us. I ran my finger up and down an old burn mark on the table, then picked at it with a thumbnail. Dad fiddled with his fountain pen, taking the top off and putting it back on again, testing the nib, unscrewing the barrel.

Rani examined the sword Dad had produced.

'Anyway,' Dad said finally, that word being the equivalent of an embarrassed cough in these situations. 'What I'm trying to say is that since I can't see ghosts, or help move them on as you can, Anton, I can contribute in other ways.'

'Go on.' I didn't like where this was heading.

'We're in dangerous waters,' Dad said. 'I can't let you forge ahead in this way. I need to step in and do what I can to put an end to this.'

'You want to turn executioner? You want to hunt down Stacey Evans and kill her?'

'I can't see any other way,' Dad said. 'She'll kill again if she's not stopped, and while she's doing it, she's affecting the city in ways that could be far more dangerous.'

'No, Leon,' Rani said. 'Anton and I have this under control.'

Dad shook his head and went on before I could object to Rani including me. 'I don't think so.' He spread both hands flat on the table in front of him and stared at them. 'Sometimes, you need to shoot your own dog.'

'What?' I squawked. I was half out of my chair. 'Where did that come from? Is this non sequitur week or something?'

'I can't let you do it, Anton. Sometimes, a man needs to shoot his own dog.'

'Aargh! Repeating it doesn't make it any better! What are you? A character in an old western movie?'

'I—'

'That's so dumb, "A man's gotta shoot his own dog." No he doesn't! Why not save the dog? Get it the right treatment, an operation, whatever.'

'It's not your dog, Leon,' Rani added gently.

'No, but it's my own son who's involved.' He took a deep breath. 'And I made him get involved.'

I put my hands on both sides of my head and squeezed. Dad carried so much guilt.

'You're not to blame, Dad,' I said. 'You didn't force me into this gap year. I agreed.'

'After pressure,' he said. 'I didn't let up easily, did I?'

'Well, no. But I wouldn't have given in either, if I didn't have some sort of leaning this way.' If I wasn't attracted to the complexities of ghosts and ghost hunting. Hadn't I heard someone say that recently?

He adjusted the top button of his waistcoat. 'I suppose not.'

'So get that out of your system, please?'

His face fell.

'Come on, Dad, you don't need redeeming,' I said. 'Not in my eyes.'

He winced. 'Am I that obvious?'

'Again, not to anyone else. I just thought about how I'd be feeling and it was easy to guess.' I stifled a yawn. 'What I most need is to have you around, for support and advice. No one else can do that like you can because no one knows me like you do.'

Dad was silent for a while. 'A parent always wants to help, to spare their children from harm.'

'I know. I appreciate it.'

'And you're eighteen and telling me this?'

'It's a sign, isn't it?' Rani said. 'That your parenting has worked.'

We both looked at her, then at each other.

'I've turned out okay,' I said. 'Is that what you're saying?'

'You wouldn't be committed to ghost hunting if Leon had been deficient in his child raising.'

Committed? Me? I was just about to throw the whole thing in!

Wasn't I?

'It wasn't just me,' Dad said. 'His mother, his aunt, his stepmother, too.'

'You're the one who's here,' Rani said. 'And you, Leon, wouldn't be putting yourself forward in your son's place if you weren't being consistent with the lessons you gave him.'

Dad picked at some non-existent lint on his sleeve. 'So, I'm being relegated to the sidelines?'

I pulled myself together. 'If I tell you that you're back-up, it's going to sound too obvious a make-up, right?'

Dad smiled. 'I can live with it.' He clapped his hands together and smiled. 'So, no more talk of quitting, then?'

The Moment of Truth – another one. I knew that I wanted to quit, but I also wanted to continue. I knew I wasn't real, top-grade ghost-hunting material, but I also knew that Rani was right about the thrills. Yes, ghosts – some ghosts – terrified me. But finding them, tracking them down, cornering them was an adrenaline hit, and doing the job right was satisfying on a very deep and personal level. The trouble was, the world outside ghost hunting was appealing too. Whatever choice I made, the other one was going to look mighty desirable.

But it wasn't just about me. Other people were part of this. Not just Dad, but Mum and Aunt Tanja and all the Marins ever since ever. And Rani, too, and Bec. And all those people out there who I was saving from the ravages of ghosts, I had to take them into consideration.

Responsibilities. I had responsibilities.

'I guess not.' I sighed. 'Your cunning plan of distracting me with fascinating ghost-hunting and personal stuff so that I'd be committed before I realised it worked a treat.'

'You smelled a rat?'

'I knew what was going on. I also know that I might not be cut out for ghost hunting, but I'm stuck with it. That won't stop me thinking I should quit next time I'm facing a nasty customer.'

'You wouldn't be sane if didn't,' Dad said.

'We all have second thoughts,' Rani said. 'We'd be stupid not to.'

'Now,' I said, moving right along before we turned into a sit-com magic moment, 'I've been wondering about the cryptic question that Stacey asked us when we met her.'

Rani nodded. 'She wanted to know why we'd visited her holy place,' she explained to Dad.

I gave the forehead a good old smack. 'Her holy place. The crash site. The roadside shrine.'

'Of course. She knew we'd been there,' Rani said. 'We know that she commands ghosts. What if she set a Watcher there?'

It made sense. The idea of anyone interfering with the place where her family died would make Stacey Evans furious – but she couldn't keep an eye on it herself. She could set a Watcher to do the job. Or two, possibly, with one ready to find Stacey with news of activity around the site. People like Rani and me, for instance.

'We'll have to be double super extra careful, then,' I said.

Dad tapped the table. 'Are you ready, Anton?'

I weighed this up. 'I think I am, Dad.'

In the car, Rani didn't turn on the engine. 'Before we get going, I want to say I'm sorry about the things I said.'

'All the things?'

'Most of them.'

'Me too, but I think I have a case of déjà vu with this saying-sorry business.'

'But if we're here, apologising to each other again, that means we're able to sort things out.'

'We're adulting like champions.'

'Let's see if we can keep it up.'

Rani drove with her usual flair. We barrelled up the highway like a perfectly on the speed limit bullet.

CHAPTER 25

We pulled off the highway and I surveyed the crash site, in daylight this time. The recent rain had added an extra touch of gloom to the flower arrangements, the mementos, the photographs. The morning was bright and clear, blue sky with no cloud, and the scarred tree with its tributes was sombre, depressing, devoid of joy.

The car rocked as big trucks whooshed past on their way north while on the other side of the shrine, equally big trucks were heading for Melbourne.

'Can you feel anything?' I asked Rani as I stroked my pendant.

She shook her head. 'Any Watcher out there would be extremely faint in this daylight.' She touched the side of her nose with a finger, almost as if she was trying to straighten the slight crookedness. 'We're putting it off again, aren't we?'

'You bet. This place gives me the willies.'

'The willies. You *really* need to update your vocabulary.'

'Blame old episodes of *Doctor Who*.'

'I was brought up in England and even I don't talk like that.'

'And now *you're* putting it off.'

'I am. This place gives me the willies, that's why.'

I threw the car door open. Outside, traffic was steady on the highway. Plenty of big trucks, B-doubles, mixed in with cars and 4WDs and utes. Some of the occupants might have caught sight of the shrine and wondered who had died there. Maybe they spent a moment feeling sad and valuing what they had. I hoped so. It's more likely, though, that they were worrying about getting where they were going.

'Look to our flanks,' Rani said. 'Any potential threats?'

'Not that I can see.'

'If there were an ambush, where would it be?'

I pointed. 'Behind the central tree, the one with all the stuff around it.'

'You're getting the hang of this.' She held up her wrist with the bracelet on it. 'Any indication of ghost presence now?'

My pendant was quiet on my chest. 'I can't feel anything.'

'No Watcher, but no Evans family ghosts, then,' Rani said. 'Thank goodness.'

I was *really* glad that there wasn't even a hint of a potential ghost anywhere near the crash site. That would have made the whole thing messed up in a big way, and since it was already a horrible mess we didn't need any more.

I crunched over the gravel and then had to skip around the

puddles the rain had left. Then I realised that these puddles were mostly in what had been tyre tracks – the heavy, braking, swerving tyre tracks that had taken the Evans's car on its last, fatal journey.

I stopped and shuddered.

Rani saw the direction of my gaze. 'Oh.'

'Yeah, I know that people die every day, in circumstances even more tragic than this, but this one really bites.'

'It does. It's so common, something like this, that we forget how it hurts those left behind.' She rubbed her hands together. 'I think she would rather have died in the crash as well.'

'Probably.'

'Road accidents affect so many people, so often.'

'Accident,' I repeated. I shoved my hands in the pockets of my jacket. 'I've never understood that. When I spill my cup of coffee, that's an accident. When I bump someone's arm so they spill their coffee, that's an accident. A road smash where people are killed or maimed and lives are ruined, that's something more than an accident.'

Rani touched me on the arm. 'I'm going to suggest something radical in these ghost-hunting times. Let's not split up.'

'Good idea.'

Side by side, we drew closer to the crash tree. Some of the more recent floral tributes had started to rot, while the oldest had been swept aside. Others had fallen over. Rani crouched and righted one of them, a large bunch of carnations in a vase, then she wiped her hands. 'Anything?'

I had one hand on my pendant, and I'd been casting

around. I felt a very low level ghost presence. 'Not sure. Let's do a circuit.'

It took a while, but when we were about ten metres away from the crash tree, my pendant twitched and I stopped. 'I've got something.'

'You too? My bracelet came alive for an instant. I thought I felt something but wasn't sure.'

'It's not near the tree, though. It's that way.'

The median between the north- and south-bound traffic was still a nice healthy runway of gum trees, with scrubby undergrowth, and some rocks that probably dreamed of being boulders when they grew up. We walked towards a stand of skinny young gums. They stood out from the more mature trees around them and must have been planted much later.

As we grew nearer I started shaking my head.

'What's wrong?' Rani asked.

'What are we going to do if it's up a tree?'

'Climb, unless you have a chainsaw hidden on you.'

We were about five metres away from the stand of trees.

'I have it,' Rani breathed. 'Very faint. Ground level. No climbing required.'

'Let's box it in,' I suggested, and Rani nodded with approval.

With swift gestures, she indicated the route she'd take to the left – and that I should circle the trees to the right. I gave her a thumbs-up, which probably wasn't standard military protocol, but she got my meaning.

I could see Rani through the stand of trees, which was only four or five metres across. The ghost presence I was sensing was right in the middle, where the trunks were clustered thickest, where a tangle of greenery tried its best to wrap itself around them.

I squinted. There it was, so faint that it was hard to make out. Our Watcher. The more I concentrated, the firmer its outline grew – old-fashioned ankle-length dress, a bonnet, a soiled bandage around her throat. Early settler in the area? Traveller on the road between Melbourne and Sydney?

Then I had to put a hand out and steady myself against the nearest trunk.

Perspective. It had taken me a moment to realise how big this ghost was, and it had finally clicked that she was tiny, just above waist height. She was a kid.

I put both hands to my head and closed my eyes. Why did she have to be a little kid?

I couldn't move. I knew, intellectually, that ghosts aren't people. Head Anton was repeating this, with emphasis, loudly while Heart Anton was saying, 'But – a little kid!'

Kids don't deserve to die. Not many people deserve to die, true, but kids …

When these deaths spawn ghosts, it just makes it worse.

This one had hair that hung in twin braids down past her shoulders. She was barefoot, like a lot of ghosts, and she stood in the middle of the trees, hovering above the leaf litter, with both hands clasped in front of her and an expression on her face as if she were waiting to see the headmaster and she wasn't really sure why.

In no way did she look like Carl, but the way she was unguarded, the way she was unfinished, reminded me of him so much. My heart felt as if it was being crushed by stones.

She didn't move as I drew closer. Even though I had to lurch through the trees, she just stood there, forlorn, with that eucalyptus smell all around, sometimes dusty, sometimes green, depending on which way the air stirred.

That was the word for her, all right. Forlorn. Lost and lonely and without hope.

Rani was there, on the other side of the ghost, making her way closer. I knelt, my arms outspread. 'It's okay,' I whispered and I really, really hoped it was. I'd forgotten what we'd come for. I wanted to help this tiny one, badly, to offer her something, to give her a hug, to let her leave and seek her rest.

She shivered and closed her eyes. I reached out for her, but as I did, she reached for me.

Our hands touched. She saw me as a friend.

That confirmed that I couldn't play around with this family business. I had responsibilities, I'd worked that out – but I'd forgotten to include one group. I had a responsibility to the ghosts.

Ghost hunting wasn't something I could dabble in. I had to take it seriously because it was a serious, humbling business. These creatures, these ghosts, mostly didn't want to be here and they took it out on us. By helping them pass on I was doing them a favour, but I was doing more than that – I was giving them hope. This world, for them, was unpleasant, a struggle, a torture. I was helping them leave and, when it came to it, they were glad.

This tiny ghost, this ghost of a child knew my struggle and she understood my commitment. She saw me as a ghost friend.

Wow.

In that rush of contact, a bunch of other stuff washed over me. I saw the wild and furious Stacey Evans corralling this poor kid ghost. I saw the threat of pain and torment if the Watcher didn't do what she was tasked with. I saw that the Watcher would meet Stacey once a week, and where.

The Watcher let go of my hands, which were cold but not useless. I nodded and pressed my hands into her tiny chest. I twisted. She went in a cloud of memories of parents, a farm, a kitten, and hot, dry wind on her face, gritty enough to make her squint.

I sagged in the middle of that stand of trees while the traffic flew past on either side.

Sometime later I understood that Rani had her hand on my shoulder. We stayed like that for a while, then she gave me a tissue.

'I hate tissues.' My voice was thick. 'One decent blow and they're history.'

'I don't have a handkerchief, otherwise I'd give it to you.'

'Thanks.' I wiped my eyes, blew, and the tissue was history.

As I knelt on the ground in the middle of the trees, Rani waited for me to get myself together.

Eventually, I stood up. 'Should have realised,' I said. 'Stacey comes here to get a report from the Watcher. Watcher doesn't leave and find her.'

Rani patted me on the shoulder, then squeezed it. 'We should have worked that out.'

'Only one ghost here. More than enough.'

'It wouldn't be much of a system if the Watcher had to abandon her post and find Stacey every time someone turned up.'

'The bad news is that our Watcher couldn't tell us when Stacey will be back,' I said.

'Ghosts and time don't go well together.'

'She only knew that Stacey had come sometime in the past and was certain to be coming again.' I looked around. 'So, tactically, do we set up camp here or do you have something else in mind?'

'I have a possibility' She took out her phone and held it up for me. 'Bec found that Stacey Evans has a Facebook page, remember?'

The page was full of shared grief and tributes. They went on and on as I scrolled. I felt grubby, intruding on the heartfelt messages of loss and sorrow. 'You're hoping that a woman who has merged with a Rogue ghost and assumed magical phasmaturgical powers is still monitoring her Facebook page.'

'I'm sure she looks at it hundreds of times a day.'

'Because?'

'Look around. This whole place is a sign of obsession. She's not letting go – her whole existence is dedicated to not letting go. She won't be able to stop looking at her page.'

Rani took her phone back.

'And now you're sending her a direct message?' I asked.

'I'm writing on her page. We want her to see that what I'm posting is public knowledge.' She finished, and she wiped her hands on the sleeves of her coat. 'There. The local council and the roads authority are clearing up this site because it's a safety hazard.'

'They're not.'

'No, but she doesn't know that.' Rani surveyed the flowers, the photos and the keepsakes. 'She's going to come running.'

'And foaming at the mouth. I hope you're ready for her.'

'I hope *you're* ready for her, Mr Smart Guy.'

'You bet. I'll hit her with a zinger, then follow up with a snarky remark and, while she's staggering, I'll pummel her with a quip or two and hope that all of this covers up my abject fear.'

'I trust that you've something more useful than that.'

'I'm working on it.'

Rani flicked the hilt of her sword. 'Because, if you can't, and she unleashes Rogues on us, there's only one thing I can do, in the end.'

'Swords are for slicing.' I picked some dry leaves off the lapel of my jacket. 'You got any water in that car of yours? I'm gasping.'

'Plenty.'

'Correct me if I'm wrong, but water's another thing you girls always have around.'

'Another?'

'Tissues. Every girl I've ever known has a secret stash of tissues within reach. Usually a kilo or two, with an emergency back-up supply hidden somewhere.'

'I didn't know you were so wise in the ways of female kind.'

'I wouldn't say "wise". I'm a keen student, though.'

She raised an arched eyebrow. The archiest. 'I'm sure.'

So we sat in the car, drank some water, and talked a little. Not much, as we were both on edge waiting for the murdering magician to scream up alongside us.

Lunchtime came and went. Rani had water, but nothing to eat apart from some sugar-free gum. I eat most stuff, but I draw the line at that. You might as well chow down on a bicycle tyre.

I outlined a plan, too, the one I'd worked up while sitting there. Hey, it meant it was mmm … fresh, okay?

Rani took my plan, studied it, screwed it up and tossed it out of the window. Metaphor.

She came up with another plan. It burned down, fell over, then sank into the swamp. But the next one stayed up.

Pop culture reference.

After that, Rani spent a lot of time with a whetstone and her sword. She found it soothing. I found it soothing too. I mean, when I go into a dangerous situation involving violence and/ or vicious ghosts, I like to do it with someone whose sword is really, really sharp.

As the afternoon stretched on I began working on a back-up, back-up plan involving a travelling circus and clown disguises. Then, as it was drifting into evening, that time when the sun gets low enough to make long tree shadows stretch across the landscape, I checked the rear-vision mirror for the billionth time and caught the sight of a 4WD gunning our way.

I don't know why my stomach knotted. It might have been the way it was rocketing along. It might have been the way it was swerving and veering around the rest of the traffic on the road and the way that it had no lights when most of the other motorists were starting to turn theirs on. But mostly it was the way that when it skidded to a halt the tyres were smoking and, for a few seconds, it looked like it was going to plough right into the back of Rani's car.

Tyre smoke is nostril-singeingly bad, but I followed Rani's lead in using it to cover us while we bailed out and ran for the crash tree.

Rani took up position on one side of the tree and faced the road, making sure that the ground behind her was unobstructed. She'd need plenty of room to back away. She settled her feet in a solid stance, unsheathed her sword and waited.

In the growing gloom, I hid behind the tree. It was part of the plan, okay?

I heard Stacey Evans scream. None of this, 'You, again!' or, 'This time, prepare to meet your doom!' She just screamed as if her heart was being torn from her chest.

'Mrs Evans!' Rani called. 'We want to help you!'

Stacey screamed again and it was raw as a bleeding wound.

By this time, I'd crept around the tree. Stacey Evans was wearing a T-shirt and a pair of jeans, and she had a black leather handbag over one arm. The T-shirt was inside out and back to front. The jeans hung loosely around her hips and her hair was writhing on her head like seaweed in a storm. As Rani backed away, she tottered forward on stiff legs.

This was part of the plan, Rani backing away. It let me circle around the tree until I was behind Stacey, to her right, only three or four metres away – a quick few paces, that was all.

That was when Stacey fumbled at her handbag and pulled out a bottle of mineral water. For a second, I was almost patting myself on the back for my observation about girls and water, before she undid the cap and shook the bottle, from side to side, as if she was dislodging something thick and gluggy.

My pendant went crazy. Rogues sprayed out of the bottle, lots and lots of Rogues.

Stacey Evans had invented portable Rogues.

Rani and I had thought that Stacey might have a Rogue or two with her in the car, but the horde of spectral forms boiling out of a plastic bottle was not part of the plan.

Rani's job was to deal with Stacey's spooky bodyguards while I did my bit. Now, my view of Rani was blocked by the mass of howling Rogues, and this was looking like a really bad allocation of roles.

I thought about trying to help Rani by throwing myself on the Rogues in a senseless sacrifice but that would be, well, senseless. If I was ever going to make a sacrifice it was going to be a sensible sacrifice, for certain.

I left Rani to do what she did best. I barrelled into Stacey, knocking her flat on her face and then I sat on her. It's funny, but that was really hard. I felt like jumping up and apologising – 'I'm so sorry' – but I went ahead with our plan. I clamped her between my knees, and while her arms and legs flailed and her hair thrashed like a nest of furious snakes, I plunged my hands through her back.

Okay, so that was a risk based on Rani's observation that Stacey Evans hadn't felt quite there. And what was the worst that could happen? I'd break a finger, she'd turn on me and I'd get Rogue-slapped?

Yeah, well, the worst that could happen was the worst that could happen.

The reality not exactly as anticipated. When I ease into ghost substance, there's no resistance, really. Maybe about the same as walking through fog. Pushing my hands into Stacey's substance wasn't like touching a ghost, or touching a human; it was like trying to push a finger through plasticine. There was an added 'Ick!' factor because I was, sort of, pushing through her flesh.

Double ick.

I did it though, while she kicked and screamed and tried to reach back to claw at me, and I tried to pin each flailing arm with a knee. I clenched my teeth and strained, little bit by little bit, and pushed. 'Steady,' I gasped. 'It's okay.'

I groped for the Rogue that had possessed Stacey, and

that's when I nearly fell off her. The sense of two beings at war inside her was nausea-inducing. One was lost and calling for help. The other was red hot and raging, cackling at the freedom it had found and almost exploding with glee. I sought for it. I grasped it. I clutched it and then wrenched as hard as I could.

Stacey screamed, then she spasmed beneath me in two great heaves and went still.

I shook my head, carefully. Rani!

She had backed against a tree, ten metres away. She was still fighting a swarm of Rogues.

They hadn't disappeared when I'd ended the Rogue's possession of Stacey Evans. That part of the plan had just gone out the window and been replaced by panic. On my part, at least, while Rani fought like a demon.

Awkwardly, I rolled off Stacey. She was breathing, but not. I fumbled around and checked the pulse at her neck – first aid training – and it was strong. And now she felt like a human being, not a fuzzy, doughy half-human/half-ghost thing.

Her hair had stopped writhing, too.

For a second or two I stayed there on all fours, panting. I struggled to my feet while traffic hissed past on either side of us, with drivers and passengers oblivious to the battle going on in the shadowed woods in the middle of the road.

Rani was in full Company of the Righteous ghost-hunting superhero mode. She was screened, partly surrounded by trees, but the Rogues had spread. Some were working their way through the trees – really, *through* the trees – to try to take her from the rear – but Rani was making it hard. She moved like a whirlwind, and her sword was never still, shearing and chopping and slashing like a high-quality kitchen machine. German, probably. Maybe Swiss.

The Rogues weren't taking a backward step, or a backward drift, either. They lacked her single-minded deadliness though. They tangled with each other in their rabid fury – Stacey Evans's portable-ghost magic had crammed dozens into that water bottle. A heap of Rogue parts grew in front of Rani's feet as she methodically dissected them, but they kept coming and coming and coming.

Rogues know no fear except the stuff they generate themselves.

Desperately, I took a few steps, then had to prop myself against a tree for a second to gather my breath again. I turned my stagger into a charge, hoping that the ground was free of anything that could trip me.

So I wasn't the sort of reinforcement Rani would have preferred. I wasn't a paladin, or a robot mercenary, or a Jedi Knight, but there was no way I was going to stand around while she fought the good fight and was buried underneath a wave of Rogues. I could do something. If I timed it right I could plunge my hands into the back of the nearest and dissipate it. Maybe two before they realised I was there. Then, while they turned on me, it'd give Rani a breather, maybe.

Sometimes when you don't know what to do, you just do something.

I ended up charging a Rogue at the rear of the pack. I got a numb shoulder out of it, all icy deadness, but it made the Rogue twist around in time to meet my hands plunging at its chest. It was the quickest easing I'd ever done. Wrench, extract, next.

Dizzy and having trouble staying upright, I was getting ready to have a go at the next Rogue when it was my turn to get shouldered aside. I reeled, bounced off a tree, and grabbed at it, panting.

Stacey Evans stumbled past me and plunged into the mass of Rogues.

In the middle of the roiling translucent mob, Stacey wasn't wild-eyed anymore. Her hair was flat and still. She was pale and haggard, and huge dark rings were under her eyes.

She saw me and she gave the saddest smile I've ever seen, full of loss and pain and longing. She mouthed, 'I'm so sorry.' Then, before any of the Rogues could react, she flung her arms wide and opened her mouth.

She inhaled the Rogues.

In one long moment that went on and on, Stacey Evans drew in all the Rogues that were attacking Rani. I couldn't feel anything, but the Rogues were caught in a hurricane. It tore at their substance, shredding them as they resisted, ripping at their ghostly clothes and their ghostly substance. They howled and gibbered, but their ghastly noise became the terror they tried to create. As a mass they were drawn towards the woman who had lost her family, and one by one they disappeared into her mouth.

The last Rogue struggled and dug in, clawing at the air, but it was finally ripped from its intangible hold and whirled away.

Stacey staggered as if struck, then clamped her mouth shut. She put a hand to the side of her face and swayed a little. Her eyes found mine. This time, she said it aloud: 'I'm so sorry.'

Then she collapsed.

Rani was there first. Her sword was sheathed when she dropped to her knees. 'She's dead.'

CHAPTER 26

Rani and I had just reached the car when the first of a fleet of 4WDs pulled up. They were all black with darkly tinted windows and when Emil Sabry slid out of the lead car I groaned. After that serious ghostly encounter, what I wanted was a doughnut van and a massage chair, not a gang of brain-sucking nasties.

Sabry waited until he was surrounded by his flunkies and then strolled over. They had no weapons visible, but I had no doubt that if things got serious, they'd pull all sorts of mayhem-making machinery from their boxers.

Sabry eyed me, then Rani before he took in Stacey Evans's body.

'So, I'm too late for her.' He shrugged. 'You two are small consolation but you'll have to do.'

'I'm no one's consolation,' I growled. 'I'll be a shortfall, a make-up, a supplement, but a consolation? Never.'

Sabry looked at me as if I was a rotting fish. 'Has anyone told you how tiresome you are, boy?'

'Maybe,' I allowed. 'Has anyone told you that attaching diminutives like "boy" to other people is a sign of having a small penis?'

He flapped a weary hand at his flunkies. 'Take them.'

Rani's sword appeared as we backed away. For what it's worth, my fists were up too, but then Rani peered at the highway. 'No traffic,' she muttered to me. 'Get ready to run.'

'What? Put on shorts and singlet?'

She didn't get a chance to answer. A trio of helicopters swooped in from the east, up and over the slight rise on the far side of the highway, skimming the trees in the median, then banking enough to allow the foremost to blow up one of the Malefactors' black 4WDs.

Orange and red lit up the night. Smoke erupted. The second 4WD blew up and then, one after the other, the rest followed. Rani and I ran for the trees. Sabry and his gang did too, but we had a head start – and we knew the territory a little better than they did thanks to our previous scoping out of the terrain.

We ducked and dived through the bush and whenever I came across a handy stone I pelted it at Sabry and his bully boys, which made them angry enough to pull out pistols, so it wasn't one of my brighter ideas.

They'd only fired a couple of shots when one of the helicopters roared in and hovered above us, spotlighting the area. A loudhailer bellowed. 'Sabry! Call off your troops!'

I crawled out from the rock we were hiding behind.

'Hi, Commander Gatehouse,' I called as I waved. 'Timing!'

Commander Gatehouse climbed down from her helicopter, which had landed next to the line of burned-out Malefactor 4WDs. She was wearing a duster, *Firefly* style, and a khaki-coloured scarf. Her boots looked so tough she could have stood in lava while humming a tune.

Sabry strode forward with his flunkies. 'This is our business. You need to leave, Gatehouse.'

We circled around the Malefactors and drew close to Commander Gatehouse. She inspected us, but addressed Sabry. 'That's a brave statement from someone who is in as bad a position as you lot are.'

'Oh, Gatehouse, don't be like that. You won't do anything to us, not with what I know.'

Gatehouse snarled. It was good; a real bared-teeth, deep-seated growl. 'Don't tempt me. What you know dies with you.'

'Hardly. I've made arrangements.' Sabry gazed at the empty highway. 'I should have noticed that you blocked off traffic.'

'Not for long. The civilians will be getting impatient.'

'Then we'd better sort this out quickly.'

Gatehouse jerked a thumb at us. 'You're not taking them, anyway, if that's what you're thinking.'

'Not at all. In fact, we were just passing when we saw these fine young people and wondered if they were stranded.'

'You were going to offer them a lift.'

'Of sorts, yes. Sadly, our transport is in no condition for that now.'

I couldn't stand it. 'Enough. Please, before I lose the will to live.'

Sabry sniffed. Commander Gatehouse wrinkled her brow. 'Anton?'

'Don't banter, you two,' I said. 'Just don't. You've both got tin ears for it.'

'Tin what?' Sabry said.

'It doesn't matter,' Rani put in. 'How did you get here?'

'The same way he did, I expect,' Gatehouse said, glancing at Sabry. 'We were monitoring Stacey Evans's Facebook page.'

Sabry sniffed again. 'I have people to do that sort of thing for me.'

'I warned you,' I said to him. 'One more and I'll report you to the Banter Police.'

He gave me the rotting-fish look again, then glanced at his wrist. 'Oh, is that the time? We must be off. It's a long walk back to town.'

'You're not wearing a watch,' I pointed out. 'Hey, aren't you two worried about this sort of confrontation in public? What will the punters think?'

'Standard cover exists for these eventualities,' Rani said.

'Film crew,' Gatehouse said. 'Location scouting.'

'Mining company,' Sabry said. 'Geologic survey.'

'Oh,' I said. 'You've done this sort of thing before.'

Gatehouse stood aside and let Sabry go. She stared at his back. 'For longer than I like to remember.'

CHAPTER 27

There's this Indian restaurant in Fairfield, near the railway line and the giant-sized wooden dog. Even though it's out of the way, Dad and I have been going there for ages, ever since it opened as a tiny little takeaway. Now it's all settled and established, and going back there is like visiting an old friend. Not too many surprises, but guaranteed good times. Chicken Tikka Jalfrezy, mmm.

It has a private room.

Since Rani had called this meeting, she was there first. When Dad, Bec and I arrived we all made a pact: no discussion about the topic of the night until after we'd eaten. So we chatted. Dad was pretty bouncy as he'd just had a letter (a letter!) from Judith saying she'd be home in a couple of weeks. Rani and Bec tried to organise Dad into a board games night by promising that they'd teach him Codenames. I asked Bec if she knew what the tip on the end of a shoelace was, and when she admitted she didn't I informed her that it was an aglet, which she agreed was pretty cool. And then we had to explain to Rani about the offbeat knowledge challenge.

I put my hand on my heart. '"Real knowledge is to know the extent of one's ignorance". Oscar Wilde.'

'No it wasn't,' Rani and Bec said together.

'Might have been Confucius,' I admitted.

'*Pulp Fiction* tomorrow,' Rani reminded me. 'With Bec. We'll enlighten you.'

'And show you how to dance like Travolta,' Bec said. 'It'll be cool.'

Commander Gatehouse rolled up. She was looking reasonably civilian. I think it was the Doc Martens instead of knee-high boots. 'And who is this?' she asked, pointing at Bec.

I stood. 'Ahem. Commander Gatehouse, this is Rebecca Kellar, a vital member of our team. Bec, this is Commander Diane Gatehouse of the Company of the Righteous. She forgets her manners sometimes.'

'Your flippancy will catch up with you one day, Anton,' Gatehouse said to me.

'Not if I catch up with it first,' I said. No, it didn't make sense, but it was quick.

She rewarded me with a puzzled but gruff look. I think the gruff was a default, so I counted the puzzlement as a win.

'There's a place for you at the head of the table,' I said, stating the obvious. It was the only vacant seat.

'Rani, Leon,' she said after she sat. 'I'm sorry, Ms Kellar, for my rudeness. I was taken aback, that's all.'

'Bec is my friend,' Rani said. 'And she's here because she can bring something to this discussion.'

Gatehouse smiled a little. 'I had a feeling your invitation was to more than a dinner.'

'I'm pleased to meet you, Commander Gatehouse,' Bec said. Best-behaviour Bec. 'I've heard a lot about you.'

Gatehouse glanced at Dad, who hadn't said anything. He was sitting there in his best jacket – a nice brown houndstooth that I would borrow sometimes if it wasn't too small for me – with his arms crossed. His expression was meant to be neutral, I think, but mostly he looked mildly seasick.

'And I've read a lot about you too, Commander Gatehouse,' Bec said.

'The Marin family archives,' Dad explained. 'You feature in some of the more recent records.'

'Nothing intimate, I hope,' Gatehouse said.

Dad smiled a little. 'That's in my personal journal.'

'Don't look at me,' I said to Rani and Bec. 'I didn't even know Dad kept a personal journal, let alone read it.'

Gatehouse grunted. 'But this meeting isn't about me. Tell me, Rani, what *is* it about?'

'It's about me and my future.' Rani waved to one of the hovering waiters. 'But the first item on the agenda is eating. Let's order.'

After sorting out preferences, Dad and I did most of the ordering because we knew what was best in this place. Bec chimed in since she'd been here with us plenty of times before. While we waited for the food, the conversation moved to the cosplay event coming up.

Gatehouse had never heard of cosplay. Rani and Bec were happy to remedy this information deficit.

While they were battering Gatehouse with their enthusiasm, I thought about Rani.

We'd spent a lot of time together. We'd had ups and downs. She'd saved my life, effectively, a couple of times and I'd done what I could to help her quest of investigating ghost-hunting alternatives. I liked her but it was muddled because I didn't know what she thought about me.

Sad, isn't it, to be reduced to such a tired old cliché? I had an inkling, though, that sometimes clichés are clichés because they reflect a common experience, which is pretty profound, if I say so myself.

But it left me no wiser.

Best shot I had was to aim at being a better Anton. To listen more than I talk. To be honest. To treat other people as people, not just sounding boards for my own cleverness. If I did that, and things worked out well between us, that'd be solid.

Or something.

In the week since our showdown with Stacey Evans and the Malefactors, Rani, Bec, Dad and I had been trying to document everything that had happened. It opened up all sorts of avenues for further research, which made Bec, in particular, excited.

They spent hours examining Dad's cache of arms, too,

and much delight came out of that, I can tell you. Rani even started giving Bec swording lessons, at which I thought my oldest friend was going to explode with happiness.

In between, I cornered Bec and asked her to look up some extra info for me. When she came back with the answers, I spent an afternoon crossing town to find Grender's mum.

She hadn't heard, and I had to break it to her. She was stony-faced, at first, and swore a lot, saying she hadn't seen him for two years and he never contacted her anyway. And then she cried. A lot.

I made her tea and I talked to her. By that, I mean I listened. She talked about when Grender was little, and the more she spoke the less like a greasy weasel he seemed. In her stories, he was just a kid and did kid stuff. Then he grew up. She thought she'd lost him, years ago, and now she had.

After a couple of hours, she pushed me to the door and said she never wanted to see my face again. Then, just before she closed it, she wanted to know if I'd visit her sometime.

I said I would.

After the samosas, the pakhoras, the kebabs and the chicken tikka entrées, Gatehouse's eyes were going a little glassy at the intricacies of the anime and manga characters Bec and Rani were describing for her. After our mains – curries and dahls of all sorts with lots of naan (of course) – Gatehouse was ready to surrender under a barrage of details about the strengths and weaknesses of various conventions, and warm thoughts about the inclusive and sharing nature of the cosplay crowd.

Gatehouse was made of tough stuff, though. She hunkered down over her gulab jamun and asked questions about gender representation and commercial interests.

Dad and I stayed out of it and ate delicious Indian desserts, until Gatehouse waved a sticky spoon at Dad. 'And do you approve of this, Leon?'

'What's not to approve? Cosplay is good-natured, harmless fun.'

'That implies you've been to one of these events.'

'I've been to a few.'

I stared. 'I didn't know that.'

'There's a great deal you don't know, Anton. Probably more than you do know.'

I knuckled my forehead. 'Why am I thinking that the last few weeks have been purposely designed to teach me this?'

'The universe, Anton,' Gatehouse said, 'isn't here to teach you things. It is available for you to learn from, though.'

'Bec, can I get that on a T-shirt, please?'

'Not a problem.'

Gatehouse dabbed at her mouth with a napkin. It was a dainty gesture for such a blunt person, but who's to say that military leaders involved in a centuries-long war against spectral entities can't have high standards of dinner etiquette?

Rani was watching her mentor carefully. She pinged a spoon against her glass of water. 'I think it's time to move to the main item on tonight's agenda: my future.' She took a deep breath. 'I want to stay here and continue ghost hunting.'

I wanted to cheer, but instead I settled for a special, inner hurrah.

Gatehouse gave a little flicking gesture with her finger. 'You're looking for resistance from me?'

'You did order me to undergo re-training.'

'Hrmph. The events of the last few weeks have demonstrated that you belong to this world.' She scratched her ear. 'The paper you presented on this new Rogue behaviour has been well received, too.'

'Ma'am?' Rani said cautiously.

'All things considered, though, the Company is important to the safety of the world, but it is a hidebound organisation, mostly looking backward to the past rather than forward.'

'I'm more than aware of that,' Rani said. 'I hope to change it.'

'That's my hope too,' Gatehouse said.

'You want to change the Company?'

'It needs it.'

With really bad timing, Dad chose this moment to butt in. 'Looking backward instead of forward is one reason the Marins split from the Company,' he said. 'Of course, we realised this two hundred years ago ...'

'Believe that if you wish, Leon,' Gatehouse said. 'It's much more comforting than accepting that recalcitrant hotheads who wouldn't follow orders simply took their toys and stormed off.'

Rani tapped her spoon against her glass again, then she pointed it at Dad and Gatehouse in turn. 'Enough.'

Dad and Commander Gatehouse shared a look that was so complex that I started to feel queasy. Antagonism was there, certainly, and irritation, but also something that could only come when people have known each other well, and for a long time.

Rani went on. 'Commander, I'd like to put a proposal in front of you.'

'I don't think so.' Gatehouse pointed at Dad. 'In fact, I have to thank you, Leon, for reminding me how different we are and how this whole meeting was a mistake.'

Dad went to speak, but Rani silenced him. 'And that's the sort of closed-minded attitude that's going to bring us all to ruin.'

Gatehouse was half out of her seat and on the way out of the restaurant. 'Eh?'

'Look.' Rani pointed at the window. 'The world out there is what we have to deal with. Shops, trains, cars and people in a city full of ghosts. The Company of the Righteous can't faff around and ignore it, not if it wants to have any chance of success. And it can't pass up the opportunity to work with those who may come to the fray with a different background.'

Slowly, Gatehouse sat down again. 'In my way, I've been trying my best to bring about change. It is difficult.'

'And who was it who told me – many, many times – that the worthwhile is almost always difficult?'

'The higher orders of the Company are more impossible than difficult, but I take your point.' Gatehouse smiled a cold smile. 'We have some young people, too, who speak like you and Anton. They aren't happy either.'

'Hey, I'm full of smiles,' I said. 'Small family business, flexible, able to change quickly.'

'Speak for yourself,' Dad said.

'You're changing,' I pointed out. 'A few years ago, Bec wouldn't have got a look-in at our operation, let alone got her hands on our records.'

Rani turned to Gatehouse. 'Bec is digitising the Marin family archives. Soon searching, cross-matching and identifying trends and movements in ghost sightings will be much more efficient.'

Gatehouse's eyebrows shot up. 'Impressive. That's the sort of approach some of our disaffected young people have been talking about. You think it could be useful, Leon?'

'It already has been,' Dad said. Whether he actually meant it or if he was scoring a point off Commander Gatehouse, it didn't really matter. Win.

'That's the sort of thing I'm proposing,' Rani said. 'I could be a pilot project, a Company officer charged with helping to modernise the organisation.'

'God knows we need it,' Gatehouse said. 'The Trespassers aren't afraid to use modernity to further their ends.'

'To help achieve this modernisation,' Rani added, 'I want to be appointed as a liaison officer with another ghost-hunting organisation.'

'You wouldn't have a particular organisation in mind, would you?'

'The Marins.'

Dad got in first. 'You want to work with us?'

'Whatever happened in the past,' Rani said, 'it's now time to unite.'

Gatehouse spread her hands on the table and examined them. 'To heal the rift?'

'That may be difficult,' Dad said, 'since what prompted the split in the first place hasn't been addressed.'

Gatehouse glared, but Rani stepped in. 'Working together is a first step in that direction.'

Gatehouse settled. 'That sounds reasonable. Are you reasonable, Leon?'

Dad was backed into a corner, but he made one last effort to assert himself. 'Why is Rani coming to us? Why not Anton go to you?'

'I think that the Company of the Righteous can spare me,' Rani pointed out. 'Without Anton, the Marin family business might suffer.'

Dad harrumphed at that. 'You're right, of course. Makes sense.' He sighed. 'We'd be happy to take you on, Rani. More than happy.'

'I'm hoping that she can learn the Marin family approach to ghosts,' Gatehouse said meaningfully. 'If she can get to the bottom of this, it might be important to everything that we do.'

'We'll do our best,' I said.

'One more thing,' Gatehouse said. 'Rani will need somewhere to live.'

'Don't I have somewhere to live already?' Rani said, bewildered.

'Not for long. Your parents are being recalled.'

'What? Why?'

'They're needed elsewhere in the organisation,' Gatehouse said.

Rani looked stricken. 'Do they know this?'

'They're already packing.'

'They haven't said anything to me.'

'They will. Before they leave.'

'You can come and live with me, Rani, if you like,' Bec said. 'I've been looking for a place of my own, but having a flatmate could be fun.'

Rani brightened a little. 'Are you sure? That'd be brilliant.'

'Sorted, then,' Bec said, grinning.

I clapped my hands together. 'Let's celebrate. Hands up if you want coffee. Now who wants tea?' I waved to the waiter. 'Tea for five, please.'

Bec stared at me. 'You're having tea, Anton? By choice?'

I sat back in my chair and smiled. 'People change.'

CHAPTER 28

Oh, and I went to the cosplay convention with Rani and Bec, as promised. Bec and Rani were sensational. I repeat, sensational. Very, very photoworthy.

Me? I went as a Captain Jack Sparrow/the Doctor mashup.

And I smashed it.

ACKNOWLEDGEMENTS

This book is a departure for me as, instead of being set in the past or in an imaginary land, it's contemporary and local. That's why I'd like to acknowledge the support that Melbourne has given me. Creature comforts and the necessities of life for a writer have been provided by Coffee Mio, for my freshly roasted coffee beans, the very stylish Lords of the North barber shop for my taking care of my hair, Officeworks for those important items of stationery, Bunnings because Bunnings, the Westgarth Theatre for important diversions at time of need, and the Melbourne Football Club, which, over the years, has demonstrated the pain and the triumph that is at the heart of great stories.

And huge kudos to Craig Phillips for his sensational cover illustration and Ruth Grüner for her superb designing. The whole team from Allen & Unwin deserve all the thanks all the time – Jodie Webster and Kate Whitfield made this a better book, and who can ask for anything more?

ABOUT THE AUTHOR

Michael Pryor is one of Australia's premier science fiction and fantasy authors. He has more than a million words in print, having published more than thirty-five books and over fifty short stories. Michael has been shortlisted seven times for the Aurealis Awards and seven of his books have been CBCA Notable Books. For more on Michael and his books, go to www.michaelpryor.com.au.